THE INCIDENT AT FIVES CASTLE

CLARA BENSON

Copyright

ISBN: 978-1500217891
clarabenson.com

Cover design by Yang Liu waterpaperink.com

ONE

'SO, AS YOU can see, it's rather a delicate matter,' said Alexander Buchanan, the Foreign Secretary.

Henry Jameson, self-effacing and owlish in his round spectacles, gave a cough that was meant to denote agreement.

'If this Klausen chap really has come up with the goods then this could be the most enormous boost for our side,' went on Buchanan. 'I don't need to tell you that. Your agents have been keeping an eye on what's been happening over there for long enough, and what they've learned doesn't exactly fill me with hope.'

'No,' agreed Jameson, 'although we seem to be safe for now. Until their powers that be can get hold of that final link in the chain, it's all so much hot air, so to speak. I heard from our top man in the region just last week: he is quite certain that the information we have is correct.'

'You mean that the latest tests have proved unsuccessful?' said Buchanan. He nodded. 'It's only a matter of time, though. I know of at least three other countries who are working on the same thing. Of course, they're far behind us at present, but they'll catch up soon enough. There are plenty of brainy fellows in the world, and one of them is bound to hit upon the solution sooner or later.'

'Well, Klausen seems to think he's done that already,' said Jameson.

'Then why the devil couldn't he tell us about it straight out, instead of engaging in all this hole-and-corner stuff? It beats me.'

'Ah, but he's always been very protective of his work. There's a lot of professional jealousy among these scientists, you know. I gather he's terrified that someone will steal his ideas and take the credit for them.'

'But surely in an instance such as this, it's far more important for the cleverest men to work together?' said Buchanan. 'Why, it's for the good of the nation, if not the world! We don't want to go through another war, now, do we?'

'Of course not, but there's no reason at present to suppose we will,' said Jameson. 'And, of course, the ten-year rule is still in place.'

'Hang the ten-year rule!' said the Foreign Secretary. 'That's all about saving money, as you well know. We can't afford to keep the Armed Forces in the luxury to which they'd become accustomed. But with a weapon like this—why, don't you see? It would be the ultimate threat. The other side wouldn't dare start another war if they knew we had something of that kind. Think of the money that could be saved if we never had to re-arm at all.'

Henry Jameson glanced at the great man. Sandy

Buchanan was a brilliant thinker and politician who had risen rapidly to his current position of eminence. It was thought likely that he would one day become Prime Minister. His greatest quality was his ability to look ahead and see all possible outcomes of an event, which gave him a great advantage in negotiations with foreign powers. It was no coincidence that none of his friends would play chess with him. If Buchanan, in the middle of peace-time, was already showing agitation about a possible future war, then it was wise to listen to what he said.

'But the other side will get it sooner or later,' said Jameson. 'As you said, it's only a matter of time.'

'That's true, of course,' replied Buchanan, 'but if both sides have it the result is the same: stalemate—always assuming we get there first. The real problem is if they get there before we do. *We* can be trusted to behave responsibly, naturally, but if they get it before us—well, who's to say they won't decide to test it out on us just for the fun of the thing?'

'Oh, quite, quite,' said Jameson.

'So, then, it's vital that we hear what Klausen has to say for himself—and vital that it's kept secret. We don't want anyone getting wind of it. I think you know whom I'm referring to, Jameson.'

'Naturally,' said Henry Jameson, who knew the politician was not talking about foreign powers now.

Buchanan went on:

'We've already had enough trouble from the Opposition over that spying affair. Questions in the House, and worse!'

'Yes,' said Jameson. 'The public don't like the thought of spies in our midst.'

'And certainly not in the Cabinet Secretariat,'

agreed Buchanan. 'We never did establish to our satisfaction whether Golovin was acting alone, although he swore he was the only one.'

'Hmm,' said Jameson, who had his own ideas on that subject.

'Ogilvy's reputation never recovered, of course, and he had to resign, and we only just won the by-election by the skin of our teeth. Burford is a good man, although of course he's young yet and can't replace someone of Ogilvy's experience. If, after all that, the Opposition were to find out that we want to develop a weapon of this kind when there are spies supposedly all around us—and, moreover, when we are meant to be cutting expenditure on arms, well—' he paused expressively.

'I understand,' said Jameson. 'Don't worry—I will make certain the matter remains confidential.'

'It ought to be easy enough,' said Buchanan. 'Strathmerrick is sound, absolutely sound, and I have been to Fives at this time of year before, so nobody will suspect anything untoward. A New Year's house party in a castle in a remote part of Scotland—why, what could be more innocent?'

'Quite,' said Jameson. He selected a sheet of paper from the sheaf he held in his hand and passed it to the Foreign Secretary. 'So then,' he said, 'here is a list of the people who will be present at Fives Castle besides us and the American Ambassador.'

Buchanan glanced over the list and rubbed his chin in thought.

'Mostly family, I see,' he said. 'The Earl and Countess, of course, and their daughters. Those girls are a handful—especially Gertie—but they're innocent enough. Claude Burford, of course. A clever young man, that. He knows what he's about. He's engaged to the eldest girl. Very suitable. The Ambassador and his wife. Gabriel Bradley—now, who's that? Oh, of course, the Ambassador's secretary. I believe I've met him before. Miss Letitia Foster—she's a governess and sort of companion. Slightly dotty old thing—been with the family for years. Klausen, when he turns up. Ah.' He paused. 'Who's this? Frederick Pilkington-Soames. I don't think I know him.'

Jameson coughed apologetically.

'I'm afraid he's a reporter,' he said. 'For the *Clarion*, no less.'

'A reporter!' exclaimed the Foreign Secretary in dismay. 'That's the last thing we need. Why the devil was he invited?'

'I believe he is a friend of Lady Gertrude's,' said Jameson. 'I understand the young ladies are accustomed to inviting their friends to stay more or less whenever they like, so it would have looked rather suspicious to forbid him from coming.'

'Surely there must be something we can do to keep him away? Can't we get him sent to cover an important story here in London? Who's his editor?'

'I shouldn't recommend that,' said Jameson. 'They're a tenacious lot at the *Clarion*. If they get the slightest hint that we don't want them there they'll be all over us like a plague of rats. No, best pretend we've no objection to his presence. We shall just have to be very careful to give the impression that there's nothing doing. After all, even politicians take time off now and again.'

'I suppose so,' said Buchanan doubtfully. He moved on to the next name on the list.

'Mrs. Angela Marchmont,' he read. 'And who might she be? I seem to recognize the name.'

'She's another friend of Lady Gertrude's, I understand,' said Jameson, 'but we used to know her very well here, too.'

'Oh yes?' said Buchanan, with a keen glance.

'Yes. As a matter of fact, she rather distinguished herself during the war. She was the secretary of Bernstein, the American financier, for several years, and happened to be in Belgium when the war started. Under the guise of an American neutral, she helped a number of soldiers and prisoners to escape into Holland. She was nearly captured several times—was even arrested and questioned once—but they never got anything out of her. We wanted to put her forward for a bravery medal, but she was horrified at the very idea, and said she'd done no more than anyone else would have done in her position.'

'An American?' said Buchanan.

'Oh no, she's English through and through,' Jameson assured him. 'She is the younger sister of Sir Humphrey Cardew.'

'Cardew?' said the Foreign Secretary. 'He's in the Ministry of Labour, isn't he? I know him, all right. Pompous ass. So she's his sister, is she? I suppose if she's anything like him she must be a stiff-backed tartar—all creaking whalebone, moth-balls and disapproving sermons, eh?'

Jameson laughed at the idea.

'Quite the contrary,' he said. 'At least, she wasn't anything like that when I last saw her ten years ago. As a matter of fact she was rather delightful. She went back to America after the war and disappeared for a while, but she returned to England a year or two ago and has been amusing herself ever since by helping my brother solve murders.'

'Oh, *that* Mrs. Marchmont,' said Buchanan. 'Yes, I've read about her. Isn't she something of an adventuress? Can she be trusted, do you think? What about Mr. Marchmont? Where is he?'

'I've no idea,' said Jameson. 'I know nothing about him.'

'Hmm,' said the Foreign Secretary doubtfully. 'I'm not so sure about this as I was. Here we are, trying our best to organize a discreet little meeting in a remote place, with no chance of anyone finding out about it, and now I find that we are to spend three or four days in the company of a reporter and an amateur detective—the very people who are most likely to stick their noses in!'

'Can't be helped, I'm afraid,' said Henry Jameson. 'We shall just have to be as circumspect as possible. If it's any comfort, I doubt anyone will be interested in what we are getting up to—they'll be far too concerned with sleeping off all the Hogmanay food and drink.'

'I hope you're right,' said Buchanan. 'I should hate anything to go wrong.'

'Don't worry, it won't,' said Jameson.

TWO

THE COUNTESS OF Strathmerrick regarded herself mournfully in the glass on the wall and assessed the lines on her face. She was sure that several more had appeared since yesterday. A still-fine woman, Lady Strathmerrick was nonetheless highly conscious that she was no longer young, and she was more disturbed by this than she cared to admit. Naturally, with three grown-up daughters and two young sons, one should by now have given up caring about one's appearance, but Lady Strathmerrick felt obliquely that it was her duty to maintain as far as possible the clear-skinned prettiness and serene, smiling demeanour which had first brought her to the attention of the public during her first wildly successful season almost thirty years ago, and which had captured the hearts of several eligible suitors at the time. With such children, however, this was impossible. Each day brought new horrors and more grey hairs.

Priss, of course, could hardly be called a horror. The eldest daughter, she had inherited her mother's looks and more, and was nothing less than a beauty. But that, in itself, was a problem. Lady Strathmerrick was loath to admit it, but it caused her pain to be seen in company with the luscious, rosy-cheeked Priss, to be compared with her and to be reminded of what she herself had lost. Clemmie, her youngest daughter, was still in the throes of the sullen, secretive stage, spending hours at a time shut in her room, doing who knew what—worshipping the devil, perhaps? Or—worse—planning a career on the stage? Gus and Bobby, meanwhile, at ten and eight respectively, seemed to break a bone or sprain an ankle at least once a week. That was normal for small boys, she supposed.

But none of them caused Lady Strathmerrick quite so much worry and consternation as her second daughter. Gertie, she was sure, was responsible for at least nine-tenths of the lines upon her face and for the grey hairs that sprang unbidden from her head in increasing quantities. It was Gertie who, as a girl of seven, had climbed onto the roof of Fives Castle with a pair of home-made wings constructed from broom-handles and bed-sheets and declared her intention to become the first woman to fly. She was caught just in time, but a sound beating failed to deter her. Aged fourteen, she had taken her mother's passport and, dressed in her mother's best fur stole and lipstick borrowed from Priss, had set off alone to visit her cousins in Paris—just to see if she could do it, she said. If there was a society party or smart dinner at which it was reported that the guests danced frenziedly on the table, or an attempt at Chinese plate-spinning was made, or some unfortunate young man just down from Cambridge was ejected from a window bereft of his trousers, it was certain that Gertie was there. Only two months ago she had been arrested and brought before the magistrates after an affray at a night-club which had apparently involved an assault with a cold sausage (the Countess had never quite managed to discover exactly what had happened in that instance), and now she wanted to invite two friends of whom Lady Strathmerrick knew nothing to Fives Castle for the New Year celebrations.

'But must they come, darling?' she said to Gertie's reflection in the glass, although she already knew it to be a lost cause. 'Your father has invited his dullest friends from work to be there, and they will be poring over a lot of dry papers and sitting in conference half the time. It won't exactly be entertaining.'

'But that's exactly why I invited them,' said Gertie. 'Fives is all right for children, I suppose—I mean, it was all jolly good fun when I was small—but it's as tedious as anything these days when there's just us there. Priss is simply awful company now she's engaged to that silly ass Claude—'

'Don't call him that, dear,' said Lady Strathmerrick. 'He's a fine, upstanding young man.'

'He's still a silly ass,' said Gertie. 'And I can't get a word out of Clemmie any more, not now she's decided she wants to go to university and spends all her time with her nose in a book.'

'Is that what she's been doing?' said Lady Strathmerrick in some relief, although going to university was little better than going on the stage, according to her view of the world.

'Yes, didn't she tell you? She wants to be a physicist like Madame Curie.'

'Oh,' said Lady Strathmerrick vaguely. 'I suppose that's not too bad.' In her mind a physicist and a physician were the same thing, and a woman physician was, of course, a nurse. Girls often wanted to be nurses. Clemmie would throw herself into her new enthusiasm for a few months, and then would no doubt move on to other interests.

'It's a bore, and so is she,' said Gertie. 'I want someone to play with.'

'But who are these friends?' said her mother. 'They're not part of that horrid night-club set of yours, are they? So loud. And they break things.'

'Oh, no, they're not like that at all,' Gertie assured her. 'Freddy is an awfully talented journalist and Angela—well, Angela is a darling. You'll adore her, I promise.'

Just then, a pale-faced woman of indeterminate age drifted absently into the room. She was untidily dressed, and was carrying a sheaf of papers and a pen. Another pen was tucked behind her ear. She wandered over to the window, seemingly unaware of the other two occupants of the room, then stopped short and scribbled a note. This was Miss Foster, formerly the family governess and now a companion to Lady Strathmerrick.

'Hallo, Miss Fo,' said Gertie. 'How's the book going?'

The woman paused in her writing and glanced up.

'Hallo, Lady Gertrude,' she said. 'My book is going rather well at present, thank you, although I am having a little trouble with a scene in which the illegitimate son of the King of Prussia disguises himself as a woman in order to obtain a secret audience with the Infanta Francisca of Spain.'

11

'Letty, do you know anything about these two friends of Gertie's?' said Lady Strathmerrick, who was uninterested in the sartorial plight of the King of Prussia's son.

'Which two friends?' said Miss Foster.

'Freddy and Angela,' said Gertie. 'They're coming up to Scotland with us for New Year. I'm sure I've told you all about them.'

'Are they the ones with the triplets?' said Miss Foster.

'Oh no, they're not married,' said Gertie. 'At least, not to each other.'

'What?' cried Lady Strathmerrick in horror. 'We can't have that!'

'No, no,' Gertie hastened to assure her. 'It's not like that at all. They're not a couple. Freddy is my pal and Angela is my pal and Freddy is Angela's pal and we're all pals together, that's all. Besides, Angela is rather older than Freddy and I, and I don't suppose she's at all interested in little boys. Anyway,' she went on, 'if there's any funny business going on I should rather think it's between Freddy and Priss.' She saw her mother's alarmed face and said hurriedly, 'I'm only joking! I promise you, there's nothing at all you need worry about.'

Lady Strathmerrick had heard this countless times before, but had never yet won an argument with her daughter. She subsided with a little bleat.

The telephone-bell rang in the hall, and shortly afterwards a grave manservant entered to tell Lady Strathmerrick that her husband had called from the House to say that he would be late for dinner. Lady Strathmerrick sighed and the manservant withdrew. Shortly afterwards, the drawing-room door opened again to admit an extremely pretty girl accompanied by a formal young man who had the air of being rather pleased with himself.

'There you are, dears,' said Lady Strathmerrick. 'And how was the picture?'

'Rather a bore in the end,' said the girl. 'After the first five minutes I realized I'd seen it before, but Claude insisted on our sitting through it.'

'My dear girl, we'd paid to get in,' said the young man. 'If there's one thing I can't stand, it's wasting money. And besides, I hadn't seen it myself.'

'But I wanted to leave,' said Priss sulkily. 'We never seem to do what *I* want.'

'Well, the next time we find ourselves watching a film you've already seen, I promise we'll go if you like,' said Claude Burford with a laugh.

Priss tossed her head but did not reply.

'Who are all these important people coming to Fives, Claude?' asked Gertie. 'Father won't tell me—he said I wouldn't be interested, but I'm sure something's up.'

'Nonsense. Nothing's up,' said Claude. 'And your father was right: you won't be interested at all. It'll just be a lot of men talking about dull business stuff. Nothing you girls need worry about.'

'But who?' Gertie found Claude's air of superiority maddening.

'Well, the Buchanans are coming. And Aubrey Nash and his wife—the American Ambassador, you know. And perhaps a civil servant or two. Oh, and there'll be a Danish professor called Klausen. Really, it couldn't be less interesting.'

'I see,' said Gertie. 'Yes, it does sound rather dull. At least there will be a couple of women, at any rate, so perhaps it won't be a complete dead loss. We shall have to see what we can do to liven things up a little.'

'There's to be no livening up of anything,' said Lady Strathmerrick. 'Letty, tell her.'

'Oh, goodness,' said Miss Foster, who in seven years as part of the Strathmerrick household had never yet managed to get any of her charges to do as she asked. 'I think you ought to listen to your mother, my dear. I think we should all like a nice, peaceful family party at Fives Castle, without any excitement.'

'Excitement?' said Gertie. 'There's no fear of that.' She sighed. 'Don't worry, Mother, I promise I shall be on my best behaviour. I shall smile sweetly at everyone and pass the salt and look demure and not swear—out loud, at least. And afterwards I shall go upstairs into the attics and scream out my boredom where no-one can hear me.'

'Don't be silly,' said Priss. 'You know you'll enjoy it, really. You always do.'

'Perhaps it will snow,' said Gertie. 'That would be fun. I haven't been tobogganing in years.'

'I'm sure you will find plenty of things to do,' said her mother. 'We shall all have a nice, quiet time of it and return to London quite refreshed.'

'I do hope so,' said Miss Foster. 'I don't like too much excitement.' She drifted out of the room.

'No fear of that,' said Gertie again.

THREE

ANGELA MARCHMONT APPLIED her lipstick with care, and was just about to put on her hat when the telephone-bell rang.

'Hallo, Mrs. M,' said a familiar voice at the other end of the line. 'All ready, then?'

'Hallo, Freddy,' said Angela. 'Yes, I was about to set off.'

'Good,' said Freddy Pilkington-Soames. 'I was just calling to make sure you weren't going to funk it.'

'Why on earth did you think I was going to funk it?'

'Because I saw your face when Gertie attacked you and insisted on your coming. You wanted to say no but couldn't think of an excuse on the spot.'

Angela laughed.

'That's true enough,' she said. 'I'm not in the habit of turning up to stay at the homes of people I barely know. As it happens, however, Lady Strathmerrick personally sent me a very kind invitation, which made me less uneasy about it. She also mentioned that the American Ambassador and his wife will be there, and that clinched the thing, as they're old friends of mine whom I haven't seen in years.'

'I see,' said Freddy. 'Angela, is there anyone in the

15

world you *don't* know?'

'Oh, probably,' said Mrs. Marchmont. 'Besides, I might ask the same thing of you.'

'I am known and beloved by everybody, naturally,' said Freddy. 'That's why I get invited everywhere. Not like my friend St. John, who has become *persona non grata* ever since he went all militant. He was desperate to come to Fives with us as he's been mooning after Gertie ever since I introduced them a few months ago. She thinks he's an idiot, but he won't listen to reason. He just keeps on sending her silly poems and making sheep's eyes at her in the hope that one day she'll notice what a dashing fellow he is and go and live with him in a grimy hovel in Whitechapel.'

'I do hope you're going to behave yourself,' said Angela. 'I've seen what mischief you and Gertie can get up to in combination.'

'Of course I'm going to behave myself,' said Freddy. 'I shall be a paragon of virtue. Difficult to be otherwise, really, in the presence of the parents and family of one's friends.'

'Are they all as—er—lively as Gertie?' asked Angela curiously.

'No, nothing like it,' said Freddy. 'The Earl and Countess are nice enough but pretty staid, all told. Priss is lovely to look at—and doesn't she know it! But she's engaged to a bright young politician, so there's no fun to be had there.'

'I should think not,' said Angela.

'Then there's a younger sister, Clemmie. She's about eighteen or nineteen. She's nowhere near Gertie's equal for tricks, but she shows promise for the future. The last time I saw her she was at the sulky stage and wouldn't smile. Apparently, she's taken it into her head to study science, and who knows, she might even make a decent fist of it. She's got brains, all right. Then there are two younger boys, Gus and Bobby, neither of whom is old enough to be of any interest to us. The American Ambassador, though,' he said thoughtfully. 'Yes, Gertie mentioned him. That's rather interesting, now I come to think of it.'

'Why?' said Angela, and repeated her question when he did not reply.

'Because I have the feeling that something is afoot, Watson,' he said.

'Really?' said Angela. 'Of what nature, exactly?'

'Oh, political, naturally. You know Sandy Buchanan is going to be there, don't you?'

'Yes, but why is that important? Surely Foreign Secretaries are allowed to visit their friends at New Year just like everybody else?'

'Of course they are, but why should he be going there at the same time as the American Ambassador? Are they going to discuss important matters of state?'

'Perhaps you ought to ask him,' said Angela. 'I don't see anything particularly suspicious in it myself. Great men tend to spend time with other great men. Did Gladstone and Disraeli have tea together, I wonder? I shouldn't be a bit surprised if they did.'

'They loathed each other, by all accounts.'

'Did they? Well then, I expect they glared at each other over sherry and made pointed remarks. Anyway, even if they are going to talk about matters of state, why should that interest us? It will probably just be negotiations about the order of precedence at official banquets or something—deadly serious to them and awfully dull to the rest of us.'

'You're probably right,' said Freddy. 'Perhaps I have spent too much time lately cultivating my natural suspicion.'

'I think you have. But even a reporter must take a few days off now and again, you know.'

'I suppose so,' said Freddy. 'Very well, I'm glad you're coming, at any rate. I shall be setting off soon myself, so I dare say I'll see you this evening at dinner.'

He saluted her and rang off. Angela put on her hat, summoned her maid, Marthe, and prepared to leave.

'Are we all set, William?' she asked, when they arrived downstairs to where her chauffeur was waiting with the Bentley.

'Yes, ma'am,' the young man replied cheerfully. He held the door open for her, and then he and Marthe got into the front seats and they set off for the North.

For the first few miles, Angela sat in silence while William and Marthe conversed politely in the front. Angela was glad of that, as the two had a somewhat prickly relationship in general. William would have been glad to be friends, but Marthe considered herself to be a cut above him and tended to be frosty. Today, at any rate, they seemed to be getting on.

The Bentley ate up the miles and by mid-afternoon, sooner than Angela would have thought possible, they were crossing the border into Scotland. There was still some way to go yet, for Fives Castle was in the southern part of the Cairngorms, many miles to the North of Edinburgh. As they left that city behind them, Angela noticed that the air grew colder and fresher, and she thought she could detect the scent of pine needles. The sky had gone a flat, dingy grey, and there was a closeness to the atmosphere, despite the cold.

'I do believe it is going to snow,' she remarked. 'I hope you have both brought plenty of thick clothes with you. I don't know how warm these Scottish castles are.'

William's expression said that he was not afraid of a bit of snow, while Marthe shivered and pulled her coat more closely around her.

'Yes, *madame*,' she said. 'I have heard that Scotland is as cold as the North Pole, and so I made sure to pack my warmest things. And yours too.'

'Oh, good,' said Angela, and fell silent again, wondering, not for the first time, whether it had been a good idea to accept Gertie McAloon's invitation. Angela had, almost by accident, done the girl a good turn a few months ago during the Gipsy's Mile case, and Gertie in her gratitude had been keen to make Mrs. Marchmont's closer acquaintance. But Angela knew very little of the Strathmerrick family, except that the Earl was something important behind the scenes in the Government, and that they all spent some part of each year at Fives Castle. Freddy was going, and that was something at least; and it would be nice to see Aubrey and Selma Nash again after several years, but Angela could not help feeling something of an interloper, despite Lady Strathmerrick's kind invitation.

It was getting dark now, and the trees overhead made it even darker. The road narrowed and began to wind gently through the pine woods. William was driving slowly, mindful that he was unfamiliar with the place. Here and there the motor's head-lamps briefly caught a deer, or a rabbit, or some other animal as it darted off into the forest. Then it began to snow.

'You were right, ma'am,' said William, as the first large flakes drifted down all around them, looking rather like scraps of torn paper that had been thrown up into the air and were now bobbing back down to earth. The snow fell gently at first, then more and more thickly. It began to lie on the road and on the grass verges. Soon enough, the trees were resplendent in thin silvery coats and Angela was becoming concerned.

'Is it far, do you suppose?' she said.

'I don't think so,' replied William. 'As a matter of fact, I was expecting to see the entrance a while back. Ah—here we are.'

The road was now bounded to their right by a high stone wall. It ran for a mile or so, then curved away from them, and they saw that they had arrived at the gates of the Fives estate. William turned the Bentley in and past the gatekeeper's cottage, and proceeded slowly along the narrow, winding road, which rose and dipped through the trees. There was not enough snow yet to cause the car any difficulties, but Angela was glad they had arrived when they did. If it continued at this rate then it would surely be two or three feet deep by morning.

The Bentley crested the brow of a small hill and emerged from the trees, and they had their first view of Fives Castle, which stood out in sharp relief against the eerie, darkening sky. In spite of herself, Angela was struck by the grandeur of the building. There are some Scottish castles which hardly deserve the name, and could be more appropriately defined as large houses, but that was by no means the case here. With its frowning bulk, its turrets, its crenellations and its hundreds of windows, many of which were lit up, there was no doubt that Fives Castle inhabited its name and description comfortably—indeed, it seemed to Angela that had someone set out to build something that could be held as a model for the ideal of a Scottish castle, he could not have made a better job of it. William and Marthe had fallen silent and were gazing at the enormous mass that loomed ahead of them. At last, Marthe murmured something in French which Angela did not catch, although to judge by the girl's expression she was unwillingly impressed.

'What do you think, William?' said Angela.

'Well, it sure is big,' said William. 'I'd like to say something more poetic but that's the first word that comes to mind.'

Angela laughed.

'And to mine too,' she said.

'It is very big,' said Marthe. 'I hope it is also warm. I have noticed that the English are very fond of cold rooms. Me, I like to sit by the fire.'

'My, but the snow is coming down thickly,' said Angela, as the flakes swirled and flurried about them. 'I shouldn't be a bit surprised if we were snowed in by tomorrow.'

'I'd like that,' said William. 'I've never been stuck in a castle before. It would be an adventure. Do you suppose they have any ghosts here?'

'Ghosts?' said Marthe. 'I do not like ghosts.'

'Don't worry, Marthe,' said Angela. 'There won't be any ghosts. And if we do get snowed in it is more likely to be very dull than anything else.'

'I guess you're right,' said William.

FOUR

THE BENTLEY NOW drew to a halt before the castle's massive oaken doors, which despite the weather were thrown open to reveal a glimpse of a dimly-lit entrance-hall beyond. The doors were framed by a grand portico, which was flanked by two stone lions. A manservant emerged with an umbrella and opened the door of the Bentley to allow Angela to descend. She hurried into the shelter of the portico with thanks, and the servant directed William and Marthe around to the servants' entrance. At that moment, a long, gleaming Daimler drew up, which must have been following close behind them. Angela paused as she recognized the occupants of the car. Someone had evidently recognized her too, for the door was flung open and a woman sprang out without waiting for assistance. She was swathed in furs and sported a cunning hat which did not quite hide the expensively-styled golden hair beneath. Even wrapped up as she was, it was clear to see that she was impossibly glamorous.

'Why, it's Angela Marchmont!' she exclaimed delightedly. 'Aubrey, look who's here! Angela, you never told us you were coming. How simply marvellous! Look, Aubrey!'

Aubrey Nash now joined them, smiling broadly, and greeted Angela with less effusiveness but no less pleasure, gazing into her eyes and pressing her hand warmly. He was tall and broad-shouldered, in the way of Americans, with a quiet, thoughtful manner. Angela had known them well a few years ago when she was living in New York, but had not seen them for some time as Aubrey had been posted abroad.

They stood for a few moments under the portico, inquiring about each other's health, families and recent doings, while the manservant hovered politely.

'Oh, but this weather is filthy,' said Selma at last. 'I swear, darling, much as I just love your fine nation, I'm sure the cold and the wet will be the death of me.'

'Then let's get inside,' said her husband.

Once safely indoors, they found themselves standing in a large, square entrance-hall, from the centre of which rose a magnificent carved staircase. Straight ahead, on the first half-landing, was an enormous Gothic window of stained glass. It was dark at present, but Angela imagined the window would look spectacular in daylight. The dim electric lights (the place had been modernized, at least) revealed that the walls were hung all around with shields, swords, halberds, flags, coats-of-arms and other heraldic symbols, as well as the usual assortment of heads removed forcibly from wild animals without their unfortunate owners' consent. A particularly bad-tempered looking stag glared at them from a wall to their right. There was even a suit of armour standing to attention at the bottom of the stairs, although the man who had worn it some four hundred years earlier must have been a good few inches shorter than Angela.

They had barely divested themselves of their outer garments when there was a clattering noise from above them and Gertie McAloon came hurtling down the stairs. She arrived breathlessly just as another woman emerged more sedately through a door that led from the hall. There was a strong resemblance between the two of them, and Angela recognized the older woman as Lady Strathmerrick, whom she had glimpsed briefly once a few months earlier. The Countess greeted the American Ambassador and his wife with affection, then turned to Angela and held out a hand.

'How do you do?' she said, with a touch of reserve which did not escape her daughter. 'You must be Mrs. Marchmont. I am Lady Strathmerrick.'

'Hallo, Angela, I'm so pleased you could come,' said Gertie. 'Mother, now I insist that you be kind to my friends. They're not all dissipated inebriates, you know. Many of them—perhaps even most—know perfectly well how to behave in polite company.'

A pained look passed fleetingly across Lady Strathmerrick's face at Gertie's blunt insistence on making public what had been said in private, but she affected not to notice the inference.

'Have you met Mr. and Mrs. Nash?' she said.

'Oh yes, we're old friends,' said Angela.

'Indeed?' said Lady Strathmerrick in surprise. She seemed to unbend slightly at this discovery.

'Do come and have a cocktail,' said Gertie, rather contradicting her previous statement. 'Or there's tea if you'd prefer.'

Angela thought it politic to take the safer course. 'I

should love some tea,' she said with more enthusiasm than she really felt, and was rewarded with an approving glance from the Countess.

'Is Gabe here?' said Aubrey Nash.

'Yes, he arrived a little while ago,' said Lady Strathmerrick. 'He's shut up in the study with my husband and the gentleman from the civil service but they should be along shortly. The rest of us are in the West drawing-room.'

She led them out of the entrance-hall and into a long, brightly-lit gallery bordered on one side by windows that presumably looked onto the garden, although given the near-darkness outside, it was difficult to tell. Along the wall of the gallery hung portraits of twenty generations of McAloons and their consorts and children, as well as one or two portraits of Kings and Queens that Angela remembered as having seen in books.

Gertie was talking brightly, nineteen to the dozen. She appeared to be on her best behaviour and Angela guessed that her mother had given her a stern talking-to in advance of the party's arrival.

'Most of the formal rooms are shut up in winter,' she was saying. 'They're dreadfully cold and damp pretty much all year, except in the height of summer, and they're just not worth heating up except when we have a really large party. The ball-room will be opened up tomorrow, though, for the dance.'

'The dance?' said Angela.

'Oh yes,' said Gertie. 'Every year at Hogmanay we hold a dance for the servants and the tenants and anyone who cares to come from the village. It's all great fun. Everybody stuffs themselves and jumps about and has a jolly good time, and all the young men fight over who gets to dance with Priss. She hates it but has to put a brave face on it and pretend she's enjoying herself.'

'It sounds delightful,' said Angela. 'I shall look forward to it.'

They now entered a large, comfortable drawing-room which was evidently the one favoured by the family, for it had the air of being well-used. Although it was smart and tastefully decorated, Angela noticed that the carpet was somewhat worn, and that some of the chairs and sofas sagged a little. One armchair was firmly occupied by an elderly retriever, who evidently considered it to be his rightful property: he made no attempt to move as the guests arrived, but merely cocked an eye and an ear at them and carried on with his nap.

A young man with a complacent demeanour rose from a sofa as they entered, and stood to polite attention. This was Claude Burford, whom Angela remembered hearing of as a rising politician. He shook hands with her, and Angela had the strangest feeling that he was looking at her and attempting to gauge whether or not she was a person of any importance. Evidently he was unable to decide, for a frown of puzzlement crossed his face briefly, which pleased her, since she much preferred not to be so easily read.

'This is my eldest daughter, Priscilla,' said Lady Strathmerrick.

'Hallo, Mrs. Marchmont,' drawled Priss, not bothering to stand up. She was both exquisitely beautiful and exquisitely bored and made no attempt to hide the fact. The Countess gave her an exasperated glance but said nothing.

'Claude and Priss are going to be married,' said Gertie. 'Isn't that right, Priss? I'll bet you can't wait for the wedding, can you? Won't it be fun to be a politician's wife?'

Priss glared at her younger sister but did not respond to the needling. Instead, she said, 'Give me a cigarette, Claude, will you?' The young man gave her a meaningful look, and she sighed and said sulkily, 'Oh, very well, I shan't, then.'

'Good girl,' he said. 'You know how the constituents hate to see a woman smoking.'

'The constituents aren't here, though, are they?' said Priss. 'Why should they care what I do at home?' Before Claude could answer, she tossed her head and entered into determinedly polite conversation with Selma Nash.

Gertie gave Angela a wink, and Angela wondered what it was all about. For an engaged woman Priss seemed to lack a certain enthusiasm for the state, and even appeared to hold her betrothed in contempt. Had there been a row? She sipped her tea and wondered how the next few days would turn out.

Lady Strathmerrick seemed to be warming to Angela, now that she had found to her relief that Mrs. Marchmont was not a bright young person who was likely to get up to mischief, but rather an elegant and sophisticated woman close to middle age who was perfectly capable of conversing without using incomprehensible slang. Not only that, she was friends with the American Ambassador and his wife, as well as, apparently, a number of other people of notable importance. That, to Lady Strathmerrick, indicated that Angela was probably All Right, and gave her some cause for relief. She now introduced

Angela to Miss Foster, a woman with untidy hair and a vague manner who had once been governess to the children.

'She was no better at controlling them than I was, though,' said the Countess with some impatience, 'and so we gave up and sent them to school.'

'I'm afraid that's true,' agreed Miss Foster mournfully. 'I fear I am better suited to the life of a companion than a governess.'

'Not that you're much company lately,' said Lady Strathmerrick. 'If you'd only spend less time on that silly novel of yours, perhaps you'd have more time for me.'

She spoke carelessly, in the manner of a superior to a dependant, but Miss Foster did not seem to take offence.

'Do you write?' asked Angela. Miss Foster brightened up.

'Oh, yes,' she said. 'Indeed I do. I don't mean to say that my poor efforts will ever be worth publishing, but I find a great deal of satisfaction in putting pen to paper and expressing my very deepest thoughts. There is something almost sublime in the sound of the syllables of the English language, and I must confess I find it quite thrilling to think that by committing my words to paper, I am giving them something in the nature of immortality. To think that people might read my little stories and poems long after I am gone!'

'You write poetry as well, then?' said Angela.

Miss Foster puffed up and preened a little.

'Not to say *poetry*,' she said modestly. 'I merely dabble in light verse. Perhaps you would like to hear some?' She glanced towards a large notebook which sat on a nearby table.

Angela's attention was just then caught by Gertie, who, unseen by Miss Foster, was shaking her head frantically, eyes wide open in horror.

'Er—' began Angela.

She was rescued at that moment by the entrance of a cross-looking girl of eighteen or so, who without waiting for preliminaries said, 'I say, it's coming down a blizzard out there. It looks as though we're going to be snowed in soon. Has everybody arrived now?'

'Oh dear,' said Lady Strathmerrick. 'No, we're still missing Mr. Pilkington-Soames and the Foreign Secretary.'

'And Professor Klausen,' added Claude Burford smoothly.

'Well, they'd better get a move on,' said the girl, who Angela guessed to be Clemmie, 'or they won't manage it at all. The snow is already three feet thick down in the glen. At this rate, nobody will be able to get here for the dance either.'

'Rubbish,' said Gertie. 'Nothing would keep them away. It's the high-light of the year for most of them. They've been looking forward to it for weeks.'

'I do hope we don't get any gate-crashers as we did last year,' said Clemmie. 'We were turning them out of dark corners for weeks afterwards. MacDonald says he's already seen a suspicious-looking character hanging about the place today. He ran off when he was spotted, though.'

'Well, if he was a gate-crasher then he was a pretty inept one,' said Gertie. 'The dance isn't till tomorrow.'

'Dear me,' said the Countess. 'Do you think we ought to send out a search-party for the remaining guests? I should hate them to get stuck in the snow.'

'No need for that, Lady Strathmerrick,' said a voice from by the door and they all turned to see Sandy Buchanan and his wife entering the room. Angela recognized him immediately: he was the darling of the newspapers because of his sociable nature, and he and his young wife were frequently photographed attending the opera, or the ballet, or the opening of a new art gallery, or the summer parties of the rich and well-born.

Buchanan greeted everyone heartily, pressed Lady Strathmerrick's hand and clapped Claude Burford on the back. As he shook hands with Angela she again had the queerest feeling that she was being assessed, for the Foreign Secretary gave her a searching glance and looked deep into her eyes. Then came a little nod and a twist of the mouth, and Angela wondered what he had seen and whether he had approved of her. She had the feeling that he was not so easily shut out as Claude.

Eleanor Buchanan was much younger than her husband, and wore her hair back from her face, which threw her thick, dark eyebrows and high cheekbones into sharp relief. She would have been strikingly attractive were it not for an intense, watchful manner and unsmiling expression which put one rather in mind of a wild animal that sees enemies all around it. The Foreign Secretary had entered into conversation with Aubrey Nash, and she looked towards the two men warily, her fingers playing unconsciously with a gold locket she wore around her neck. Angela thought she had never seen anybody so tense, and did her best to put her at ease, although she did not seem to be having much success, for Mrs. Buchanan replied in monosyllables and glanced to her right and left as she spoke, and Angela soon gave it up and left her to herself.

It was getting late and the Countess was beginning to make noises about dressing for dinner when Freddy Pilkington-Soames swung into the room as though he owned the place. He made a bee-line for Lady Strathmerrick, bowed slightly and gave her his most winning smile.

'Hallo, Lady S,' he said. 'It's awfully good of you to invite me. I believe we've met once before—it was a year or two ago, at the Derbyshires' house, wasn't it?'

'Oh—ah,' said Lady Strathmerrick, caught off guard by his familiar courtesy. 'Yes, I believe I remember it. How delightful to see you again.'

Freddy then proceeded to ruin the good impression he had just made by turning to Priss and saying, 'Hallo, Priss. You're looking as ravishing as ever—far too good for that ass Claude. When you've divorced him you can marry me. How about it?' He then turned and started theatrically as he pretended to see Claude Burford for the first time. 'Oh, sorry old chap—I didn't see you there.'

'I resent that,' said Claude, who had no sense of humour. 'Priss is not going to divorce me. It's simply absurd of you to suggest such a thing. If you were any sort of gentleman you'd apologize to her now.'

But Priss had perked up at Freddy's entrance and merely said, 'Don't be ridiculous, Claude. Freddy's baiting you, as usual. And you fall for it every time.'

Freddy smirked.

'I'm sorry, old bean,' he said. 'Priss is right—I was just teasing. I instruct myself continually to be a model of decorum but somehow I can't stop myself from doing it when the opportunity presents itself.

Lady Priscilla,' he said with a formal bow to Priss, 'please accept my humble apologies. I won't do it again. Now I dare say you'd like to have me soundly thrashed.'

'Idiot,' said Priss, who was eyeing him with some interest. Angela noticed that Selma Nash was also giving the young man covert glances from under her lashes. She sensed trouble—never too far away when Freddy was about—and resolved to keep well out of it.

'Where are Gus and Bobby?' said Lady Strathmerrick when Freddy had greeted everybody and given Angela a particularly significant leer. 'Clemmie, dear, would you mind going to fetch them? They were supposed to be here by now.'

Clemmie sighed and went out.

Freddy said, 'I say, I hope you've got plenty to eat and drink here. The snow was coming down so thick and fast that I had to abandon my car halfway up the drive when it got stuck in a dip. I don't think anybody else will manage to get here tonight—or tomorrow either, if it keeps coming down like this.'

'Do you mean we're trapped here?' said Eleanor Buchanan, and there was a strange note in her voice that might have been fear or something else entirely.

Gertie looked up in surprise at her tone.

'Don't worry,' she said. 'We've been snowed in before, and it's rather good fun. Why, we were stuck here for two weeks once—do you remember, Priss? We did run rather low on food then. I half-thought we should have to start eating each other.'

'I wouldn't bother eating you,' said Freddy. 'You've no meat on you at all. Hardly worth it. Priss, on the other hand, looks far more appetizing. Quite deliciously succulent, in fact.'

Fortunately, Lady Strathmerrick was talking to Claude and neither of them heard. Priss heard perfectly but affected not to. Sandy Buchanan looked amused but his wife did not.

'I do hope it stops snowing soon,' she said. 'I should hate to think we couldn't get away.'

'My dear girl,' said her husband. 'Why, we've only just arrived and the fun has yet to begin. There are plenty of ladies here for you to talk to while we men get on with business, and there's plenty for you to do. To listen to you anyone would think you expected to be dreadfully bored by the whole thing, if you're that desperate to get away.'

'Oh, I didn't mean that at all,' she said, flushing. 'I'm terribly sorry if that's how it sounded. I just meant—well, you have to get back to London in a day or two, don't you? You have lots of important meetings.'

'Don't you worry about that,' said Buchanan soothingly. 'Now, I think we had all better go and get dressed for dinner, or we shall be late.'

FIVE

ANGELA COMPLETED HER toilette with Marthe's expert assistance, took one last critical glance at herself in the glass and left her room. She was rather pleased with her new evening-gown, which was of dark-blue silk and hugged her figure in all the right places, while cunningly-placed beading and embroidery contrived to disguise any minor imperfections in her form. She enjoyed listening to it rustle as she drifted along the passage to the head of the stairs, where she stopped for a second to make a slight adjustment to one of her gloves.

'Hallo, Angela,' said a voice, and she looked up to see Aubrey Nash standing at her shoulder. He offered her his arm. 'It always takes Selma an age to decide what to wear,' he said by way of explanation, 'so I never wait.'

His glance showed that she had made the right choice of dress. Angela smiled and took his arm, and they walked down the stairs together and into the drawing-room. They were not quite the first ones there, for two of the guests had arrived before them. Aubrey introduced her to his secretary, Gabe Bradley, a pleasant-faced young man who had spent the afternoon discussing business with the Earl. Then the other man came forward and a look of surprise crossed Angela's face as she recognized him.

'Hallo, Mrs. Marchmont,' said Henry Jameson.

'Why, Mr. Jameson!' she exclaimed, her face breaking into a smile. 'I had no idea you were going to be here.'

'I'm afraid I can't say the same,' said Mr. Jameson. 'I knew you were coming. You are looking very well, Mrs. Marchmont. How long has it been? Ten years, perhaps?'

'Oh, at least,' replied Angela. 'Now, that makes me feel dreadfully old.'

'You don't look a day older than you did then,' he said gallantly. 'I understand you have been showing the chaps at Scotland Yard how their job ought to be done.'

'Hardly,' she said with a laugh. 'I should say it's more the case that I have been getting in the way. I seem to have the most unfortunate knack for destroying evidence without meaning to.'

'You are too modest,' said Jameson. 'I know my brother admires your detective abilities greatly.'

'Oh, well,' said Angela uncomfortably. 'Perhaps in another life I should have liked to have been a detective, had I been a man. As it is I am forced to satisfy myself by meddling in things that don't concern me.'

They were soon joined by the other guests and members of the family, and the conversation became more general. Finally, Angela was introduced to the

Earl of Strathmerrick, very formal in his dinner-suit, who shook her hand and listened to her name as though he had never heard it before. His manner was distant and he glanced over her as though she were not important—or was it perhaps her imagination? Angela suddenly wondered why she was so conscious of being judged, and decided to stop thinking about it.

At dinner, Angela was seated between Aubrey Nash and Henry Jameson. The Ambassador was talking to Lord Strathmerrick, so Angela and Henry talked merrily, in the way of old friends who have not seen each other for many years. Henry was married now, she learned, and had a growing brood of children. The little ones were all very fond of their Uncle Alec, the inspector, who was rather wedded to his job at Scotland Yard and showed no signs of settling down. Angela agreed that it was difficult to find time for that kind of thing when one was busy solving crimes.

Henry then turned to talk to Clemmie, and Angela had a few moments to observe what was happening around the table. Gertie was sitting next to the Foreign Secretary and giggling at his amusing story of a recent encounter with an important French politician. Lady Strathmerrick, meanwhile, was doing her best to cheer up Mrs. Buchanan, who was picking miserably at her food. Freddy had somehow wangled himself a seat next to Priss, and she was looking rather like the cat that had got the cream. As the two of them flirted discreetly, Angela glanced at Claude Burford, who was also sitting next to Priss, and saw that he was staring across at the Foreign Secretary and completely ignoring Miss Foster, who was sitting on his other side. Sandy Buchanan was just finishing his anecdote, and as he concluded, Claude burst out laughing and said, 'Oh, I say, that's very good, sir.'

Freddy said, 'Pass the salt, Claude, old thing. Priss wants it, but you're ignoring her.'

'Am I?' said Claude. He passed the salt to Priss and then went back to hanging on the Foreign Secretary's every word. Eventually, he seemed to remember that he ought to be paying attention to his fiancée, and turned towards her. This gave Selma Nash the opportunity to engage Freddy in conversation.

'Have you ever seen snow like this?' said someone at last.

Gus and Bobby, the Strathmerricks' two youngest children, who had until then been concentrating on their food in respectful silence, perked up immediately at the mention of snow.

'I dare say you'd like to go out and build a snowman tomorrow,' said Sandy Buchanan to the boys, with a twinkle in his eye.

'Oh, yes, sir,' said Gus immediately.

Bobby, his younger brother, nodded.

'You can help us if you like,' he said to Gabe Bradley, who was sitting opposite him.

'Don't bother Mr. Bradley with your nonsense, Bobby,' said Claude. 'He has important work to do.'

But Gabe laughed.

'Why, I should love to,' he said. 'That is, if I can. I don't get much of a chance to play these days, I'm afraid, and I may be wanted tomorrow. But if I get a moment, why, nothing will keep me away—you'll see!'

'Let's all go out,' said Gertie.

'We shall see, dear,' said the Countess.

Shortly afterwards the ladies retired to the drawing-room, and Freddy tactfully followed suit, suspecting that the men had business to discuss that could not be disclosed before him. He sat down by Priss, while Gertie and her two brothers began a noisy game of beggar-my-neighbour and Clemmie took up a book and buried herself in it. Selma Nash and Eleanor Buchanan struck up a conversation about the ballet, at which the latter seemed to forget her customary wariness and became almost animated, while Lady Strathmerrick bickered gently with Miss Foster.

Angela wandered over to the window and stood by it for a while, gazing out onto the terrace. The light from the drawing-room made it difficult to see, so she drew the curtain further across the window recess to shut out the glare. The snow was still falling thickly and had begun to drift against statues, urns and ornamental walls. What looked like a small fountain was almost entirely covered and had become an amorphous mass of curves, with the occasional protruding black shape in places where the snow had not settled. As Angela stared out, she thought idly of the past few hours. It was an interesting gathering, with an intriguing mixture of people, and she had begun to enjoy herself despite her previous reservations. Most importantly, she felt that she had acquitted herself well with the Countess, who had been rather stiff at first but was now beginning to unbend.

'There you are,' said Freddy, who had come to join her behind the curtain. 'How are you getting on? Not too bored, I hope.'

'Not at all,' said Angela. 'Everyone seems very pleasant.'

'Yes, there are lots of good-looking men for you to exercise your charms on,' he said. 'And women, of course,' he said as she threw him a glance. 'I don't mean to say I consider you to be some sort of man-eater.'

'I should think not,' said Angela in some surprise at the idea.

Freddy went on, unabashed, 'You were getting on rather well with that American fellow at dinner.'

'Of course I was,' said Angela. 'I told you, I've known him for years. *And* his wife,' she said with some emphasis.

'I wonder what happened to the other chap who was supposed to be coming,' said Freddy. 'What is he? A Swedish professor, wasn't it?'

'Danish, I believe,' said Angela. 'I doubt he'll make it here now, in this weather.'

'I wonder why nobody mentioned him.'

Angela glanced at him sideways.

'By the way, Freddy, I think you're right,' she said. 'I think something secret is going on at Fives.'

Freddy was all attention.

'Oh?' he said. 'Why is that?'

'Because Henry Jameson is here.'

'The civil servant? Is that his name? Any relation to our friend the inspector?'

'They're brothers,' said Angela.

'Good Lord, I had no idea,' said Freddy. 'Is he important?'

'He is, rather. He's very high up in the Intelligence service.'

'Are you sure?' said Freddy, picturing the owlish

Henry Jameson to himself and shaking his head in perplexity. 'How do you know?'

'As a matter of fact, I worked for him during the war,' replied Angela.

'You? I thought you were in America then, running through rich husbands and living a life of idleness and ease.'

'I don't know where you get your ideas from,' said Angela. 'My home *was* in America, but I didn't spend the whole war there. And I have not "run through" any husbands at all,' she added with dignity.

'So you worked for Intelligence?' said Freddy. 'Typing up secret memorandums and what-not in an office, eh?'

'Something of the sort,' said Angela dryly. 'Anyway, from what I remember, Henry Jameson was not the type of man to travel about the country unless the country required it of him. If he's here at a house party in Scotland with the Foreign Secretary and the American Ambassador, then you can be sure something is going on.'

'I see,' said Freddy. 'I wonder what it is, then. I mean to say, it requires no great stretch of the imagination to see that Nash and Buchanan might occasionally find themselves at the same do, but I can't see why on earth this Intelligence chap should be here at the same time. And then there's the Danish professor. What was his name?'

'I don't remember,' said Angela.

'Perhaps he has something to do with it.'

'Well, they're not likely to tell us anything, are they?' said Angela. 'Especially not when the *Clarion's* most inquisitive reporter is sneaking around the castle with his notebook.'

'I am briefly off duty, having found other means of entertaining myself,' said Freddy.

'Ah, yes,' said Angela. 'Don't think I haven't noticed you foisting yourself onto Priss.'

'I haven't foisted anything onto anyone,' said Freddy. 'No foisting has taken place. I never foist. Both parties are entirely and wholly willing. And that ass Burford needs taking down a peg. I don't know what she sees in him.'

'Oh, *I* see,' said Angela. 'You're doing it to annoy him. Why?'

'I'm not *just* doing it to annoy him, but I do have a score to settle with him. We were at school together, you know, although he was a few years older than I. He was just the same then: perpetually sucking up to the bigger boys in order to gain advantage. And he was a terrible bully to the smaller boys. I fagged for him and he used to kick me mercilessly. I don't suppose he even remembers it.'

'Poor you,' said Angela sympathetically, and then gave him an odd look. 'Somehow I can't imagine you suffering that kind of thing for long,' she said. 'I should have expected you to do something about it.'

'Oh, I did,' he assured her. 'I set fire to his bed one night while he was in it. I'd be obliged if you wouldn't mention that, though, as they never found out who did it, but the police got involved and things were rather unpleasant at school for a while.'

Several remarks came into Angela's mind at once, but she contented herself with merely saying, 'But that means you've already settled the score, doesn't it?'

'Not really,' said Freddy. 'Some rotter woke him up just in time and he got out completely unhurt. I shall always remember it, though. I was a poor, motherless child and nobody came to my rescue.'

'Don't be silly,' said Angela. 'Your mother is alive and well and very fond of you.'

'Nevertheless, we Pilkington-Soameses have long memories,' he said darkly. 'We are like elephants—we never forget.'

'So, let me see,' said Angela. 'In order to get revenge for something that happened many years ago when you were both children, you are now bothering the fiancée of a respectable junior Member of Parliament.'

'Bothering? Nonsense,' said Freddy. 'She's hardly beating me off. Why, anybody can see the poor girl is bored to tears by him. I shall let a little light into her jaded life and bring a smile to her face once again, if only for a day or two.'

'Well, I wash my hands of the whole thing,' said Angela. 'Don't associate me with your schemes. I am already doing rather well in convincing Lady Strathmerrick that I am not some sort of adventuress—which I believe was her earlier conviction. I have brought my most respectable frocks and am determined to behave as demurely as a nun.'

'Yes, you look very nice,' said Freddy approvingly. 'I should think you'll pass all right. But look, your hair has got caught in your earring. Let me get it out for you.'

He moved nearer, and Angela inclined her head towards him as he attempted gently to extricate the offending curl from the little diamond drop. They were standing in this attitude of concentration, his face close to hers, when Lady Strathmerrick, who wished to look out of the window, suddenly joined them behind the curtain.

'Oh! I beg your pardon,' she exclaimed in embarrassment. 'I—I didn't realize anybody was here.'

It was quite evident what she thought they were doing. Angela and Freddy turned in surprise, and Angela, to her horror, felt herself going red.

'It's quite all right, Lady Strathmerrick,' she said hurriedly and somewhat confusedly. 'Freddy was just helping me with my earring.'

Even to her own ears it sounded feeble. The Countess darted her a glance of disbelief and withdrew before anything else could be said, leaving the two of them standing there, staring after her.

SIX

ONCE THE LADIES and Freddy had retired to the drawing-room, the rest of the men relaxed a little. Port was handed round and cigars were lit.

The Earl of Strathmerrick, while of little actual importance in the real business of government, was known for his impressive acumen in bringing the right people together at the right time, and acting as a sort of go-between for key events in the national and international sphere. It was at Fives Castle that an important treaty had been signed which, it was thought, had prevented another war from starting immediately after the last one had ended. It was here, too, that during three days of talks between two great men, one of them had agreed to abandon his ambitions and allow the other a free run at becoming Prime Minister in return for an unspecified reward. Most people were unaware of the Earl's reputation, but to those in the know, if Lord Strathmerrick invited people for a weekend at Fives Castle it was a sure sign that something important was afoot.

This vital auxiliary of world affairs now lit his cigar and gave a cough.

'Filthy weather,' he began. 'When did you say Klausen was going to arrive, Jameson?'

'He didn't say,' replied Henry. 'He was very vague about the whole thing.'

'Well, it may be too late now,' said the Earl. 'I gather the road is impassable already. Why do these scientific chaps have to be so damned secretive? It's all very well keeping it from the world at large, but if he's going to convince us that he really has come up with the goods, then he's going to have to do better than this. How do we know he's really going to turn up and that this isn't all some kind of childish joke on his part?'

'Come now, Strathmerrick,' said Sandy Buchanan. 'I don't think there's any cause for concern yet. Klausen is merely demonstrating a healthy sense of caution—not unreasonable when one's dealing with something as potentially explosive as this.'

Aubrey Nash laughed shortly.

'Yes, "explosive" is the word, all right,' he said.

'Tell me, Nash,' said Buchanan. 'What do your superiors think of it all?'

'Oh, they're very interested indeed,' the Ambassador assured him. 'Of course, this whole thing has been arranged at the last minute, so they had to put me onto it as there was no time to send someone over from the Department of State—but make no mistake, if Klausen's discovery can be proved to be the real thing, then they will be very keen to come in with the British Government on the development side—very keen.'

'What is the nature of this weapon, exactly?' said Claude Burford. 'I mean, I know it's some kind of powerful explosive, but I don't quite understand how it's meant to work.'

'Oh, neither do we,' said Buchanan with a laugh. 'We are having to take Klausen on trust. All I can tell you is that he has been conducting experiments on certain chemical substances with the aim of breaking them down into their constituent atoms. I believe he has been attempting to make these atoms react to each other in such a way as to create energy. Beyond that, however, I'm as much in the dark as you.'

Gabe Bradley now addressed the Foreign Secretary: 'If this weapon is as powerful as Professor Klausen seems to think, then I guess the United States and Great Britain won't be the only countries to be interested in it, is that right, sir?'

'Yes,' said Buchanan. 'We already know of two or three other countries that are working on the same thing. According to our intelligence sources, one country in particular—I think we can all guess which one—has come close to a solution. It's vital that we get there before them—all the more so, as we know that until recently someone here was informing them of our progress.'

'Ah, yes,' said Aubrey Nash. 'The famous Whitehall spy scandal that blew up so spectacularly last year.'

'And cost Ogilvy both his ministry and his seat in Parliament,' agreed Buchanan. 'His constituents would never forgive him for his part in allowing a spy to operate so close to the heart of the Government, practically in full view of everybody. He pleaded incompetence, of course, but there were mutterings at the time that he must have been involved himself, which is nonsense, although I must say he didn't exactly cover himself with glory. His wife was very ill at the time, however, so that must be his excuse for not paying attention to what was happening right there under his very nose.'

'They caught the fellow, though,' said Claude.

'Yes, but not before he'd passed on who knows what highly confidential information to his superiors,' said Buchanan. 'It was all extremely embarrassing for the Government and quite frankly it's a wonder we survived the scandal.'

'Are you quite sure the whole thing was cleared up?' said Aubrey Nash. 'I seem to recall there was some suggestion that this spy, whatever his name was, was not working alone.'

'We're as sure as we can be, which is not very,' said Henry Jameson frankly. 'Golovin was clever—he knew his job all right, but he swore he was a lone agent.'

'And you think he may have passed on news of Klausen's work?' said Nash.

'It's possible,' said Jameson, 'although he can't have passed on anything of great importance in that respect, since even we don't know very much about it. Klausen didn't want to reveal all until he was quite sure of his facts.'

'And now he is?'

'So he says,' said Jameson. 'He told us only last week that he'd finally confirmed his theories. He was terribly excited about it and wanted to share the news immediately. That's why this meeting was arranged at such late notice. I'm sorry if you had to cancel your other plans.'

Aubrey Nash waved his hand.

'Don't worry about that,' he said. 'We had nothing planned that couldn't wait. This is much more important.'

'I only hope he manages to get here, then,' said the Earl. He looked worried.

'I'm sure he will,' said Jameson. 'Besides, he promised to telephone if there were any difficulties.'

'What if he doesn't come, though?' said Gabe Bradley. 'It's a pity he didn't let us have a copy of the documents before the meeting.'

'Oh, he did,' said Sandy Buchanan, and the other men looked at him in astonishment. Henry Jameson was sure the Foreign Secretary was enjoying the sensation he had caused.

'Then why didn't you say so?' said Nash. 'We might have taken a look at them in preparation.'

Buchanan shook his head.

'Klausen entrusted me with a copy on sufferance, only because I insisted that it would be better for security purposes if he did—and on condition that I show the documents to nobody before he got here.'

'But surely that doesn't matter now?' said the Earl. 'Why, we are all here for the express purpose of looking at them.'

'True,' said Buchanan. 'But as Klausen explained to me, the documents themselves are completely useless without his presence, since they are so advanced in nature that only he or someone equally qualified can explain them. Believe me,' he went on in response to their protests, 'if I thought it would do any good I should go and get them now, but it won't. I've looked at them, and can't make head or tail of them. They seem to be in some kind of code, for one thing.'

'This Klausen fellow must have a sort of morbid persecution complex, to go to all these lengths,' said the Earl.

Jameson shook his head.

'I don't think so,' he said. 'You know, don't you, that he was invited by the other side to work for them? When he said no they made threats against him—threats which were pretty vague but which convinced him that his life was in danger. That was a few years ago when he was a brilliant young scientist and before he won the International Prize for physics, but for some time he never travelled anywhere without a bodyguard.'

'Why should his life be in danger, though?' objected Gabe Bradley. 'Surely what the other side want is his knowledge and expertise? They're hardly going to kill the goose that lays the golden eggs.'

'He feared he was in danger of being kidnapped,' said Jameson. 'The other lot aren't above drugging people and spiriting them away to work on their scientific projects, you know.'

'Well, that may or may not be the case,' said the Earl. 'And if it is, and if Klausen is intercepted and carried off en route to Fives Castle, I only hope you've put the papers in a safe place, Buchanan.'

He spoke half-jokingly, but the Foreign Secretary nodded seriously.

'Yes,' he said. 'They are locked securely away. Nobody will be able to find them without searching very carefully for them.'

'Well, then,' said Aubrey Nash, 'all we can do now is wait for him to arrive—if he ever does.'

Sandy Buchanan stood up and walked over to the window. It was still snowing thickly.

'Don't worry, he will,' he said.

SEVEN

THE NEXT MORNING Angela was already dressed and was just brushing her hair in front of the glass when there was a knock at her door.

'May I come in?' said Gertie, peeping into the room. Her cheeks were pink and her eyes were shining with the light of exercise. 'The boys came and dragged me out of bed early this morning,' she explained. 'We've been building a snowman. I say, Angela, it's the most gorgeous day—simply stunning. The snow is three feet thick in places.'

She ran over to the window and looked out, and Angela joined her. As Gertie had said, it was a beautiful day. The early sun gleamed off the thick covering of white and threw everything into sharp relief. It had been too dark to see much the day before when she had arrived, but now Angela saw that Fives Castle was set on the ridge of a hill, looking out over a deep glen carpeted with fir trees. Below her window was a grand terrace from which a flight of steps led down to a sloping lawn. The whole of the landscape before her was hidden under a counterpane of crisp white. Out on the lawn she saw Gus and

Bobby capering about a half-finished snowman, throwing snowballs at each other. She could hear their distant yells of laughter and was very tempted to join them.

'I actually came in to cadge a cigarette,' said Gertie. 'Father's had me under penance ever since that bust-up at the Copernicus Club, and I've had to promise not to smoke as he doesn't approve of it in women, so when I'm at home I'm reduced to begging from others.'

'Claude doesn't seem to approve of it either, I notice,' said Angela, handing her cigarette-case to Gertie.

'Oh yes, he's a frightful stiff,' said Gertie. 'He's always telling Priss what to do.'

'Do you think he and Priss are entirely suited?' said Angela hesitantly.

Gertie shrugged.

'You wouldn't think so, would you?' she said. 'But Priss seems to think they are. She accepted him, after all. Come on, let's go and have some breakfast and then go out.'

She seemed uninterested in her elder sister's happiness or otherwise in marriage, so Angela gave it up and followed Gertie from the room.

After breakfast, wrapped up in their warmest things, they went into the garden, where Gus and Bobby were still running about with shrieks of delight. They had been joined by Clemmie, who had shed her customary cross expression and was enjoying herself as much as her brothers.

'We've finished our snowman,' said Bobby to Angela. 'He's looking a bit lop-sided, though. Gertie ran off and we couldn't reach to get his head on properly.'

'Let's put it right, then,' said Angela. She set to work then stepped back to judge the effect. 'There—that's a bit better, isn't it?'

'Oh, yes,' said Gus.

'But this snowman is looking awfully lonely,' went on Angela. 'I think what he needs is a snow-woman to keep him company.'

'A snow-woman! A snow-woman!' yelled Gus and Bobby, and set to work with alacrity.

With five of them helping, it was not long before a second snow-figure was standing next to the first one.

'She's a beauty,' said Angela, gazing at the snow-woman who, despite their best efforts, was afflicted with an unsightly hump.

'She needs a hat!' said Gus, and the two boys ran off into the castle in search of suitable attire for their new creation. Meanwhile, Gertie took another of Angela's cigarettes and went behind a tree to smoke it, so as not to be seen from the castle windows.

'I don't see why Priss is allowed to smoke while I'm not,' she said grumpily.

'Because Priss behaves herself,' said Clemmie.

'Don't be ridiculous,' said Gertie. 'Of course she doesn't.'

'Well then, at least she doesn't get caught,' said the younger girl.

'That's true enough,' said Gertie with regret. 'I've never learned the knack of keeping my sins a secret. I always seem to commit them in full view of the world. Perhaps I ought to take a lesson from Priss, then.'

'She was being a bit obvious last night at dinner, I thought,' said Clemmie.

'What do you mean?' said Gertie.

'Why, flirting madly with Freddy, of course.'

'Oh, Freddy,' said Gertie dismissively. 'Everyone flirts with Freddy. And Freddy flirts with everyone. In fact, I ask you, is it even possible to speak to Freddy without flirting with him?'

'Difficult,' Clemmie acknowledged. 'You were pretty obvious too, though, with Sandy Buchanan.'

'Nonsense,' said Gertie.

'Yes you were. You were hanging on his every word and simpering like an idiot. She used to have the most awful crush on him, you know,' said Clemmie to Angela. 'She was distraught when he got married.'

'That's true enough,' admitted Gertie. 'I thought after his first wife died I might be in with a chance, but no such luck.'

'Isn't he a little old for you? He must be at least fifty,' said Angela in some amusement.

'I like older men,' said Gertie dreamily. 'They're so masterful and capable.'

'And he obviously likes younger women—just not you,' said Clemmie unfeelingly.

'I wonder where he found her,' said Gertie. 'Eleanor, I mean. Do you know anything about her? I don't. What does he see in her? She's like a wild animal watching out for predators—all narrow eyes and sudden glances. What's bothering her?'

'Us, probably,' said Clemmie. 'We were a bit loud at dinner last night.'

They paused to watch as a procession of servants passed along the terrace, carrying chairs and tables.

'Are they for the dance?' asked Angela.

'Yes,' said Gertie. 'I dare say we shall be wanted later on to help.'

'How many people are you expecting?' said Angela.

'I don't know, in this snow,' said Gertie, 'but with the servants and the people from the village it might be anything up to a hundred or even a hundred and fifty. You'll have to join in, of course, as will the rest of the party. You ought to see Father doing a reel, Angela—it's quite a sight.'

'I shall look forward to it,' said Angela.

Just then they heard a voice hailing them, and they turned to see Aubrey Nash and Gabe Bradley coming across the lawn to join them accompanied by Gus and Bobby, who were laden down with scarves and hats.

'I wonder what happened to the Danish professor,' said Angela. 'He was supposed to arrive yesterday, wasn't he?'

'Perhaps he got buried in a snowdrift and expired of cold,' said Gertie.

'Who's that?' said Clemmie.

'Some professor or other. Klausen, I think his name was,' said Gertie. 'Perhaps we ought to send out a search party.'

'Professor Lars Klausen? The famous physicist?' said Clemmie suddenly.

'I've no idea,' said Gertie. 'Why, do you know him?'

'If he's the same one then yes, of course I know him. Why, everyone has heard of him. Don't you remember? He won the International Prize for physics a couple of years ago, for his work on atomic structures.'

Gertie made a face expressive of an utter lack of interest in atomic structures.

'Oh, but he's brilliant,' said Clemmie enthusiastically. 'Is he really meant to be coming? Why didn't anybody tell me? His theories are absolutely the latest thing.'

'Well it doesn't look as though he's coming now, does it?' said Gertie. 'The road is impassable. Hallo, Mr. Nash,' she said as the others came up. 'Have they set you on to clearing the drive?'

'I can do that if you like, Lady Gertrude,' replied Aubrey Nash pleasantly, 'but first of all, I hear there's a snowman in a state of some embarrassment.'

Gus and Bobby sniggered as Gabe placed a shabby old bonnet from some fifty years earlier on the snow-woman, and they all spent the rest of the morning outside, in a general mood of rising hilarity. After an energetic snowball fight there then began a particularly silly game of tag, involving complicated rules invented by Gertie, during which even Angela found herself giggling like a girl. At lunchtime they all returned to the castle, pink-cheeked and laughing, to find Lord Strathmerrick striding about in the entrance-hall, barking orders to the servants and looking cross. He gave the newcomers an impatient glance and hurried off somewhere.

'What's wrong with Father?' said Gertie when they got into the drawing-room. 'He's not looking too happy.'

'Oh, he's probably cross about the telephone,' replied Lady Strathmerrick. 'It seems the snow has brought the telegraph lines down, and the telephone isn't working.'

'Then we must be completely cut off, I guess,' said Gabe. 'The road is impassable and there is no means of communication from the castle to the outside world.'

'Oh, it's not quite that bad,' said Gertie. 'The road's only impassable by motor-car, but there's a path through the trees behind the castle and it ought to be easy enough to get to the village on foot— especially on skis. It's less than half a mile away, after all. As I said, we've been cut off before and it's never that bad. And I'm sure they'll get the lines fixed soon.'

'It won't be today or tomorrow, though,' said Lady Strathmerrick, 'and I think that's what your father is concerned about. We are still one guest short, remember, and I think he is a little worried that the professor might have got stuck in the snow on the way here.'

Gus and Bobby looked at each other, wide-eyed, but said nothing.

They made a quick luncheon, for the household was busy with preparations for the dance that night, then most of the men disappeared in twos and threes into various rooms, presumably to discuss important matters of state.

'I believe I shall take a turn out of doors,' announced Freddy. 'What could be pleasanter than to be the first to tread in virgin snow? There's something unaccountably satisfying about planting one's feet into a blanket of shining white, hearing the crunch underfoot and looking back at the single trail of crisp footprints that bears witness to one's pioneering spirit. If man ever travels to the moon, I imagine he will feel very much the same.'

Gertie snorted.

'Ass,' she said. 'What time did you get out of bed? The rest of us have been out in the garden all morning and churned all the snow up already. You'll have to go to the West meadow if you don't want to see anyone's footprints but your own.'

'Then I shall go to the West meadow,' said Freddy, unperturbed. He rose and went to put on his boots. Angela bumped into him in the hall just as he came downstairs, and he looked about him mysteriously, put a finger over his lips and drew her into a little recess.

'What have you found out?' he said in a stage-whisper.

Angela was surprised.

'What about?' she said.

'Why, about the secret meeting, of course,' he said.

'Nothing,' she replied.

He clicked his tongue impatiently.

'And you call yourself a detective?' he said.

'I don't, as a matter of fact,' said Angela, but he was not listening and went on:

'This time of year is terribly slow for good stories. I want to find out what's going on here so I've got something for old Bickerstaffe when I get back to the *Clarion* offices. In spite of my astounding successes recently, I'm still considered something of a raw, untried junior, and I want to establish myself firmly in his good books.'

'But if it's something of national importance, ought you to be publishing it in that rag of yours?'

'The *Clarion* is a highly-respected organ,' said Freddy with dignity.

'Of course it is,' said Angela kindly.

'And naturally we wouldn't publish anything that was confidential. But don't you see? This has nothing to do with what appears in the paper. I just want Bickerstaffe to know that whenever something of interest is going on, Frederick Pilkington-Soames Esquire is there on the spot, notebook in hand.'

'Oh, I see,' said Angela. 'You don't care about publishing a story. You're just anxious to cut a dash with your editor by showing him that you know something he doesn't.'

'*Précisément*,' said Freddy. 'And it's for that reason I need your help. You wouldn't want to see the son of your oldest friend lose his job through a dearth of material that was not his fault, now, would you?'

Angela made no comment about his description of Cynthia Pilkington-Soames as her oldest friend.

'But what am I supposed to do?' she said.

'Why, just keep your eyes and ears open, and see what you can find out. Your pal from the Intelligence service would be a good place to start.'

'If you think I am going to try and pump Henry Jameson for information on matters of national security you are very much mistaken,' said Angela. 'Besides, if he knows his job—and I happen to know he does—he will be as close-mouthed as an oyster.'

'Well, then, what about this Nash fellow? You ought to be able to get something out of him for old times' sake, at least.'

'What exactly do you mean by that?' said Angela.

Freddy smirked and tapped his nose.

'I know more than you might think,' he said, then as Angela regarded him with suspicion, continued, 'as does Selma Nash.'

'What?' said Angela. She was not pleased with the turn the conversation had taken.

'Oh, she and Aubrey have no secrets from one another. They are quite the open couple. She knows all about his life before they were married. You were quite friendly with him before he met Selma, weren't you?' He spoke carelessly but there was a mischievous glint in his eye.

'Hmm,' said Angela, who liked her private concerns to remain private. 'That is none of your business. And anyway,' she went on, to detract attention from herself, 'what's all this "Selma"-ing? You've only just met her, and it's already "Selma" this and "Selma" that.' Freddy coughed but did not reply, and Angela shook her head in mock-exasperation. 'How long have you been here?' she said. 'Eighteen hours? That was fast work.'

'Time is immaterial when it comes to the sphere of the human heart,' said Freddy with a sentimental sigh.

'Idiot,' said Angela. 'Isn't one woman at a time enough?'

'Selma is jolly nice. And clever too. Not as nice or as clever as you, of course,' he said, giving her nose a playful tweak.

Lady Strathmerrick happened to be passing in company with Eleanor Buchanan just as he did it. The Countess pursed up her lips when she saw them, but walked on without comment. Angela slapped Freddy's hand away crossly.

'Will you stop it?' she hissed. 'I believe you did that on purpose.'

Freddy opened his eyes wide.

'What an extraordinary suggestion,' he said. He turned and looked after the two women thoughtfully. 'Now, that's another thing we might investigate.'

'What do you mean?' said Angela.

'Eleanor Buchanan. What has she got to be so suspicious about? You must have noticed that tense manner of hers. I wonder what it's all about.'

'I don't know,' said Angela.

'Then we must try and find out. I shall leave that in your capable hands.'

Selma Nash could just then be seen descending the stairs, wrapped up in furs and wearing a pair of thick boots.

'I'm all set,' she called to Freddy.

Freddy bowed.

'Just coming, my lady,' he said, then lowered his voice. 'Go and be nice to Aubrey,' he said. 'I'm sure he'll be overjoyed, and Selma doesn't mind sharing.'

'Freddy, you really are the limit,' said Angela, hardly knowing whether to laugh or frown. Freddy wagged his eyebrows at her.

'Well, it's your decision,' he said. 'Do as you please. In the meantime, we're off to make some footprints in the West meadow.'

He joined Selma and they went out together arm-in-arm.

EIGHT

WHEN FREDDY AND Selma had gone, Angela was left standing in the entrance-hall, wondering what to do with herself. Everyone, it seemed, had disappeared on business of their own, leaving her alone. Priss, Gertie and Clemmie had been pressed into helping set up the ball-room for the dance that evening. Angela briefly contemplated offering to help, but decided that she would be more likely to get in the way than anything else. What to do, then? She looked out through the great double doors of the castle. It was a crisp, bright afternoon and the snow was very tempting. She decided to go out and explore.

A few minutes later she descended the stone steps under the portico and struck out down the drive, with the vague intention of finding a suitable spot from which to gain a good view of the castle. It seemed to her that the best place would be the top of a nearby hill, but between here and her objective the road dipped and rose steeply, and she feared that her way would be blocked by snowdrifts. She tramped through the snow for several minutes, relishing the silence, which was almost complete save for the sound of her own breathing and the crunching of her boots, but soon found that she had been right about the impassability of this route when she unexpectedly sank up to her knees.

'Oh dear,' she murmured, as she extricated herself with difficulty and grimaced at the unpleasant wet and icy sensation that was now intruding itself into her boots. 'Rather foolish of me, really.'

She scrambled back to safety and hobbled over to a nearby tree, where she balanced on one foot at a time and emptied the snow from her boots.

'Perhaps it will be better to keep to the beaten track after all,' she said to herself. 'I don't want to get buried in a snowdrift.'

She made her way back up the drive and onto the lawn, where she caught sight of a figure, swathed in shawls and wearing a rather odd broad-brimmed hat, who was standing and regarding the two snowmen with interest. It was Miss Foster. She looked up as Angela approached.

'Hallo, Mrs. Marchmont,' she said brightly. 'Are you enjoying the snow?' As Angela assented, she went on, 'I am not fond of it myself, but I am a little stuck on my latest chapter, and so I thought a turn in the fresh air might provide food for my imagination.'

'And has it?' said Angela with a smile.

'Not exactly,' said Miss Foster. 'The first thing I saw when I came out was these two snow-figures, which distracted my thoughts from my work and sent my mind wandering down an entirely different path, since they put me in mind of a pair of tragic lovers, doomed to die together under the heat of the sun.'

'I hadn't thought of it like that,' said Angela, 'but I suppose you're right.'

'All very romantic, of course,' said Miss Foster, 'but a little beside the point, since I am at present trying to solve a very different problem. I am trying to think of a way in which my heroine might escape from a locked room without leaving the door open and alerting her captors to her flight.'

'A lock-pick fashioned from a hair-pin?' suggested Angela.

'Yes, I had thought of something similar. Unfortunately, however, in the previous chapter the lady was struck down by a dangerous bout of fever which almost killed her, and therefore had all her hair shorn off, leaving her without the need for hair-pins.'

'I see,' said Angela. 'That's rather inconvenient for the purposes of your story.'

'Yes,' agreed Miss Foster, 'and I can't change the part about the fever because it is essential to the plot and explains why she was unable to meet her lover on the battlements as she promised. He is now under the impression that she has thrown him over for the evil Sir Willoughby Edgerton, and has gone off in despair to fight at Culloden. No,' she went on, 'I believe she will have to escape through the window, even though she is being held at the top of the North tower, one hundred feet above the ground. Perhaps I can have her climb down the ivy.'

'What is the name of your story?' asked Angela politely.

'*Lucinda of the Isles*,' replied Miss Foster. 'It is a historical novel set during the Jacobite Rebellion.'

'And do you hope to have it published?'

Miss Foster gave a genteel little laugh and put her

hand to her mouth.

'Oh, Mrs. Marchmont, you flatter me,' she said. 'I am a mere amateur. I don't deny that it is a dream of mine one day to see my works in print, but that day is far in the future. My talents and skills are simply not up to the task at the moment.'

'Does no-one read your stories, then?' asked Angela, and immediately bit her lip, suddenly fearful that Miss Foster would take the opportunity to press one of her works upon her with an exhortation to read it. But Miss Foster did not appear to have such a thing in mind.

'Oh, yes, I do have a select group of friends who read what I write, and for whom I return the favour,' she said.

'A kind of writers' circle, do you mean?' said Angela.

'Yes,' beamed Miss Foster. 'That's exactly it. We communicate by correspondence, mostly, although once or twice a year we do meet for an evening of literature and poetry, with perhaps a glass or two of home-made elderberry wine. No more than that, though,' she finished, wagging her finger playfully.

'Naturally,' said Angela, suppressing a shudder at the thought of home-made elderberry wine. 'And do you criticize each other's work?'

'Oh yes,' said Miss Foster. 'That is an essential part of the arrangement. Each of us agrees to complete one chapter every month. We then send it to another member of the circle, who reads it and gives a considered opinion on the chapter itself and its place in the story as a whole.'

'What sort of people are in the circle? Are you all women?'

'Not at all. As a matter of fact, the idea was thought up by a man. Mr. Adams runs a small publishing house in London, and he began the circle with the idea of helping aspiring authors polish their talents, and perhaps become good enough one day to be published.'

'I see. I would say that that was very kind-hearted of him, but I should imagine he has another motive too,' said Angela with a smile. 'No doubt it is of benefit to him to watch over your progress—for then he may get some new books to publish.'

'Indeed, you are right,' said Miss Foster. 'However, even if nothing happens in my case, it is an enormous privilege to receive criticism from such an expert.' She gave a little sigh, and went on, 'It's a pity the snow is so deep. My latest chapter is almost ready to send off. No matter, though—perhaps I can make some changes in the meantime.'

The sound of loud, childish voices was heard in the distance just then, and the two women turned to see Gus and Bobby running towards them, carrying an odd assortment of objects.

'We're a search party,' announced Gus breathlessly in reply to Miss Foster's inquiry. 'We're going to hunt for Professor Klausen. He's got lost.'

'I dare say he's buried in a snowdrift somewhere,' said Bobby. 'He's probably freezing to death. We're going to rescue him before he gets encased in the ice like a woolly mammoth.'

'Goodness,' said Angela. 'We don't want that, do we?'

'Don't you think it's more likely that the professor saw the weather and decided to remain at home rather than try to get to Fives Castle?' said Miss

Foster more practically.

'It's possible, I suppose,' said Gus doubtfully, 'but it's probably best to make sure.'

'Would you like to come, Mrs. Marchmont?' said Bobby, who had taken rather a liking to Angela.

'Why, I should love to,' said Angela, judging that she had better tag along in order to make sure the boys did not get into any difficulties.

'Oh, good,' said Gus. 'We've got all the equipment we need, I think.'

'So I see,' said Angela, trying not to laugh, for the boys were indeed laden with the most extraordinary assortment of tools and ironmongery. Gus had a length of rope coiled around his waist and held a torch in one hand and a coal shovel in the other, while Bobby carried a hammer, some nails and an axe. 'Why do you need a hammer?' she said.

'Once we've dug him out we'll need to build him a shelter,' Bobby explained. 'We'll cut some wood with the axe and build a den for him. I've got some matches in my pocket too, so we can light a fire.'

'The snow is very deep,' said Angela. 'You'll have trouble keeping your balance with your hands full like that. Suppose you leave some of it behind. We can come back for it if we need it, but you'll need your wits about you for a while and it won't help if you're loaded down.'

The boys were eventually persuaded to leave behind everything but the rope, the torch and the matches, and they prepared to begin. Miss Foster murmured something about being expected by Lady Strathmerrick and returned to the castle.

'Which way shall we go?' said Angela. 'I suppose the obvious place to search is along the drive, but I tried to go that way a few minutes ago and got stuck. We'd need skis to search properly in that direction. Shall we try somewhere else first?'

Gus thought for a moment.

'There's the path through the woods,' he said. 'It goes to the village. He might have come that way, I suppose, but wouldn't he have had a motor-car if he was coming from London?'

'He might have left it in the village and done the last half-a-mile on foot,' suggested Bobby.

At length it was agreed that they would try that way first, and they set off. The path led through a tunnel of bare-branched trees which was bounded by a fence on one side and a dark, rushing stream on the other, and their progress was delayed for some minutes as the boys occupied themselves with throwing sticks into the water and trying to overturn an interesting-looking rock.

'Look out for signs,' said Gus as they reluctantly moved on. 'He might have tied his handkerchief to a fence-post, or left a trail of breadcrumbs. That's what I should do if I were lost in the snow.'

'There's no use in looking for footprints, anyhow,' said Bobby. 'Why, this whole path has already been trampled all over by people coming from the village to help get things ready for this evening.'

'That's true enough,' said Gus, staring in disgust at the many sets of footprints which indicated that a steady stream of people had passed towards the castle that day. 'They've ruined any chance we might have had of finding the professor's tracks.'

'And wouldn't someone have found him by now if he'd come along this way?' said Bobby. They stopped and stared at each other uncertainly.

'Perhaps we ought to try somewhere else, then,' said Gus.

'Oh, but look,' said Angela, who had seen something just ahead. She pointed.

'Oh!' said Bobby. 'Footprints!'

In this particular spot the stream moved away from the path to take a sharp detour around a large alder tree. Most of the footprints continued straight along the footpath towards the castle, but one set broke away and crossed the snow towards the stream.

The three of them gazed at the marks. Judging by the size of them, they had been made by a man.

'Look,' said Angela. 'They continue on the other side of the stream. He must have tramped about a bit here while he held onto the tree for balance and used that rock as a stepping-stone.'

The boys were excited.

'It must be the professor!' exclaimed Bobby.

'And look, he fell in the stream!' said Gus. He pointed to the other bank. There, the mess of tracks did indeed indicate that whoever it was had jumped from the snow-covered rock to the other side and then slipped backwards into the water.

'He must have got soaked,' said Angela.

Bobby snorted.

'What a duffer,' he said, and before Angela could stop him, leapt lightly onto the stepping-stone and then to the other side of the stream. Gus followed.

'I don't know if I can do that,' said Angela, in some embarrassment. 'I'm not as sure-footed as you two.'

'Oh, but it's easy,' Bobby assured her, jumping back and forth several times to demonstrate.

'I could tie the rope to this tree here and throw it

across to you, in case you lose your balance,' suggested Gus, after a moment's thought.

Angela agreed to this, and Gus immediately fastened one end of the rope to a sturdy-looking tree that overhung the water.

'There,' he said. 'That's fast enough. Now, look out.'

He threw the line across the stream to Angela, who caught it and, taking a deep breath, sprang as lightly as she could onto the stepping-stone, and then to the other bank without mishap.

'You see, you didn't need it after all,' said Bobby kindly. 'If you got a little more practice you could do it as easily as we do.'

'I dare say you're right,' said Angela. 'Now, which way did he go?' She did not suppose for a second that the tracks really did belong to Professor Klausen, but she was caught up in the game now and was curious to know where they led.

'This way,' said Gus, who was busy coiling the rope around his waist again.

On this side of the stream the woods grew more thickly, shutting out much of the light—which in any case was starting to fade as the afternoon advanced. Here and there the ground was less thickly covered or even bare where the snow had been unable to penetrate through the trees, but even so, it was still easy enough to follow the tracks of their mysterious quarry. In some places the footprints headed one way only to turn back on themselves after a few yards as the man came up against an impassable thicket or other obstacle, but always they headed in the same general direction: towards Fives Castle.

'I wonder why he came this way rather than

keeping to the path,' said Bobby.

Angela thought the tracks most likely belonged to a poacher or someone of the sort, but she merely said, 'Perhaps he had a fancy to take a more circuitous route to the castle, in order to get a better view of the place before he arrived.'

Bobby looked unconvinced.

'But the best view is from the other side of the stream,' he said. 'You can't see anything from the wood.'

This was true enough, and Angela was forced to admit her theory was unlikely.

'I think the professor got lost in the dark,' said Gus. 'It would have been pitch-black last night, and he might easily have wandered away from the path.'

'I don't think the dark is to blame,' said Angela. 'These footprints were made after it stopped snowing—and most likely some time today. Didn't you notice that they were on top of all the other tracks back there? That means whoever it was came along the path after all those other people who were heading for the castle.'

'Oh, yes,' said Bobby. He looked at her, impressed. 'That's rather clever of you, Mrs. Marchmont. I should never have thought of that.'

'It's starting to get dark,' said Gus. 'We'd better get a move on if we want to find the professor and get back in time for tea.'

They tramped on through the trees. After a short while the woods began to thin, and soon afterwards they came out into a meadow and saw the castle, standing proudly before them on the ridge of the next hill. It was certainly a grand sight. The snow was deep again now that there was no shelter, and it was easy enough to follow the footprints. They led around the edge of the wood to a little hut, which was secured with a rusty bolt.

'Look!' said Bobby. 'He must have tried to get in.'

'Didn't manage it, though,' said Gus, glancing at the tracks, which led off again across the meadow.

'No,' said Angela. 'This bolt is rusted solid.'

'What's that on the ground?' said Bobby suddenly. 'It looks like blood.'

'So it does,' said Gus excitedly. 'Perhaps he's desperately injured.'

'Hardly,' said Angela, as she regarded the two or three red spots at her feet. 'There's not enough blood for that. I think he probably just grazed his hand trying to draw the bolt back.'

'Oh,' said Gus, disappointed.

'Still, though, I imagine he was in a bad enough mood, after falling into the water and then skinning his knuckles,' said Angela, by way of consolation. 'At any rate, we know now that he passed this way very recently. Those bloodstains are quite fresh.'

'So they are,' said Gus. 'Let's hurry. Perhaps we can catch him up.'

They pressed on, moving quickly now in excitement, for they sensed they were about to find the object of their quest. The tracks headed on doggedly in a straight line towards Fives Castle, and for some way they were the only footprints to be seen. After fifty yards or so, however, the trail was crossed by two other sets of prints, which led off together into the distance, away from the castle. Bobby tramped over to look at them.

'I wonder who this is,' he said. 'Look—one set is much smaller than the other.'

'Probably a man and a woman, then,' said Gus.

'Where are we?' said Angela suddenly.

'In the West meadow,' said Bobby.

'Ah,' said Angela.

'Let's see,' said Gus. He followed the new tracks for a little distance, then bent to examine them. 'They stopped here and turned to face each other,' he said. 'They must have been standing jolly close together.'

'Perhaps one of them had something in his eye, and the other one was helping him get it out,' said Angela. 'Shall we get back to the professor? I don't think these two need rescuing, and anyway it will be dark soon, so if we want to find him we'd better hurry.'

Gus ran back to join them and they carried on. After a few minutes, however, it became clear that their hunt had been unsuccessful, for they now found themselves very close to the castle and here, to their dismay, they lost the trail as it merged with hundreds of other footprints, which flattened down the snow and turned it into a grey, sodden mush.

'What a waste of time,' said Bobby grumpily. 'We've followed him all this way and he made it to the castle without us.'

Angela was thankful to be back, for her feet were cold and wet and she was thinking longingly of hot tea and buttered muffins. The three of them went inside to find Lord Strathmerrick standing in the entrance-hall with Henry Jameson. The Earl gazed vaguely at his sons and eventually seemed to remember who they were.

'We've been tracking Professor Klausen,' burst out Bobby, still full of their quest, 'but he got here before we did.'

The two men glanced at each other in surprise.

'Did he?' said Lord Strathmerrick. 'Good Lord, why did nobody tell me?' He accosted a passing manservant. 'Robert, at what time did Professor Klausen arrive?'

'He hasnae arrived yet, my lord,' replied the man. 'At least, not as far as I know.'

'Oh,' said Gus, disconcerted. 'Then whose footprints were we following?'

'I haven't the faintest idea,' said the Earl, 'but you had better go and wash before tea, or your mother will have something to say to you.'

The boys ran off, arguing loudly about where the professor had got to, and Angela went upstairs to change her things and warm her toes by the fire. She had enjoyed their little adventure, but was pretty sure that whoever they had been following, it was not the professor.

NINE

WHEN ANGELA ENTERED the ball-room after an early
dinner she found that Gertie and her sisters really had
been hard at work preparing for the dance, for the
whole place was brilliantly lit and decorated with
garlands of fir-cones, wreaths and ribbons, while a
great Christmas tree stood in the far corner, glittering
and twinkling with shiny ornaments, bows and bells.
Someone had brought in the bad-tempered-looking
stag's head from the hall and had hung it on the wall
with a hat placed jauntily on one of its antlers, and a
big, hand-written sign that said '1928!' hung round its
neck. It glared balefully around, as though daring
anyone to laugh. Around the sides of the room long
tables had been set, at which perhaps a hundred
people sat in a great state of merriment and high
spirits. They were evidently full of food and good
cheer and were now waiting for the dance to begin.

'Where did you disappear to this afternoon?' said a
voice at Angela's ear. It was Freddy.

'I have been on the trail of a missing man,' she said

mysteriously.

'Oh yes? Whom?'

'Professor Klausen.'

'And did you find him?'

'No, but I got jolly cold and wet in the meantime.' She explained about the footprints, and went on, 'I imagine they were made by a poacher, but I hadn't the heart to tell the boys—they were having so much fun, you see. And what about you? Did you have a nice walk with Selma?'

'Yes, it was most pleasant,' he replied, looking insufferably smug, 'but don't tell me you're jealous?'

Angela opened her mouth to squash him but just then there was a great commotion as the musicians began tuning their instruments and all the visitors rose to their feet as one.

'Let's go and dance,' said Freddy, taking her hand.

'Oh, very well,' said Angela, although she was not really as reluctant as she sounded, since she had rather been looking forward to this evening.

Very soon the fiddles were playing and the dance was in full swing and everyone was enjoying themselves hugely—or at least giving the appearance of it: Priss, it was true, had something of a glazed look on her face as she danced with one young farm-hand after another and tried to pretend she didn't mind it, while Lady Strathmerrick displayed the permanently wrinkled brow of a woman who was certain something was about to go wrong. All in all, however, the party was a success. Gertie danced a hilarious jig with a bewhiskered old-timer who was determined to prove he could shake a leg as well as any youngster, while Gus and Bobby, partnered with each other, joined enthusiastically in an eightsome reel. The company was riotous and the noise deafening. Angela danced with everyone who asked her, until she was quite tired out and had to go and sit down at one of the tables to get her breath back. Henry Jameson, her partner at the time, joined her, and despite her assurances to Freddy, she could not resist trying to get some information out of him.

Accordingly, she began by telling him of her adventure with Gus and Bobby that afternoon, laughing at the idea of the professor's getting buried in a snowdrift. To her surprise, however, he seemed remarkably interested in the story of the footprints, and questioned her closely about them.

'Why, you don't think it really was Professor Klausen, do you?' said Angela.

'No, no, I don't imagine it was,' he replied. 'I was just intrigued by your adventure, that's all.' He seemed inclined to change the subject, but Angela was not so easily put off. She glanced at him sideways.

'I suppose you're not going to tell me why you're *really* here, are you?' she said. Henry Jameson raised his eyebrows at her, but said nothing. 'No, I thought not,' she went on. 'You can't fool me, though. I know there's something going on. Why are all you men so concerned about this professor? I've heard you muttering together in corners about him and seen you looking at your watches. He's important, isn't he?'

Henry hesitated.

'Do you know who he is?' he said cautiously.

'Clemmie seems to think he's a famous scientist who is going to revolutionize our knowledge of how atoms work. But to be perfectly frank,' she went on confidentially, 'I don't have any knowledge to revolutionize. I gather it's all very abstruse.'

'Yes, it is,' he said. 'I don't pretend to understand it myself.'

'But he is not coming to Fives just to dance a reel, is he? And neither have you, for that matter.'

'No,' he agreed. Their eyes met in understanding, and he smiled. 'Let us just say that I shall be very relieved when Professor Klausen turns up,' he said, and would say no more on the subject.

He went off to dance with Eleanor Buchanan, and Angela remained seated. Freddy was dancing with Selma Nash. They appeared to be enjoying one another's company immensely.

'You haven't danced with me yet, Angela,' said Aubrey Nash, who had just then appeared at her side. She smiled her acquiescence and he led her to the floor. Freddy saw them and gave her a wink, which she ignored. Afterwards, Aubrey followed her out into the passage and lit cigarettes for them both. She leaned against the wall and smoked, her arms folded across her body, not looking at him. He regarded her intently.

'You're looking very well, Angela,' he said. 'It's been a long time, hasn't it?'

Angela agreed that it had indeed been a long time.

'Funny how things turn out,' he said ruminatively. 'Who would have thought that Selma and I would have got married? Or that you would have married that fellow whatshisname?'

'Quite,' said Angela dryly.

Aubrey cleared his throat.

'I guess he's not on the scene any more. That young man of yours, Freddy—' he paused.

'He's not my young man,' said Angela. 'What on earth gave you that idea?'

'Why, the way you flirt with him.'

'Everyone flirts with Freddy, and Freddy flirts with everyone,' repeated Angela smiling, as she remembered what Gertie had said earlier. 'Don't be ridiculous, Aubrey. I can assure you he's not my young man.'

'That's a good thing, then, seeing how he and Selma are getting along so well. I don't mind, you know,' he said as he saw her glance up. 'Selma and I—well, we have an understanding.'

'I see,' said Angela warily. They looked at each other in silence for a moment, then he moved a little closer and raised his hand slowly as though to stroke her hair.

What would have happened next if Lady Strathmerrick had not emerged from the ball-room just then and come upon them is a matter for conjecture. Angela once again felt herself blushing furiously as the Countess stopped dead and opened her eyes wide.

'Lady Strathmerrick,' said Aubrey smoothly. 'Why, I've been looking for you everywhere. We still haven't danced yet.'

He took her arm and bore her off into the ball-room, leaving Angela in a state of great perturbation for various reasons—not least, the fact that once again she had made a fool of herself in front of her hostess. Aubrey, too—now that was something she had not bargained for. She hoped he was not going to be difficult.

'This is all getting rather awkward,' she said to herself.

It was now approaching midnight, and things were getting a little out of hand in the ball-room as the mood of hilarity increased. As the clock began to chime, servants, tenants and house guests alike counted down in chorus, then there were loud cheers as the bells in the castle chapel rang out to mark the passing of the old year and the start of the new one. There was much raucous singing of Auld Lang Syne, followed by a solemn speech from Lord Strathmerrick which nobody listened to much, and then the ball-room began to clear as those who had come from outside set out to brave the snow, which had begun to fall thickly again, and the servants retired to their beds to sleep off an excess of cold meat, hot punch and unaccustomed exercise.

At last only the family and their guests remained behind, and one by one they returned to the drawing-room, which was mercifully cool and peaceful after the heat and deafening noise of the past few hours. Miss Foster stayed for only a few minutes and then excused herself, saying that she was really very tired, and Clemmie followed suit shortly afterwards. Lady Strathmerrick, too, was stifling her yawns but was clearly too polite to leave given that most of her guests showed no signs of flagging. Fortunately, Gertie took pity on her mother and packed her off, assuring her that nobody would be in the slightest bit offended if she went to bed. The Earl and Henry Jameson went into the study and the Buchanans and the Nashes sat down to play whist, while Priss and Freddy whispered and giggled together in a corner. Claude Burford was nowhere to be seen, but was presumed to have gone to bed.

'I'm bored,' announced Gertie suddenly. 'Let's play a game.'

'Words to strike fear into the very soul of every

right-thinking man and woman in England,' remarked Freddy. 'When Lady Gertrude McAloon of the noble house of Strathmerrick suggests playing a game, you can be sure that chaos will shortly ensue. I hope you have a fire-engine standing by at the very least, and preferably also a brigade of infantrymen.'

'What nonsense you do talk,' said Gertie. 'I propose Sardines.'

'Sardines! Sardines!' said Gus and Bobby together. They were in a great state of excitement at having been allowed to stay up with the rest of the house. Their enthusiasm was infectious, and soon Priss, Freddy, Angela and Gabe Bradley had been persuaded to join the game.

'Splendid,' said Gertie in satisfaction. 'I shall hide first. Give me five minutes and then come and look for me. I shall be in one of the downstairs rooms.'

She went out with a wicked glint in her eye, carrying something with her. The others waited five minutes as instructed, and then left the drawing-room in pursuit.

'We're supposed to split up,' said Bobby, seeing that Freddy and Priss were inclined to stick together.

'I'm no good at finding people,' said Priss. 'I need Freddy to help me.'

Bobby scowled at this unfair advantage, but soon spotted a likely hiding-place and ran off to look into it. Everyone else drifted off in different directions and Angela soon found herself alone. It was cold in the passage and she shivered, regretting her initial enthusiasm. She thought she would go and fetch a wrap from her room. As she reached the landing, she saw Claude Burford ahead of her, emerging from one of the bedrooms. He did not see her, but crossed the corridor and entered another bedroom. A second or two afterwards, another person came out of the first bedroom and walked towards the stairs.

'Oh, Mrs. Marchmont,' said Eleanor Buchanan, looking slightly flustered as she spotted Angela. 'I was just coming to fetch my cigarettes.' She held up a cigarette-case and hurried downstairs, leaving Angela to stare after her, open-mouthed. Of all the least likely things to happen, Claude Burford and Eleanor Buchanan together seemed to win the prize. Angela fetched her shawl and ran back downstairs, still shaking her head in wonder.

Now, where was Gertie? Angela glanced into one or two rooms but saw nothing that would be a suitable place to hide several people. She thought for a moment and then headed for the billiard-room, as she vaguely remembered it to contain one or two large pieces of furniture that might do. Sure enough, when she entered the dimly-lit room she heard a muffled giggle, followed by a 'Shh!' Against the right-hand wall stood a large oak chest, and for a moment she thought Gertie must be hiding inside it, but then a loud creak emanated from a battered old cupboard in the corner. Angela went across to it.

'Hallo?' she said, as she opened the door. Gertie and Gus were sitting there, among a mess of billiard-cues and tennis-shoes, in a state of suppressed merriment. Gertie was holding a bottle.

'Quick! Get in!' she hissed. Angela moved a tennis racquet to one side and squeezed in beside them. 'Now we all have to take another drink,' said Gertie. She put the bottle to her lips and suited the action to the word.

'What is it?' said Angela.

'Father's best whisky,' Gertie replied, handing the bottle to Gus, who took a gulp and grimaced. 'Don't tell him, will you?'

'Ought you to be drinking?' said Angela to Gus, out of a vague sense of duty.

'Oh, it won't do him any harm,' said Gertie, and pulled the door shut. Angela duly took a turn with the bottle, and they sat there in the pitch-darkness, silent except for an occasional shove and hissed protest on the part of Gus or Gertie. Before cramp had quite set in they were discovered and joined by Gabe Bradley, who had already had more to drink than he was accustomed to and was inclined to loll. They all took another gulp of the whisky at Gertie's urging. Gabe whispered something into Gertie's ear and she squealed and giggled. There was a sound as of a hand being slapped away. Gus hiccupped. Angela began to regret not having played whist instead.

After what seemed like an age, during which it was thought only polite to pass around the bottle several times, Freddy and Priss found them.

'Are we the last?' said Freddy.

'No, we still haven't got Bobby,' said Gertie. 'Hop in and have a drink.'

They did so. The cupboard now held six people and was becoming very stifling and uncomfortable.

'I feel sick,' announced Gus. There was a sudden movement as everyone tried to shuffle out of his way.

'Have you been drinking?' said Priss. 'Gertie, you idiot, why on earth did you let him have the whisky?'

'It's Hogmanay,' said Gertie defensively. 'It was only a bit of fun.'

'You'd better get out, old chap,' said Freddy.

'No!' whispered Gertie. 'Listen!' They fell silent;

someone had come into the room. 'It must be Bobby.'

They listened as the newcomer paused for a moment, seemingly out of breath. There was a soft thud followed by a creak. Bobby must be looking inside the oak chest first. Then came a rustle and a grunt, then another thud, this time louder, and they heard the sound of the chest lid being shut gently. Instead of throwing open the cupboard doors, however, Bobby then evidently left the room, for they heard the door shut quietly.

Suddenly an unpleasant noise emanated from Gus.

'I'm going to be sick,' he said, and burst out of the cupboard. The other hiders unfolded themselves carefully and emerged too, treading carefully around the unfortunate young heir of Strathmerrick, who was now depositing the remains of his dinner on the floor.

'You can clear that up,' said Priss to Gertie in distaste. 'It was your fault.'

Gertie, feeling rather guilty, patted her brother's head gingerly as he groaned, and looked in the cupboard for some suitable rags to wipe the mess up with. Just then the door opened again and Bobby came in.

'There you are,' he said indignantly. 'I've been searching for simply *ages*. Am I the last?' He stopped, realizing that something had happened. 'What's wrong with Gus?'

'He—er—ate something that disagreed with him,' said Freddy. 'You'd better get him to bed.'

Bobby was persuaded to escort his older brother away, and Priss and Gertie went off to fetch a mop and bucket, arguing crossly, leaving Freddy and Angela to stay or go as they pleased. Freddy stretched experimentally.

'That cupboard was jolly uncomfortable,' he said. 'I say, where has Gabe got to?' A snore revealed that Gabe Bradley had fallen asleep where he sat. 'Angela, shall we lock him in?'

'What?' said Angela vaguely. She was not thinking about Gabe. She crossed the room and lifted the heavy lid of the oak chest. She stood there in silence, staring down at what it contained.

'What on earth are you doing?' said Freddy.

She turned to look at him, the lid still open in her hand.

'I think I've found Professor Klausen,' she said.

TEN

FREDDY JOINED HER and looked into the chest. There, resting on a heap of blankets, was the body of a man. He was youngish and slightly built, with a moustache and fair hair that had begun to thin at the temples.

'Is he dead?' said Freddy.

'I should imagine so,' said Angela, pointing to the bloodstain which had spread out around a hole in the centre of the man's chest, and which looked rather like a dark wax seal. She rested the heavy hinged lid of the chest carefully against the wall, then reached in and felt for a pulse. She shook her head.

Freddy gazed at the dead man dispassionately.

'Are you sure it's the professor?' he said. 'Do you know him?'

'No, but it seems the logical conclusion to draw.'

'We'd better fetch Lord Strathmerrick,' he said, 'although I don't relish the thought of getting him out of bed at this hour.'

'He was in the study with Henry Jameson earlier,'

said Angela. 'Perhaps they're still there. Why don't you go and see?'

He went off and Angela was left alone in the dim room, gazing down at the dead man and thinking very hard. He was dressed in outdoor clothes and a pair of thick boots. Who had put him in the chest? And why had they killed him? Struck by an idea, she reached down and carefully felt in his pockets.

'Where is everybody?' said a slurred and sleepy voice behind her. Angela gave a little shriek and whirled around, then put a hand to her heart as she realized that it was only Gabe Bradley, who had evidently just woken up. He extricated himself with difficulty from the cupboard and looked about him in a dazed fashion.

'Everyone's gone to bed,' said Angela. 'Perhaps you ought to go too.'

'Maybe you're right,' he said. 'I don't feel so good.'

'A good night's sleep and you'll feel as right as rain in the morning,' she lied cheerfully.

'I guess so. Goodnight, then,' he said, and went off, staggering slightly and seemingly having no curiosity as to why Mrs. Marchmont had been ferreting about in an old chest.

Angela's head was spinning a little too after all the whisky, but she turned back to the object of her investigation. The man was lying on his back with his knees bent—presumably to allow him to fit into the chest, since it was not quite big enough for him to lie stretched out. Grimacing, Angela took hold of his right ankle and lifted his leg. It unbent easily, and she spent a minute or two examining the sole of his boot, then lowered the leg gently back into the chest. As an afterthought she looked at his hands too, and shook her head slightly.

When Freddy returned with Lord Strathmerrick and Henry Jameson, they found her standing by the window looking out.

'It's stopped snowing,' she said as they came in. 'I hope it's not too thick to get through to the village and fetch the police.'

'That might not be a problem for the moment,' said Henry Jameson, crossing the room to look inside the chest. 'Yes, that's him all right.'

Lord Strathmerrick joined him and the two men stared at the body. The Earl looked grave.

'I don't suppose he still has—?' he said quietly, throwing a significant look at the Intelligence man.

Henry bent down and felt in the man's pockets, then shook his head. The men exchanged glances, and the Earl cleared his throat.

'I—er—understand you were all engaged in some sort of game,' he said, then wrinkled his nose. 'What is that smell?' he said. 'Has somebody been sick?'

'It was Gus,' said Freddy. 'He ate something that disagreed with him. The poor little chap has gone to bed. Where are Gertie and Priss? They were supposed to bring some hot water to clean it up.'

'I saw them going upstairs a few minutes ago,' said Henry. 'They seemed to be going to bed.'

'Well, of all the—' said Freddy.

'Yes, yes, well, never mind that for the present,' said Lord Strathmerrick. 'I should like to know who put this body here. I understand you were all hiding in the cupboard. Did you see anything at all?'

Angela, uncomfortably conscious that women of her age did not generally hide in cupboards drinking whisky out of the bottle, blushed a little.

'We heard him come in,' she said. 'We thought it was Bobby and so we all kept very quiet. Whoever it was sounded as though he were carrying something heavy. He opened the chest, dumped his burden into it and then went out.'

'And you have no idea who it was?' said Henry.

Angela and Freddy shook their heads.

'Can this room be locked?' said Jameson. He went to the door. 'Ah, yes, I see there's a key here.' He turned to Angela and Freddy. 'Very well, there's nothing any of us can do at present. It's past two o'clock and I imagine you must both be tired, so I advise you to go to bed. I understand the telephone is still out of order, and as you so rightly say, Mrs. Marchmont, it will be difficult to get to the village with the snow lying so thickly, so I suggest we leave things as they are for now and try to decide what to do tomorrow morning. In the meantime, I shall lock this door so nobody can get in.'

Angela recognized the voice of authority when she heard it, and smiled, for at that moment Henry Jameson reminded her very much of his brother.

'Very well,' she said. 'We shall leave things in your hands.'

'And please,' added Henry as Angela and Freddy went out, 'don't say a word to anyone about this. I imagine the news will get out soon enough, but I'd rather it didn't come from either of you.'

They promised not to say anything and went off, leaving the billiard-room in the charge of Henry Jameson and Lord Strathmerrick.

'Do you suppose they'll clear up Gus's mess?' said Freddy as they emerged into the hall. Angela was about to go upstairs but he put a hand on her arm to stop her. 'Where are you going?'

'Why, to bed, of course,' said Angela. 'It's late and I'm very tired and—quite frankly—a little on the squiffy side after all that whisky.'

'Never mind that,' said Freddy. 'Come and compare notes.'

She followed him reluctantly into the drawing-room, which was quite empty and lit only by the dying embers of the fire. He switched on a lamp and sat down.

'Now, tell me what you found out from the body,' he said. 'Don't tell me you didn't take a good look at it when I went out, because I shan't believe you.'

'I didn't find out anything much,' she said. 'I did take a look, but I was only trying to find out whether the professor was the mysterious man whose footprints the boys and I followed this afternoon.'

'And was he?'

'No,' she said.

'Can you be certain of that?'

'I think so, yes. The professor had fairly small feet and the soles of his boots were straight-ridged, whereas the footprints we were following this afternoon had a criss-cross pattern and were much larger, and the right boot looked as though it had a nail or something stuck in it. Our quarry this afternoon must also have had a graze or a cut on his hand from a rusty bolt, but the professor had nothing of the sort.'

'So who was the man you followed?' said Freddy thoughtfully.

'I don't suppose he was anyone of interest at all,' said Angela. 'There's no reason to assume he has anything to do with this business. What I should like to know, however, is: when did the professor get here and what happened to him after he did? He must have arrived this evening—probably during the dance, or surely he would have made himself known.'

'We don't know that he didn't,' said Freddy. 'The servants might have seen him—or even one of the guests.'

'Well, he obviously never got a chance to pay his respects to Lord Strathmerrick before someone took a pot-shot at him,' said Angela.

'It seems not,' said Freddy. He felt in his pockets. 'Damn—I seem to have left my notebook upstairs.'

'You're not going to write a story?'

'Of course I'm going to write a story,' he said. 'Why, the man was world-famous. This is going to be the most enormous scoop for me—once they let me publish it, at any rate.'

Angela had not thought of it in this light. Naturally the death of the eminent Professor Klausen would be big news.

'Dear me,' she said. 'After all the trouble he took to keep the meeting quiet, Mr. Jameson must be feeling pretty sick that the professor has gone and got himself murdered. The papers will be dying to know what was going on here at Fives Castle.'

'So they will,' said Freddy. 'You are going to help me find out, aren't you?'

'We'll see,' said Angela. 'At present all I want is to go to bed.' She stood up.

'I did think Priss might wait up,' said Freddy wistfully.

Angela made an impatient noise.

'Am I imagining things, or is everybody in this house misbehaving except for me?' she said.

Freddy glanced at her sideways.

'If you feel inclined to throw yourself into the fray at all, do let me know. I'm always happy to oblige,' he said lightly.

'Don't be ridiculous, Freddy, I'm not *that* drunk,' she said, and went out.

'Crushed again,' said Freddy to the empty room. He finished his cigarette and then decided to go and risk a knock on Priss's door.

ELEVEN

'BUT THIS IS terrible,' said Aubrey Nash.

'It most certainly is,' said Lord Strathmerrick soberly.

It was early on New Year's day and Aubrey, the Earl, Henry Jameson and Sandy Buchanan had gathered in the billiard-room to discuss what to do next. They all looked very tired: the Ambassador and the Foreign Secretary had been roused from their beds after only a few short hours' sleep, while Jameson and Lord Strathmerrick had not been to bed at all. The unfortunate Professor Klausen was still in the chest, since nobody could decide where else to put him; besides, rigor mortis had now set in and it would be difficult to extricate him for a while without causing damage to the body. The lid had been lowered to give him decent concealment, and the men did their best to ignore the presence of the chest, although nobody could resist darting the occasional glance at it.

'How did it happen? We were waiting for him.

How come somebody got to him first?' said Aubrey.

'We don't know,' said Henry Jameson. 'We've spoken to the servants, and nobody saw him arrive. It's pretty clear he had only recently got here, though, given that he was still wearing his overcoat and boots when he died.'

'He must have arrived during the dance,' said Sandy Buchanan. 'It would have been easy enough to sneak in then without anybody seeing him. I suppose that was his intention—to arrive without any fanfare. Drat his secretiveness! If he'd only let us know he'd got here, he might be alive now.'

'I suppose the fellow who did it has escaped now,' said the Ambassador. 'He must have done it and then slipped out unseen and escaped through the snow.'

'I'm not so sure of that,' said Henry. 'It was snowing rather heavily when the dance ended, and all the villagers went off home very quickly. The snow had stopped by the time the body was discovered. Now, I went out at first light and couldn't find any tracks leading along the path to the village. Of course, he might have gone in a different direction, but the drive is pretty well impassable as you know, and most of the other ways out would have required him to wade through deep snow across the meadows, or to find his way through the woods in the pitch-black.'

'Might he have escaped along the village path while it was still snowing?' said Buchanan. 'His tracks would have been covered then.'

'I don't think so,' said Jameson. 'I followed the path as far as I could, but had to turn back as I came up against an obstacle: the snow has brought down a tree and a good deal of earth from the bank on one side of the path. Quite a landslide, in fact. I spoke to one of the groundsmen, and he knew all about it—said that one or two stragglers from the party had been trying to get home just after one o'clock but had found the fallen tree and had had to come back to the castle. Now, since most of the people who passed along that way last night must have done so shortly after midnight, I think we can assume that the landslide happened some time between then and one o'clock. However, according to Mrs. Marchmont and Mr. Pilkington-Soames, it was well after two o'clock when our mystery person came into the room while they were hiding in the cupboard, and presumably deposited Klausen in this chest. By that time the path to the village was blocked.'

'Are you saying that he is still here at Fives Castle?' said the Earl.

'I think there's a good chance of it, yes,' said Henry.

'Then we must start a search immediately,' said Aubrey Nash. 'If what you say is true, Jameson, then we are quite cut off, so if we hurry we may catch him before he escapes with the plans.'

Sandy Buchanan had been regarding Henry Jameson with a shrewd expression, and now he spoke up.

'Are you quite sure it *was* an outsider, Jameson?' he said.

Henry turned to him with a smile of understanding.

'Not necessarily, although we can't say it wasn't either,' he replied, and repeated what Angela had told him about her, Gus and Bobby's adventure of the day before.

'I see,' said Buchanan thoughtfully. 'So someone

came to the castle yesterday and took a somewhat circuitous and complicated route when he might have easily come straight along the path. Presumably, then, whoever it was wanted to avoid being seen.'

'I dare say it was Klausen himself,' said Lord Strathmerrick. 'I shall question the boys and ask them to describe the tracks. If their description matches that of Klausen's boots then we know it was probably him. I won't ask Mrs. Marchmont, as we don't want her to suspect that there might be a connection between this business and that of the footprints.'

'I'd be surprised if she doesn't already suspect it,' said Henry. 'She's no fool.'

'Look here, Jameson,' said Sandy Buchanan. 'What do we really know about this Marchmont woman? You tell me she worked for Intelligence during the war, but how can we be sure that she hasn't changed sides in the meantime? I mean, don't you think it's rather odd that she happened to get herself invited here just now, at a time when things are all supposed to be hush-hush?'

'She's meant to be a friend of Gertie's,' said Lord Strathmerrick, 'but as far as I can tell, they only met a couple of months ago, through this Pilkington-Soames fellow. Are you suggesting that she scraped the acquaintance in order to get invited here?'

'I shouldn't be a bit surprised,' said Buchanan. 'It would be easy enough, after all. Gertie's a smart girl but she's a trusting sort. I can well imagine that she might invite a new friend up to Fives on the spur of the moment, never dreaming for a second that she had been manipulated into it.'

Henry Jameson liked Angela, but was wise enough and experienced enough to know that attractiveness and charm did not necessarily denote trustworthiness. He considered the matter.

'All I can tell you is that her integrity and loyalty were unquestionable ten years ago,' he said cautiously. 'I don't know what she's been doing since then, but I should be surprised if she has changed that much.'

Aubrey Nash now spoke.

'Well, I guess I know her better than anyone here,' he said firmly, 'and I can assure you that she's straight up.'

'Oh,' said the Earl. 'She's an old friend of yours, is she?'

'I should say so,' said Aubrey. He coughed. 'As a matter of fact we were once engaged to be married.'

The others regarded him in surprise.

'Good Lord,' said Sandy Buchanan. 'Why didn't you say so before? When was this?'

'A long time ago. It's not important—didn't last long as a matter of fact, but I can tell you now that I'm not in the habit of getting tangled up with spies.'

'I don't suppose for a second you are,' said Buchanan, 'but have you seen much of her since your engagement ended?'

'We saw each other quite frequently for a while after I got married—she and Selma were good pals, you see. I hadn't seen much of her in recent years, though.'

'Then, I beg your pardon, but my point still stands,' said Buchanan. 'Unless you can tell us exactly what she's been doing recently, how can you be so sure she's innocent? She might have been nobbled in the meantime. The other side have all kinds of underhand methods for influencing people, you know.'

'Because I know her,' said Aubrey, 'and I can't believe it of her.'

'This is a little beside the point,' said Henry Jameson. 'We know that neither she nor Freddy Pilkington-Soames murdered Professor Klausen, because several witnesses were in the cupboard with them at the time.'

'We don't know that she didn't take the documents, though,' said Buchanan. 'You say she was alone in the room for several minutes after the body was found. She could easily have rifled through his pockets and stolen them.'

'I won't believe it,' said Aubrey stubbornly.

'Well, then, what about Pilkington-Soames?' said Buchanan. 'No doubt he could have found an opportunity to do it. It would have been the work of a moment to find the documents and take them. I must say, he looks the type. There's something rather *louche* about him, don't you think? I certainly shouldn't trust him myself. For one thing, he appears to be trying to seduce every woman in the house.' He stopped short as he realized that some of his listeners might not take too kindly to this insinuation.

'I take it you've had a good look at the body,' said Aubrey, addressing Jameson after a short pause.

'As far as I could,' replied Henry. 'It seems clear that he was shot through the heart with a small-calibre gun of some sort.'

'And nobody heard it?'

'Obviously we haven't questioned everybody yet, but there was a lot of noise last night, what with one thing and another, so it might easily have gone unnoticed. Besides, we don't know where the killing took place. Presumably it wasn't in here or the ball-room, but it might have been almost anywhere else, far out of earshot.'

'Surely not *that* far out of earshot,' said Aubrey. 'Remember he had to bring Klausen's body here to dispose of it. Dead bodies are heavy, and the farther he had to carry it, the more likely he was to be discovered.'

'True enough,' acknowledged Henry.

'We shall have to hunt for bloodstains,' said the Earl, but Henry shook his head.

'I don't suppose there are any,' he said. 'It looks to me as though the bleeding was all internal. Look.'

He opened the lid of the chest and all four men stared down at what it contained, wearing expressions that ranged from sympathy to distaste.

'Yes, I see what you mean,' said Buchanan. 'There's not much blood at all, is there? Is there an exit wound?'

'I haven't looked yet,' said Henry. 'We'll have to wait until the rigor wears off now before we can get him out and take a good look at him. Until then he can stay here. We don't want news of this getting out and spreading all over the castle if we can help it.'

Just then there was a soft knock at the door and Claude Burford entered the room, accompanied by Gabe Bradley, who was looking somewhat the worse for wear and slightly shame-faced.

'Ah,' said Aubrey. 'Our first witness. You don't look too clever, Gabe.'

Gabe muttered something about feeling under the weather, but Claude could not wait for him to finish.

'I came here as soon as I heard. Is it true about Professor Klausen?' he demanded, looking from one serious face to another as though to seek confirmation in their eyes.

'I'm afraid so, Claude,' said Lord Strathmerrick. 'And if that weren't bad enough, he doesn't seem to be carrying any documents with him.'

Claude stared.

'Do you mean to say the plans have been stolen?'

'It looks very like it,' said Buchanan.

'Unless he wasn't carrying them in the first place,' said Henry.

'Oh, but he must have been,' said Lord Strathmerrick. 'He wouldn't have come here without them, surely?'

'No,' said Buchanan. 'I think we ought to work on the assumption that he had them with him and that he was killed for them.'

No-one seemed inclined to raise any serious objections to this.

'But who killed him?' said Claude. 'Has anybody called the police?'

'We have no telephone at present,' said the Earl.

'Of course. Yes, I had forgotten. Then have you sent someone to the village? We must act as soon as possible or he may get clean away.'

The situation was explained to him and he subsided for the moment, although not without one or two injured remarks on the fact that nobody had called him earlier.

'Now, Gabe,' said Aubrey Nash. 'You are the nearest thing we have to a witness to this whole thing. Why don't you tell us what happened?'

Gabe told them what he could remember about the game of Sardines—which was not a great deal— then looked at the floor miserably and confessed that he had fallen asleep in the cupboard and had therefore seen nothing.

Claude gave an astounded exclamation.

'Just a minute,' he said. 'Do you really mean to say that six of you were hiding in that cupboard last night when this fellow came in?'

Gabe admitted that this was the case.

'And none of you saw a thing?'

'No. At least I don't think so. I certainly didn't. As I said, I fell asleep.'

'I see,' said Claude.

'Well, that can't be helped,' said Sandy Buchanan. 'And so you woke up and left the room with the others, before Mrs. Marchmont and Mr. Pilkington-Soames discovered the body, is that right?'

'Not exactly, sir,' said Gabe, looking even more uncomfortable. 'As a matter of fact there was no-one in the room except Mrs. Marchmont when I woke up. At first I didn't know where I was, and then when I realized I was still in the cupboard my first thought was to get to bed, so I said goodnight and went out.'

Buchanan and the Earl exchanged glances.

'What was Mrs. Marchmont doing when you spoke to her?' said the Earl.

Gabe hesitated, then swallowed. He was fast realizing that he had made rather a mess of things.

'She seemed to be searching inside the chest,' he admitted at last. 'She jumped and gave a little squeal when she saw me.' They were all looking at him now, and he went red.

'Didn't you ask her what she was doing?' said Lord Strathmerrick.

Gabe shook his head.

'Did you see her take anything?' said Buchanan.

'No,' said Gabe, 'but in all honesty, I wasn't

exactly seeing clearly.'

'Hmm, that's evident enough,' said the Ambassador dryly.

The Earl turned to Henry Jameson.

'Well, we've no proof of anything,' he said, 'but it all looks highly suspicious. At the very least we need to keep a close eye on Mrs. Marchmont and see that she doesn't try to get away. We must get those plans back. It would cause untold damage if they were to fall into the hands of the enemy.'

'I'm sorry,' said Gabe wretchedly. 'I swear I had no idea what was going on. I guess I messed up.'

'Well, there's no use in worrying about that now,' said Sandy Buchanan. 'The main thing is to find those documents before whoever took them makes his—or her—escape.'

TWELVE

ANGELA WOKE UP earlier than she had expected on New Year's day. She lay with her eyes closed for a few minutes, hoping to drift back to sleep, but the events of the night before would insist on crowding into her mind, driving away her dreams, and soon she was wide awake.

'Well, there's no use in lounging in bed all morning,' she said to herself. 'There's bound to be all kinds of fuss today and people running around in confusion and whispering in corners. Presumably they'll all be glowering suspiciously at me too, once Gabe has told them that I was looking through the professor's pockets—as I've no doubt he will. Very well, I shall put on my brightest lipstick and give them something worth glowering at. I only hope my eyes are not too red this morning.'

Ten minutes later she entered the breakfast-room, looking as fresh and cheerful as she could manage under the circumstances. Henry Jameson was there, toying unenthusiastically with the remains of some devilled kidneys.

'You look very tired,' she said. 'Have you been up all night?'

'I'm afraid so,' he replied.

She helped herself to some toast.

'I suppose one oughtn't to ask what has happened since we last spoke?' she said slyly after a pause.

'Very little,' he replied, 'since we appear to be entirely cut off from the village at present.'

She glanced at him inquiringly and he explained about the fallen tree.

'Then you haven't been able to call the police?' she said.

'Not yet. We shall put some of the men on to clearing the path later.'

'Later?' she said in surprise, then understood. 'Ah, of course.' Naturally they would want to hush last night's events up and keep the police out of things for as long as possible.

Henry glanced at her uncomfortably. He finished his breakfast quickly and excused himself.

'You'll find my room quite neat and tidy,' Angela could not resist saying sweetly as he went out, and she had the satisfaction of seeing his mouth twitch in a half-smile.

She sat alone for a while, gazing out of the window at the white landscape, until Aubrey came in.

'Are you all breakfasting in turns?' said Angela.

'No, I came to find you,' he said. He sat down in a chair next to her and leaned forward confidentially. 'You'd better be careful,' he said in a low voice. 'You're under suspicion.'

'Yes, I thought I might be,' she replied. 'In fact, I should be astonished if I weren't.'

'Gabe says that when he woke up—or came to, shall we say—he saw you bending over into the chest as though you were searching for something. What were you doing?'

'Why, searching the professor's pockets, of course,' said Angela imperturbably.

Aubrey sat back.

'But why?' he said.

'Why do you think?' she said. 'I was curious. It was a fatal combination of too much whisky and an incorrigibly inquisitive nature. Wouldn't you have done the same? Wouldn't *anyone* have done the same?'

'Did you find anything?' he said.

'Not a thing,' she replied. 'Well, apart from the usual odds and ends—handkerchiefs, loose change and the like. But I didn't take anything, I swear.'

'Are you sure that's all you were doing?'

'No,' she said. 'I also looked at the soles of his boots and the backs of his hands. I wanted to know if he was the man the boys and I were tracking through the snow yesterday afternoon.'

He shook his head.

'Hmm,' he said. 'Henry Jameson was right. He said you would make the connection. Was it the same man?'

'No. I don't know who we were following, but it certainly wasn't the professor,' she said. 'Might it have been the killer, do you think?'

'It's possible,' said Aubrey, 'but if it was we're going to have a hell of a job finding him. For one thing, his footprints will have been completely covered up in this latest fall of snow. And in any case—' he broke off.

'You're going to tell me they suspect an inside job,

aren't you?' said Angela. He did not reply, and she went on, 'At least I can produce witnesses to say I didn't murder him. As to whether or not I was in league with someone else—well, that's a little more difficult to prove.'

'I told them you're completely innocent, naturally,' said Aubrey.

'Did you? I'm not sure you ought to have done,' she replied.

'Why not?'

'Well, how can you be so certain I *am* innocent?' she said.

'Don't be absurd.'

'I'm not being absurd. We haven't seen each other for years. Who knows what I might have got up to in that time? Why, I might have fallen into all sorts of bad company. I might have come under the irresistible influence of a fascinating criminal. Someone might be blackmailing me into carrying out nefarious deeds. How do you know I haven't become a dope-fiend who will do anything, including conniving at murder, for her next shot?'

'Well, have you?'

'Of course not. But I can't prove it, so you really ought to assume the worst—especially in cases such as this.'

'Why are you so determined that I should suspect you?'

'Because, strange to say, I care about you enough not to want you to compromise your position,' she said. 'Think about it, Aubrey: you're the Ambassador—the highest representative of the American Government in this country. You can't afford to let your judgment become clouded. Even now you've already told me more than you ought to have. It was just your bad luck that it happened to be me who found the professor's body, but there was no need to show me that you were quite so interested in him. You've as good as told me that you're worried about something he was carrying in his pockets. I already suspected that something hush-hush was going on here, but now you've given me one more piece to add to the puzzle. How do you think your superiors will feel about it if it turns out that I *am* involved in all these goings-on?'

'You're not involved, and I was only trying to put you on your guard,' said Aubrey. 'As things stand, you're in a difficult position.'

'Thank you, but there was no need. I can take care of myself,' she said. 'And it is you who ought to look out for your position, not I.'

He took her hand in both of his.

'I know you're not guilty of anything,' he said.

'And so do I,' she said with a smile. She withdrew her hand gently. 'Don't worry. I'm not afraid. Now, you had better get back to work. I dare say you have a lot to do.'

'Don't try to run away, or anything silly like that,' he said, only half-jokingly.

'I won't,' she promised. 'I couldn't even if I wanted to. We're completely cut off, don't you remember?'

He smiled and went out, and Angela was left to her own reflections, which were less than satisfactory. Naturally, she had nothing to hide, but she was uncomfortable at the thought that half the guests at Fives Castle now suspected her of who knew what. It was fortunate that only a few people were aware of the professor's death at present, but how long would that last?

There was a strange atmosphere in the castle that morning—an odd combination of listlessness and tension, idleness and activity. Nothing seemed quite as it ought to. As the morning went on, the other inhabitants of the castle drifted downstairs one by one in varying states of health and cheerfulness. It was Sunday, but word had come to say that snow had got in through the old chapel roof and spoilt the prayer-books and the cushions, so it had been decided not to hold a service that day—and of course, there was no question of being able to get to the church in the village, so they were left to sit about the house until somebody had the presence of mind to organize some entertainment. Gertie looked particularly white-faced after the revelry of the night before, and forgot herself so far as to sit in the drawing-room for an hour, staring at the wall and smoking one cigarette after another, quite heedless of her mother's presence and disapproval. Priss looked sulky, as usual, and replied in monosyllables to Selma Nash's conversational overtures, while Clemmie was assumed to be in the library, buried in a book. Eleanor Buchanan had lost what little animation she had gained, and stood staring out of the window, toying with the gold locket she always wore around her neck, and even Miss Foster, who had gone to bed relatively early, seemed unable to make any progress with her work: she soon gave up any attempt at correcting her latest chapter and took to wandering about the place, hugging a sheaf of papers and occasionally applying her glasses to her nose in order to study the pages and rearrange them to her greater satisfaction.

Some time after eleven, Freddy finally rolled in, yawning. He dropped into a chair and sat in silence. After a few moments Angela noticed that he was trying to attract her attention. She was not in the mood to speak to him and so shook her head slightly. Eventually, spurred into a direct attack, he said:

'I say, Mrs. M, weren't you going to give me back that book I lent you? I believe you said you had it upstairs. I shouldn't ask, only I rather promised to give it to Bradley later.'

Since Gabe Bradley was not in the room he was on safe ground. Angela resisted the urge to roll her eyes and said she would fetch it. He followed her out into the entrance-hall, then opened a likely-looking door, which led into a small sitting-room that looked as though it were not in frequent use.

'Let's go in here,' he said. 'Too many people around in the hall for discretion. Now, then, tell me what you've found out.'

'You don't think they'd tell me anything, do you?'

'No, but I expected you to be up at dawn, looking for finger-prints and cigarette-ends, measuring bloodstains and what-not. Do you mean to say you weren't?'

'I believe I left my magnifying-glass and tape-measure at home,' said Angela. 'Very remiss of me.'

'You shall have to do better next time, Watson,' he said.

'I doubt they'll let us anywhere near the billiard-room from now on, anyway,' said Angela, 'since they suspect us of having had a hand in the business—or me, at any rate.'

'What? Really? Why? And how do you know?'

'Aubrey told me, but it was no more than I had

deduced myself.'

'But what do they suspect us of, exactly? Not the murder, surely? Why, there were four other people in the cupboard besides us. They know we didn't do it.'

'No, not the murder itself, but when you went to fetch help last night Gabe Bradley woke up and caught me—er—searching the professor's pockets.'

'A hardened pickpocket, by George!' said Freddy in some amusement. 'Rifling through the belongings of a dead man. You never told me about that.'

'I didn't tell you because I didn't find anything,' she said.

'But what were you looking for?'

'I don't know. But everyone seemed so on edge waiting for him to arrive that I thought perhaps he was bringing something important with him.'

'And given your finely-honed detective instinct you naturally wanted to find out what it was.'

'Naturally.'

'But Gabe saw you and thought the worst.'

'Exactly,' said Angela. 'Now they think I—and probably also you, since you were there at the time— were sent here to intercept the professor and steal this secret thing, whatever it was.'

'But they know we didn't kill him.'

'As a matter of fact, they don't. All we can really demonstrate is that we didn't dispose of his body. We don't know exactly when or where he died, and I certainly don't have an alibi for the whole of last night, do you? One of us might have killed him and left an accomplice to hide the body.'

'It all sounds rather complicated and far too much like work to me.'

'Perhaps so, but I'm just telling you what the

others will think. Look at it from their point of view: all the other guests are pretty much above suspicion, but we are practically strangers here—and they can't find out anything about us either, because we're snowed in and the telephone is cut off.'

'That's true. Will they lock us in our rooms, do you think?'

'I doubt it, but I expect they're searching them as we speak.'

'Really?' said Freddy interestedly. 'I wish you'd told me before. I could have arranged to leave something suspicious there for them to find—an odd glove, say, or a spent cartridge.'

'I shouldn't joke about it if I were you,' she said. 'They appear to be deadly serious. And, after all, a man has died.'

'True,' he said. 'That is rather unfortunate for him. I wonder what he was bringing. Are you absolutely sure you didn't find anything in his pockets?'

'Yes, of course.'

'But what were you looking for?'

'I've no idea. Lord Strathmerrick and Henry knew what it was, though. Don't you remember? They searched Klausen's pockets too. That means it must have been something small if they expected to find it on him.'

'Documents, perhaps?' suggested Freddy.

'That would be my guess,' said Angela. 'Some important thesis or piece of research.'

'Or a new invention of some sort. An industrial machine or a weapon.'

'I wonder if Clemmie would know,' said Angela. 'I may speak to her later.'

'Good idea,' said Freddy. He gave a sudden

malicious grin. 'But Angela, if you're under suspicion, why is Aubrey telling you so? Have you got him in thrall to your charms? Is he going to cast Selma aside and beg you to run off with him?'

'Good gracious, I hope not,' said Angela, in some alarm at the idea.

'But you were engaged to him once, weren't you?'

'Yes, but it was a long time ago,' she said. 'It wasn't a serious thing.'

'Does he know that?'

'Let us hope so,' she said dryly.

Freddy looked at her intently.

'One day, Angela, I am going to get you well and truly drunk and then you shall tell me all about yourself down to the very last detail.'

'Oh, I don't think so,' said Angela. 'And anyway, even if I did I'm quite sure I'd bore you to sleep. Underneath this exotic and fascinating exterior lies a very dull woman, I'm afraid.'

'Nonsense,' said Freddy. 'Why, I'll bet you've done all kinds of exciting things in your time. I shouldn't be a bit surprised if you'd left a trail of bloodied enemies and distraught lovers scattered in your wake.'

'Well, naturally I have, darling,' she said, 'but haven't we all?'

She blew him a mocking kiss and then escaped before he could ask her any more questions.

THIRTEEN

WHEN ANGELA WENT up to her room after lunch she
found Marthe attending to last night's evening clothes
with an expression of mild disgust.

'Ah, *madame*,' she said as her mistress came in. 'I
am trying to understand why your dress is covered
with dust. Is Scotland a particularly dusty country?'

'Not as far as I know,' said Angela. 'I'm sorry,
Marthe, but I'm afraid I allowed myself to be
persuaded into a game of Sardines last night. That's
probably where the dust is from.'

'Sardines? Fish?' said Marthe. 'What is this game?'

Angela attempted to explain the rules to her, and
she listened politely but was clearly at a loss to
understand why grown men and women should want
to run around in the middle of the night in an
undignified fashion, squeezing themselves into spaces
that were too small for them.

'Anyway,' finished Angela, 'we all ended up hiding
in an old cupboard in the billiard-room, which was
probably rather grubby.'

'The billiard-room?' said Marthe. 'But that is where
they found the dead body, *n'est-ce pas*?'

'What do you know about a dead body?' asked Angela in surprise.

'Why, all the servants are talking about it, of course,' said Marthe. 'They are saying that a famous scientist was shot dead and hidden in a wooden chest by a lady. Me, I do not believe a woman would do such a thing and ruin her clothes.'

'Is that what they're saying?' said Angela. 'So much for secrecy. How did they find out about it?'

'Servants know everything,' said Marthe simply.

'Not everything,' said Angela. 'They don't know who did it.'

'*Non?* Who is this lady who is meant to have shot him, then?'

Angela coughed.

'Me, I believe,' she said.

'Ah. Did you do it?' said Marthe with perfect unconcern.

'Of course not.'

'Then I shall tell them so, *madame*. And I shall not listen to them any more.'

'Oh, but please do,' said Angela. 'If they know about the body in the chest then they very likely know lots of other things that might be useful. Do keep your ear to the ground and tell me if you hear anything.'

'Such as what?'

'Well, for example, I'd like very much to know what the professor was supposed to be bringing with him to Fives Castle.'

'What do you mean, *madame*?' said Marthe.

'It appears that something was taken from his pockets, presumably by the murderer, but I have no idea what it was. Perhaps the servants know.'

'Perhaps. I will find out what I can.'

'Excellent,' said Angela. An idea struck her. 'Oh, and another thing—see what you can find out about Eleanor Buchanan, the Foreign Secretary's wife. I'm curious to know more about her.'

'I know the lady you mean,' said Marthe. 'Her maid is also French. She will talk to me, I have no doubt. Do you think she is the murderer?'

'I haven't the faintest idea,' replied Angela. 'I had thought her unfriendliness was due to shyness, but then I saw something last night that made me look at her in a different light. Perhaps it's nothing, but if it does fit in somewhere I should like to know.'

Marthe assented with a nod, then bade Angela hold still while she attacked her with a clothes-brush. Angela stood obediently, wondering about what she had seen yesterday evening. Why had Eleanor Buchanan been meeting Claude Burford in secret? Claude had struck her very much as the type to know exactly on which side his bread was buttered. He was engaged to the beautiful daughter of an influential aristocrat, and was the protégé of the Foreign Secretary himself; why, then, should he risk it all by consorting with the Foreign Secretary's wife? It made no sense, unless Eleanor Buchanan had drawn him in in some way. But that in itself was an odd idea. Angela could make no sense of it.

She left her room and went downstairs. In the hall she met Gertie, who was looking a little better after a hearty lunch. She was holding something in her hand.

'Look at this,' she said in some merriment. 'Miss Fo must have dropped it.'

It was a notebook which was scribbled over from cover to cover. Evidently it had been insufficient to contain all Miss Foster's ideas, for it was stuffed with a number of loose leaves, also covered in her handwriting. Angela took one of the sheets and read with some difficulty, for the writing was crabbed and blotted:

"'*Hie ye awa' the noo, wee Mac a' Bhiataich, for the Sassenachs are a' coming ooer the brae, ye ken,' cried the Lady Lucinda. Her long, flowing brown locks gleamed in the sunlight and she hoisted up her quivering*—'" She turned over the page. 'Oh, it seems to end there,' she said. 'What a pity. This scene must take place before Lucinda contracts the deadly fever and is forced to have her head shorn.'

Gertie took the paper from her and shoved it back into the notebook.

'Give that to Miss Foster, will you?' she said to a passing servant, then turned back to Angela. 'Isn't it marvellous? Just you wait: before you leave she'll pin you into a corner and force you to listen to the first ten chapters, all declaimed in authentic voices and accents.'

'Splendid,' said Angela.

'I say, come out for a walk in the garden, will you?' said Gertie. 'I want to blow away the cobwebs and clear my head, and it's stifling in the house. Besides, I want to talk to you about something.'

A few minutes later, wrapped up warmly, they passed through the great oak doors and walked around the castle and onto the terrace. Gus and Bobby were down on the lawn, taking it in turns to pull each other about on a wooden sledge. Gus had evidently fully recovered from his misadventure of the night before and was yelling quite as loudly and capering quite as energetically as his brother. Angela felt a twinge of envy at the resilience of the very young, and was about to mention this to Gertie when the younger woman turned to her and said suddenly:

'Come on then, tell me all about the murder.'

'Is there *anybody* in the house who doesn't know about it?' said Angela.

'Oh, probably. I dare say Mother has no idea, and I certainly shan't tell her.'

'How did you hear about it?'

'By listening at the study door,' replied Gertie shamelessly. 'You see, I was sure there was some funny business going on—funnier than the normal political stuff, I mean. It started when I came downstairs this morning. I had the most beastly headache, and should far rather have stayed in bed, but I felt bad about running off last night and leaving Gus's mess for the servants to clear up, so I was trying to get into the billiard-room to find out whether it still needed doing, but of course I couldn't because it was locked. Then Father came to the door and opened it just a crack and peered through— thinking I was one of the maids, I suppose—and practically whinnied in horror when he saw it was me and sent me packing. I pretended I hadn't noticed anything, but as soon as they all retired to the study I scooted straight along after them and applied my ear to the keyhole. I must say, I heard some rather interesting stuff.'

'What exactly did you hear?' said Angela, who was not above eavesdropping herself if the occasion required it.

'Well, some of it was a bit muffled, but I gather you found Professor Klausen's dead body in the old chest after we'd left the room—is that true?'

Angela nodded.

'Then that must be what we heard last night, when we thought Bobby had come into the room,' said Gertie excitedly. 'It was the murderer dumping the body. But how did he die?'

'He was shot through the heart, it seems,' said Angela.

'I say, how thrilling!'

'Not for him, I imagine.'

'No,' conceded Gertie. 'One ought to make a decent show of sympathy, I suppose, but I'd never met the man so it's rather difficult to be sincere in such cases. I am sorry he's dead, of course, but only in a vague kind of way. If it were Father who had been shot, naturally I'd feel differently. Anyway,' she went on cheerfully, 'apparently he was carrying something that's now gone missing.'

'Ah,' said Angela. 'Did you hear what it was, exactly?'

'Some papers, I think. I don't know what's in them, but I do know Father and Sandy are very scared that they are going to fall into the hands of the enemy.'

'Good gracious,' said Angela.

'And by the way, I rather think they suspect the enemy is you,' said Gertie. 'Or possibly Freddy. They were talking about searching your rooms. I hope you don't have anything incriminating in your trunk.'

'I don't think so,' said Angela. 'I believe my luggage is impeccable, so they're quite welcome to look through it. Besides, if I had stolen whatever it was, I should hardly be stupid enough to hide it in my room.'

'No, you wouldn't. And neither would Freddy.

Why do they think you two did it?'

'I suppose because we are the only strangers at the castle,' said Angela. She did not feel it necessary to mention that she had also been caught rifling through the dead man's pockets.

'I wonder who really did it,' said Gertie. 'I say,' she said suddenly. 'Clemmie will be distraught when she finds out that her scientific hero has met a violent and tragic end. I think she was hoping to get his autograph. No chance of that now.'

'Oh, but we mustn't tell her,' said Angela. 'It's supposed to be a secret—although I admit it doesn't seem to have remained very secret so far. I think your father and Henry Jameson want to do some detective-work of their own before the snow is cleared and they have to call the police. I rather think they are hoping to hush up the purpose of Professor Klausen's visit, too.'

'Are you sure we can't tell her?' said Gertie. 'I'll bet she can guess what these missing papers are if anyone can.'

Angela shook her head doubtfully, but was unable to reply for just then Gus and Bobby came rushing up to greet them. They were still excited by the snow and were going to build an igloo, they said.

'Are you quite recovered?' said Angela to Gus.

Gus blushed.

'Yes, thank you, Mrs. Marchmont,' he said. 'I felt a little queasy when I got up but once I'd had breakfast I was quite all right. Ugh, though,' he said with a grimace. 'I shall never drink whisky again.'

'Then the experience has been worth it for you,' said Angela with a smile. 'There will be plenty of time to appreciate a good single malt when you are older and more inclined to drink it from the glass than the bottle, but in the meantime there is lots of fun to be had that won't end in your being sick.'

'You see?' said Bobby to his brother. 'I told you she'd be all right about it. Not like Claude.' He turned to Angela and Gertie and said indignantly, 'Claude gave us a good telling-off this morning about the whisky—and I didn't even have any!'

'Dear me,' said Angela. 'How did he find out about it?'

Gus huffed a little.

'Priss told him, the sneak,' he said. 'It was a rotten thing to do, and she'd better watch out for frogs in her bed, just wait and see. I shan't forgive her in a hurry.'

'She probably didn't think, that's all,' said Gertie in some amusement. 'I don't suppose she meant to get you into trouble. What did Claude say?'

'He said we'd been very bad, and that he'd tell Father and Mother about the whisky if we didn't tell him exactly what happened last night, and then Father would give me a beating and it would serve me right. That's a shabby trick to play on a sick man, and it's not as though I was being deliberately naughty.'

Angela tried not to laugh at Gus's righteous indignation.

'What did he want to know?' she asked.

'I don't know exactly, said Gus. 'He was asking all sorts of strange questions about what we were doing in the cupboard, and what we could see and hear while we were in there. He wanted to know whether I saw whoever it was who came in and looked inside the chest, and I said, "Do you mean Bobby?", and—'

'—and I said it wasn't me,' chimed in Bobby.

'—and I said I didn't know that, and Claude wanted to know who it was if it wasn't Bobby, and I said I had no idea—'

'—but he kept on insisting that Gus must have seen something through a crack in the door, didn't he Gus?'

'Yes,' said Gus. 'I swore I hadn't seen anything and said why didn't he ask Gertie and Mrs. Marchmont if they'd seen anything, and he said he would. I don't know why he's so interested in that old chest, anyway.'

'Then he turned on me and wanted to know if I'd seen anyone wandering around the castle while I was searching for all of you,' said Bobby, and snorted in disgust. 'Of course I did. I saw lots of people, in fact. Practically everyone was still up. Mr. and Mrs. Buchanan and the Americans were playing cards in the drawing-room, and Father and Mr. Jameson were doing something in the study. Then there was some dirty-looking fellow I didn't know who had got lost on his way home from the party. And Claude was up for ages himself, so why didn't he see anything?' he finished.

Angela glanced at Gertie.

'Who was this fellow who had got lost?' she said.

'I don't know,' said Bobby. 'I bumped into him when I was coming out of the gun-room and gave him a shock. I told him he was going in the wrong direction and the door was back the other way, and he said thank you, and I said he'd better hurry before the snow got too thick for him to pass, and he sort of nodded and ran off.'

'Was he a local?' said Gertie. 'I thought we knew everybody who came to the dance.'

'I don't think so,' said Bobby, frowning. 'He didn't have a Scots accent at any rate. He spoke like one of us, but he was all dirty, as though he'd been sleeping in a hedgerow, or something.'

Angela and Gertie exchanged glances again.

'Young or old?' said Gertie.

'Young, I think,' said Bobby.

'Did you mention him to Claude?' said Angela.

'Yes, but he didn't seem very interested,' said Bobby.

Angela raised her eyebrows. Either the mention of the mysterious man had not registered in Claude's mind, or he had a reason of his own for discounting its importance—and presumably that reason was that he suspected someone else.

'What do you think?' said Gertie when the boys had gone back to their igloo. 'Could this man be our murderer, do you suppose? He doesn't sound like anyone we know. He wasn't a villager, and the only people around here who speak like us are us—if you see what I mean.'

'Yes,' said Angela thoughtfully. Gertie glanced at her.

'Come on, out with it,' she said. 'What are you thinking?'

'Just that those tracks the boys and I followed yesterday might be more significant than I thought,' replied Angela. 'I thought they were probably made by a local at first, but now I wonder.'

'Do you mean because of the man that Bobby saw?'

'Yes, and don't you remember what Clemmie said the day we all arrived, about a suspicious-looking stranger who had to be chased off?'

'Oh, yes, of course,' said Gertie. 'Perhaps it was the same man. Do you think he has been hanging around here waiting for Professor Klausen in order to kill him and steal the documents?'

'It's possible, don't you think?'

'But we've been snowed in since last night. That means he must still be here,' said Gertie.

'Yes,' said Angela.

'Let's go and find him,' said Gertie.

They looked at each other.

'We'll need a gun,' said Angela.

FOURTEEN

INSIDE THE CASTLE Lord Strathmerrick, Sandy Buchanan, Henry Jameson and Claude Burford were conferring in private.

'It's damned awkward, that's what it is,' the Earl was saying. 'Why the devil didn't somebody tell us earlier about Nash and Mrs. Marchmont? I should never have invited her had I known he had such a conflict of interest.'

'Oh, come now,' said the Foreign Secretary. 'Why, you couldn't possibly have known that Klausen was going to get himself killed.'

'No, but even so—even had everything gone according to plan, the whole situation is extremely delicate, and it's not going to get any less complicated when we have an attractive divorcée, or widow, or whatever she is, sashaying about the place, trailing former lovers in her wake. Especially when one of those former lovers happens to be the American Ambassador.'

'Do you think Nash has compromised himself,

then?' said Buchanan.

'I've no idea,' said Lord Strathmerrick. 'One would hope not, given that he has brought his wife with him. However, it's clear he's still rather sweet on the Marchmont woman and so I'm not certain we can trust his judgment.'

'Then you are quite certain she and Pilkington-Soames are mixed up in all this?' said Henry Jameson.

'I have no doubt of it myself, sir,' said Claude, addressing the Earl. 'I know very little about her, but I was at school with Pilkington-Soames and I know him of old. I've never met a more dissolute and unprincipled fellow in my life. He fagged for me at school and I never liked him—always found him to be a sneaking, insinuating little crook of a boy, and not above indulging in all kinds of unnatural activities, I'm certain, although I could never prove it. I took every opportunity to try and thrash it out of him but he always bounced back with that smug look of his. I always knew he'd go to the bad. And he and Mrs. Marchmont seem to be as thick as thieves—or worse. If she is guilty then I'm certain they're in league with each other. I've no doubt she's come under his influence and will do whatever he says.'

Henry raised his eyebrows at this picture of Angela, which he was fairly sure was nothing like the truth, but made no comment.

'Have you managed to find out whether anyone saw anything while they were all hiding in the cupboard?' said Buchanan.

'Priss didn't see anything,' replied Claude, 'and neither did Gus and Bobby. Bradley slept through the whole thing. I haven't spoken to Gertie yet, and of course there's no use in questioning the other two, since they certainly won't give us a truthful answer.'

'They say they didn't see anything,' said Henry, 'and I'm inclined to believe them.'

'Very well, then,' said the Foreign Secretary. 'I think we have found out as much as we can for the present. The men are out looking for footprints leading away from the estate—although I don't suppose they'll find any. Now, we need to decide what to do next. Is there any concrete action we can take to salvage the situation? For example, is there any way in which we can hush up the professor's death for the present? What do you think, Strathmerrick? Do you suppose the local police will be amenable to a little juggling with the truth?'

'I shall deal with that,' said Henry. 'I have the authority to issue orders to the police if national security demands it. In fact, I suggest we don't involve the local constabulary at all. We shall merely inform them that the case is a delicate one of a political nature, and that we have handed it straight over to Scotland Yard. It's a pity my brother is not here,' he went on thoughtfully. 'The case would be in safe hands with him.'

'But didn't you say he's a friend of Mrs. Marchmont?' said Buchanan.

'I understand your suspicions of the lady,' said Henry patiently, 'but I'm not sure we ought to be concentrating on her to the exclusion of all else. If it turns out that she had nothing to do with it, then the real criminal may escape in the meantime.'

'That is true,' said the Earl, who was a fair man at heart. 'Very well, let us not lose sight of all the other possibilities. If we are unable to find the criminal or criminals ourselves then we shall leave it to your brother, Jameson.'

'More important, however,' continued the Foreign Secretary, 'is this matter of the documents. As you know, I have a copy of them upstairs in my room, so in that respect they are safe. However, Professor Klausen's copy has presumably been stolen. I'm sure I don't need to impress upon you how imperative it is that we find the papers as soon as possible and prevent whoever took them from passing them on to his or her political masters. It is in all our interests that this research remain in our hands alone.'

Everyone nodded in solemn agreement.

'Jameson, have you conducted a search yet?' said the Earl.

'Yes,' said Henry. 'I searched Mrs. Marchmont and Mr. Pilkington-Soames's rooms this morning, but found nothing.'

'Are you sure they don't suspect you've been in there?'

'Oh, I dare say they know perfectly well I've been in there,' replied Henry. 'As a matter of fact, Mrs. Marchmont as good as gave me permission.'

'Did she?' said Lord Strathmerrick, somewhat disconcerted.

'Of course. She's fully aware that she's under suspicion, and I imagine she's told young Freddy that he is too.'

'In that case, if she did take the documents she won't have hidden them in her room,' said Buchanan.

'No,' agreed Henry.

'Then where can they be? We must widen the search.'

'Good God, man,' said the Earl with a laugh. 'Have you any idea what an impossible task that is?

Why, the castle itself is over two hundred thousand square feet in size, and that's not even taking into account all the outbuildings and cottages on the estate. Where would we even begin? We certainly won't find those plans by searching at random for them.'

'No,' said the Foreign Secretary, 'but if we know who took them we can narrow down the search considerably by retracing that person's footsteps since last night.'

Claude Burford coughed.

'Since we are here behind closed doors,' he said, 'might I ask whether we can be sure that the Ambassador and his secretary are entirely to be trusted?'

The other men looked at each other in surprise.

'Are you suggesting that this is a plot on the part of the Americans?' said the Foreign Secretary at last.

'Perhaps I am,' said Claude. 'It would make things rather simpler, don't you think?'

'But then that means Mr. Nash must be the murderer—or his wife,' said Lord Strathmerrick, 'and Ambassadors don't generally go around killing people.'

'Not even on the orders of their Governments?' said Claude. 'Perhaps America is keen to develop this new weapon and keep it for itself. You know how terrified they are at the mere idea of the Socialists gaining influence—they still haven't forgotten those bombings of ten years ago—and we did have that spy scandal last year, which made us look pretty bad in the eyes of the rest of the world. Perhaps they have decided we are not to be trusted and want to cut us out of the thing altogether.'

There was a pause as everyone considered this new idea.

'I can't believe the Americans would do such a thing,' said Buchanan finally. 'Why, we're practically their closest allies. Can you imagine what a fearful scandal there'd be if they did do it and it all came out? And besides, our scientists are the cleverest in the world. They can't do without us if they want to see the thing developed any time in the next twenty years.'

'Well, then,' said Claude, who was reluctant to let go of his theory, 'could the Ambassador be working for a foreign power?'

This idea was pooh-poohed even more firmly, and he was forced to subside.

'I know I am repeating myself,' said Sandy Buchanan, 'but we are running short of time. Even if we don't find out who *took* the papers, we must find the papers themselves—and quickly, before they can be spirited away from the castle and passed on. Please, I urge you—if you have any idea of where they might be hidden, then act on it immediately.'

Henry Jameson now spoke.

'What about your copy of the papers?' he said to Buchanan. 'I confess I am a little uneasy about all this. I think now would be a good time to bring them downstairs and lock them in the safe here in the study. I should hate to lose this second set. Even if we can't make head or tail of it, there are presumably people who can—the professor's colleagues at the university, for example. We don't want to lose such vital research.'

The Foreign Secretary hesitated for a second. He liked to act alone, but was forced to acknowledge that this was not the moment to do it.

'Very well,' he said. 'I shall go and fetch them now.'

He went out, and the others waited. After five minutes he returned, white-faced. It was immediately apparent that something had happened.

'The papers,' he said, aghast. 'They're gone!'

FIFTEEN

MEANWHILE, ANGELA WAS not sashaying but rather tramping with difficulty—and a nose that *would* run—in the direction of the East meadow in company with Gertie. Here the ground rose gently before them and there were fewer drifts, and so they made rapid progress. They reached the top of the incline and turned back to gaze at an unprepossessing view of the side of the castle, its walled kitchen garden and one or two tumble-down cottages.

'Might he be in one of those?' said Angela.

'No,' said Gertie. 'They're occupied, but there are some empty buildings over this way. I thought he might be in one of them.' She looked at Angela, who had her hand in her pocket. 'May I see it?' she said.

Angela glanced around cautiously and brought out a revolver. It was a dainty little thing, almost toy-like, but nonetheless deadly.

'Perhaps I ought to have brought Father's shotgun with me,' said Gertie, examining it with interest.

'I think this will be enough,' said Angela. 'We don't

want to kill anyone—only bring him in.'

'Why didn't they find it when they searched your room? I should have thought they would have pounced on it with glee and locked you in the turret immediately if they had.'

'Yes, I rather thought so too, so I gave it to William this morning, to look after for me,' replied Angela.

'Clever of you. You don't suppose it was used to kill the professor?' said Gertie suddenly.

Angela shook her head.

'That was my first thought, but I've checked it and it's still fully loaded,' she replied. 'Besides, I didn't exactly advertise the fact that I had it with me, so I don't see how the murderer would have known about it.'

Gertie pointed the revolver into the distance and shut one eye.

'I wonder if I could hit anything from here,' she said, then handed it back. 'Have you ever shot anyone with it?'

'Not with this one,' said Angela. 'I did shoot a man with its twin once, though.'

'Good Lord. Did you kill him?' said Gertie.

'Not with the gun,' said Angela shortly.

'Well, I'll be damned,' said Gertie, impressed, and would have asked more questions, but something in Angela's manner told her that further inquiry into the matter would not be welcomed, so instead she said, 'And to think I thought that Hogmanay was going to be deadly dull! I never dreamed for a moment that we'd be tracking down a murderer.'

'Neither did I,' said Angela.

'I must say, it's all jolly exciting. You must come

again for next New Year, Angela.'

'I don't suppose I'll be invited,' said Angela dryly. 'Your father thinks I am a foreign spy and murderer's accomplice, and your mother thinks I am setting traps for every man in the house.'

'Oh, that's quite tame compared to what they think about some of my other friends,' Gertie assured her.

They came to a stile and crossed it.

'This is the East meadow,' said Gertie. 'There's a barn and a couple of other buildings over there by those trees. I vote we take a look inside.'

'What did MacDonald say about the man he chased away the other day?'

'Not much; only that he wasn't a Scot as far as he could tell.'

'I wonder if it is the same man, then. It's certainly possible.'

'Why do you think he came?' said Gertie. 'Did he mean to kill the professor all along, do you suppose, or did it happen accidentally when he was trying to get the documents off him?'

'You'd have to ask your father or Mr. Jameson about that,' said Angela. 'I imagine they've had plenty of opportunity to examine the body by now and draw some conclusions.'

Gertie made a face.

'They won't tell me, though, will they?' she said. 'We girls always get left out when there's anything exciting happening. Not this time, though. We'll find him, just you wait and see.'

'We don't know that he hasn't escaped across the fields,' said Angela.

'What, at two o'clock in the morning in the dark, and with three feet of snow on the ground? Why, he'd have frozen to death if he tried it. No,' said Gertie, 'I'm willing to bet that he's still somewhere here on the estate, hiding.'

'If he had any sense, he'd have hidden in the castle where it's nice and warm,' said Angela, and Gertie paused uncertainly.

'I say, I never thought of that,' she said. 'Do you really think he might be there?'

'There would be less chance of him dying of cold if he were,' said Angela, 'although of course there's always the risk that he might be caught.'

Gertie looked towards the barn in the distance and then back towards the castle.

'Well, we've come all this way,' she said. 'We may as well carry on.'

They did so, crunching across the field towards the little group of outbuildings, which stood about a quarter of a mile away by the side of a small patch of woodland. There were no footprints but their own in the meadow, so if the murderer had escaped that way then he must have done so while it was still snowing.

As they approached the barn, they glanced at each other and with one accord slowed their pace and lowered their voices.

'Look!' said Angela suddenly.

'Footprints!' hissed Gertie.

From the look of the snow outside the barn, it was evident that someone had been there, for several sets of footprints led into and out of the building. Going away from it, the tracks led in more than one direction, but most of them headed towards the little pine wood nearby. Angela crouched down and examined them briefly, then held up one finger to Gertie to indicate that they all belonged to the same person. She looked about her; there was no sign or sound of anyone nearby.

Gertie pointed into the barn with an inquiring expression. Angela shrugged and brought out the revolver. She placed her finger over her lips and together they peered through the slightly open door. The barn was perhaps half-full of baled hay, all piled high in a single mound. The two women crept as silently as possible around the stack, looking about them carefully, but there was no-one to be seen.

'There's nobody here,' said Gertie at last. 'He must have left before we arrived.'

'He *was* here, though,' said Angela. 'Look—he made himself a bed.'

It was true: a heap of loose hay on the floor before them indicated that someone had attempted to make himself comfortable and ward off the cold.

Gertie shivered.

'He must have been freezing,' she said. 'I wonder who he was.'

'Whoever it was, he's been wandering around Fives since yesterday, at least,' said Angela.

'How do you know?'

'From his boots. It's the same man Gus and Bobby and I were following yesterday,' said Angela. 'I recognized the footprints. The right boot has a nail stuck in it.'

'Well, that seems to fit,' said Gertie after a moment's thought. 'He first tried to get in on Friday and was chased off by MacDonald. Then he came back yesterday along the path from the village, and this time got into the castle and was seen by Bobby while he was wandering around. He shot Klausen and dumped his body in the chest, then escaped across the meadow while it was still snowing and decided to shelter here for the night and escape the next day.'

'If he's a stranger, then I wonder how he knew where to put the body,' said Angela.

'Oh, he probably wandered around looking for somewhere likely, and finally happened upon the chest,' said Gertie. 'It was just unfortunate for him that we happened to be hiding in the cupboard.'

'Ye-es,' said Angela doubtfully. She was just about to say something else when there was a sudden noise behind them like a gasp, and they whirled round to find themselves face-to-face with the most extraordinary apparition. It was dark and dishevelled, with wild hair sticking out from under a filthy deer-stalker. A muffler covered the lower part of its face, leaving only a pair of wide eyes visible, and its grubby, crumpled clothes were covered in bits of hay.

'Oh!' said Gertie.

The apparition recovered immediately from its shock and darted out of the barn.

'Quick! After him!' said Angela.

Gertie needed no prompting: she was already halfway to the door. They emerged into the daylight, squinting, and looked about them breathlessly.

'There he is!' cried Gertie, and was off like a shot, following the man as he stumbled as fast as he could across the meadow. Angela thrust her gun into her pocket and set off too, describing a large arc in an attempt to cut off his escape. She was too late, for he looked behind him and saw what they were doing. He immediately changed direction and headed to his left, back towards the castle. He reached the stile they had just crossed and vaulted over it, Gertie following not far behind.

'Stop!' she cried, but he paid no heed. Instead of running back in the direction of the castle, however, he followed the fence to the left, his objective apparently the wood behind the barn. Gertie followed doggedly but he was gaining on her little by little. Soon he would be lost in the trees.

Angela, meanwhile, had seen what he was doing, and doubled back, intending to enter the wood from the other side and perhaps cut off his escape that way. She reached the barn and stopped for a second to get her breath back. There was no sense in wearing herself out in useless pursuit of a quarry who was undoubtedly faster than she, and so she stood there for a few moments, thinking and listening. She heard Gertie shouting something; the noise seemed to be coming from behind her, so she crept to the back of the building to try and see what was happening. Here, the fence ran between the barn and the pine wood. Angela was over it in a moment, listening and watching. All was silent, save for the hoarse 'raark' of a crow in the distance and the whistling of the wind in her ears. He must be hiding in the wood.

Quietly, stealthily, she stepped forward, taking her gun out of her pocket again as she did so. Here, under the shelter of the trees, the snow lay less thickly on the ground, but even so it was still difficult to move without making a sound. But if she was making a noise then so must he be. She cocked the revolver and edged forward cautiously, glancing about her as she did so. It was all very well having a gun, but he almost certainly had one too, and the last thing she wanted was to make a target of herself. Suddenly, there was a flapping of wings and a cracking of twigs as a bird took flight with a great commotion, and

Angela whirled around with a little gasp of fright. Quickly, she slipped behind a tree and looked towards the source of the noise. What had scared the bird away? She decided to find out. Taking a circuitous route, she quickly reached the spot she was aiming for and paused, taking cover behind a small, bushy-branched pine. Then her heart nearly leapt out of her mouth, for her knee bumped against something soft which gave a muffled shriek and jumped to its feet in front of her. Angela raised her gun in panic, but then lowered it immediately and lifted her eyes to the heavens, breathing deeply to calm herself.

'Damn you, Angela,' whispered Gertie in relief. 'I almost died of fright!'

But Angela had placed her finger over her lips and was indicating a spot a few yards ahead. There, with his back to them, was their quarry. He was crouched down in the shelter of some bushes, and was evidently under the impression that his pursuers were somewhere in front of him. Angela and Gertie exchanged glances and crept across to him.

'Don't move,' said Angela sharply.

The man started and turned, and would almost certainly have attempted to run off had he not seen the lethal-looking pistol that was being pointed at his head by the taller of his two pursuers.

'Don't shoot me!' he cried in terror. 'Gertie, it's me!'

He pulled down the muffler that covered the lower part of his face and Gertie gave an exclamation.

'St. John!' she said. 'What on earth are you doing here?'

SIXTEEN

St. John Bagshawe sat in a comfortable easy chair in Freddy's bedroom, dressed in Freddy's silk dressing-gown and a spare pair of pyjamas that someone had dug out, and took a bite of buttered muffin with a great sigh of satisfaction.

'I say, these are simply marvellous,' he said, 'especially when one's had nothing to eat but liquorice and snow for the past twenty-four hours.'

He looked up at Gertie, Angela and Freddy, who were all standing and watching him with varying degrees of exasperation and curiosity.

'St. John,' said Freddy, 'why are you here?'

'Why, to see Gertie, of course,' said St. John, quite unabashed. 'You wouldn't invite me up here for New Year, Gertie, so I decided to come off my own bat.'

'But why didn't you simply knock on the door?' said Gertie. 'I should hardly have turned you away in the snow. Tempting as it might have been,' she added as an afterthought.

'I know that, and that's what I was counting on,

but it all went rather wrong. You see, I didn't want to look *too* obvious, so I'd planned to pretend I was on a walking-tour of Scotland. I was going to come here and pretend to get lost in the grounds, then accidentally bump into you and pretend that I hadn't realized I was so near Fives. Then you would have to ask me to stay—or at least invite me to the dance, and I should accept and everybody would be happy.'

'Says you,' said Gertie. 'What went wrong?'

'That fierce-looking man of yours with the two-foot-long whiskers and the Scots accent you could cut with a knife, that's what,' said St. John. 'He caught me while I was mooching about on the terrace, and chased me off. At least, I think that's what he was doing—I couldn't understand a word he was saying, but he pointed his shotgun at me so I took the hint.'

'MacDonald,' said Gertie. 'So that *was* you, then.'

'Yes. Then it started to snow so I went back to the village, where I'd been staying, and tried again the next day. The snow was a lot deeper than I expected, but plenty of people had already gone along that way so it was obviously passable. I got to the castle—'

He paused to take another bite of muffin and a sip of tea.

'Why did you leave the path?' said Angela.

'How do you know that?' he said, looking up in surprise with his mouth full.

'We were following your footprints,' she replied. 'We thought you were someone else.'

'By Jove,' he said, and stared at her for a second, his cup suspended halfway to his lips. 'Yes, I did leave the path. Unfortunately for me, I spied old Whiskers coming towards me and didn't want to risk a second encounter, so I jumped over the stream—fell in, as a matter of fact—and struck out across the meadow. Then I got rather lost for a while.'

'I thought as much,' said Angela. 'We tracked you to the old shed. You cut your hand trying to get in.'

He glanced at the back of his hand, which was grazed, then looked at her in admiration. 'It's almost as though you were there,' he said. 'Yes, I got soaked when I fell in the stream and I wanted somewhere to wring my trousers out. The bolt was rusted, though, so there was nothing doing. Tell me then, what did I do next?'

'I don't know,' said Angela. 'We followed you as far as the castle entrance but then lost your trail.'

'Yes, I did get that far,' he said, 'but by that time I'd started to realize that my story was going to look a bit thin. I mean, it's all very well bumping into someone by accident when you're out in dry weather, but I was hardly likely to be out hiking for the fun of it in three feet of snow, with the castle practically cut off, was I? So I thought the best thing to do would be to ask Freddy for advice.'

'If you had, I'd have told you to go home,' said Freddy.

St. John stuck his chin out.

'At any rate, I was freezing cold by then so I slipped in through the front door when nobody was about. I thought I'd find you lounging about somewhere and would be able to attract your attention. There didn't seem to be anybody around, though, so in the end I slipped into an empty bedroom on the second floor and decided to wait for the dance to begin. I knew it would be a noisy affair and thought I'd be able to gate-crash discreetly.'

Gertie was eyeing him in exasperation.

'Why didn't you, then?' she said.

'I fell asleep,' he replied. 'My bed at the inn is dreadfully uncomfortable, you see, and I'd hardly slept a wink the night before, so I expect I was pretty tired. I woke up at about eleven o'clock and thought I'd be in time to throw myself into the last of the festivities, but then I caught a glimpse of myself in the glass and realized that in my present state I was hardly likely to recommend myself, so I—er—stayed where I was,' he finished lamely.

'After all that!' said Gertie.

'What happened then?' said Angela. 'At what time did you leave the bedroom?'

'It must have been shortly after twelve,' he said. 'I wanted to slip out with the rest of the crowd and get back to the inn.'

'Bobby says he saw you,' said Gertie.

'Is that the little boy? Yes, I got a bit lost, and he told me how to find my way out.'

'But why did you decide to go and sleep in the barn?' asked Freddy.

'I didn't mean to,' replied St. John. 'I had intended to return to the inn, but I found that a tree had come down and blocked the path. I was pretty sick, I can tell you. There seemed nothing to do but return to the castle, but by the time I got back the front doors were locked, and so I thought I'd better try and take a different route back to the village. I got as far as the barn and decided to give it up and spend the night there. It's no fun sleeping in a haystack in the middle of winter, so I had a rotten time of it and was just about to have a second try at getting back when you two started chasing me about and pointing guns at me,' he said with an injured air.

'Oh, don't mind Angela,' said Freddy. 'She's from America, where every woman is required by law to carry a six-shooter in her garter at all times.'

'I'm sorry, Gertie,' said St. John. 'I know I've made rather a fool of myself, but it was only because I couldn't get your attention in any other way. I mean, I wrote you all those poems, but you sent them back. I thought women liked poetry and that sort of thing.'

'Poetry? Is that what you call it?' said Gertie with a sniff. 'Plain rude, I should say. It seemed to consist mainly of a list of all those parts of the body one generally tends to conceal from public view. And there were one or two verbs that I had to go and look up in the dictionary. Where you learned *those* words I don't know, but I'll bet it wasn't in church.'

'For shame, St. John,' said Freddy with a smirk as his friend went pink in the face.

'I shouldn't have minded so much, but it didn't even rhyme,' went on Gertie, whose literary tastes were unsophisticated.

Angela wanted to return to the matter at hand.

'Did you happen to see anybody apart from Bobby while you were wandering around the castle after midnight?' she asked St. John.

'A couple of people, yes,' said St. John. 'As a matter of fact, I saw *you* going up the stairs, and then shortly afterwards a woman with dark hair came downstairs.'

'That must have been Eleanor Buchanan,' said Angela. 'We did pass each other.'

'And there was a middle-aged woman in a dressing-gown, too. She was making notes on some paper and talking to herself as she walked. She was on her way upstairs, and she bumped into a pillar and apologized to it.'

'Miss Fo,' said Gertie. 'Anyone else?'

'I don't remember. Look here,' he said in sudden puzzlement, 'why are you asking all these questions? Anyone would think I'd come to steal the silver, the way you're going on. I came to see Gertie and made a mess of things, and now I suppose I shall have to slink off back to the inn without even an invitation to dinner.'

He looked up hopefully, but Gertie was not inclined to indulge him.

'Have you got a gun?' she said abruptly.

'A gun?' said St. John. 'Of course I haven't got a gun. I wanted to impress you, not shoot you.'

'He might have buried it in the snow,' said Freddy. 'That's what they'll say.'

'What on earth are you talking about?' said St. John. 'That's what *who* will say? I don't have a gun, I tell you.'

'Ought we to tell him?' said Gertie.

'I think it's only fair to let a man know when he's in danger of being hanged,' said Freddy, who was enjoying his friend's discomfiture immensely.

'*What?*'

'There was a murder here last night, Mr. Bagshawe,' said Angela. 'Someone was shot dead last night, presumably while you were still here in the castle. I should start thinking carefully about your alibi if I were you, since your presence here at the vital moment looks suspicious, to say the least.'

St. John gazed around at them all in alarm.

'But who was killed?' he said. 'I didn't do it. Freddy, you believe me, don't you?'

Freddy assumed a look of deep and sincere regret.

'It looks bad for you, old chap,' he said. 'We've all been eliminated from the investigation. That just leaves you. Can you prove where you were at the time of the murder?'

'Oh, leave him alone, Freddy,' said Gertie. 'St. John, you're an ass, but I don't suppose you had anything to do with this. Unfortunately, *they* don't know that, so you'd better start praying that they find the real guilty party, and quickly.'

'Would someone please explain to me what is going on?' said St. John. '*Who* was killed?'

Angela gave him a brief explanation of last night's events and he sat there, open-mouthed.

'Oh, but that's absurd,' he said at last. 'Of course I had nothing to do with it.'

'Unfortunately, your recent—er—political activities indicate otherwise,' said Freddy.

'What have my political activities to do with it?' demanded St. John.

'You're a Communist, aren't you?' said Freddy.

'And proud to be one,' said St. John, drawing himself up.

'Proud enough to betray your country if the other side came calling?'

St. John hesitated.

'Well, I don't say I'd go that far. No, of course I wouldn't. I'm as patriotic as the next man. But I should like to see Britain become a truly Communist state, and that's what we're fighting for—the right for every man to earn a decent wage and live his life in dignity.'

'What about every woman?' said Angela sweetly.

'Er—' said St. John. 'Yes, of course. Women will have a vital part to play, naturally. It will be the job of every woman to support her man in the fight, and all that. But you wouldn't want them taking all the men's jobs, now, would you? No,' he said, warming to his theme, 'women are much better suited to the part of staunch supporter and helpmeet. Your glory is not to be gained on the battlefield, but at home, creating a calm and comfortable haven for the menfolk to return to after a long day fighting the good fight.'

'That sounds awfully dreary,' said Gertie. 'I'd much prefer to join in the fighting, if it's all the same to you. But anyway, this is all beside the point. Don't you see? Everyone knows you're a filthy Bolshevist, so you're the obvious suspect for the murder.'

There was a pause as St. John digested the truth of this.

'What shall I do, then?' he said in dismay. 'You must help me get away from here. I don't want to be arrested.'

'You can't,' said Freddy. 'We're cut off by the snow.'

'Well, then, you must hide me somewhere until the snow melts and the road is cleared.'

'Don't be silly,' said Gertie. 'You shall stay here and face up to things like a man. Besides, you don't want to miss dinner tonight, do you? The New Year's feast at Fives is famous. You'll be telling people about it for years to come.'

'Oh?' said St. John, perking up a little.

'Yes, and this year's is going to be an especially good one. There's to be lobster and truffles and partridge and pheasant and three whole turkeys and mutton cutlets and roast beef and lots and lots of champagne,' said Gertie all in one breath. 'And then if you've still got room we've got jellies and meringues and ices and strawberry creams.'

St. John gave a little moan of longing. The muffins had done little to fill the hole in his stomach.

'It does sound rather good,' he said. 'The food at the inn is pretty rotten. May I really stay?'

'Of course,' said Gertie. 'I shall break the news to Father, and Freddy shall lend you a suit.'

Freddy wrinkled his nose.

'Not before he's cleaned himself up,' he said. 'I'm not letting you anywhere near my best togs while you're still caked in three inches of muck.'

'Of course not,' said St. John, who had quite recovered and was looking forward to the prospect of a lavish dinner in company with Gertie. 'I shall take a hot bath forthwith.'

'A bath?' said Freddy. 'Communists don't do anything as wasteful as taking baths, surely? Oughtn't you to stand on your principles and make do with a wipe-down with a cold sponge instead?'

'Under a Communist government everyone will be able to take a hot bath whenever they like,' said St. John. 'That's the whole point. You see—'

'Oh, do can it, old chap,' said Freddy. 'Hose yourself down in whatever way you please, then come downstairs and we'll throw you to the lions. As Angela says, you might want to work on your alibi in the meantime.'

St. John shut his mouth with a snap, and the others took the opportunity to leave the room.

SEVENTEEN

LORD STRATHMERRICK LOWERED himself into his chair with a sigh and gazed at Henry Jameson across the desk. There was still an hour until the feast began and the two men were sitting in the study, sampling a bottle of excellent sherry. The Earl had intended to offer Henry some of his best whisky, but on investigating the drinks cabinet had discovered that there seemed to be none left, although he was sure there had been almost a full bottle last night. He would have to speak to the butler about it. At present, however, he had more pressing concerns on his mind. He coughed.

'So, then,' he began. 'We're in rather a hole, it seems.'

'Yes,' said Henry.

'Not only have we lost poor old Klausen, we have also lost his copy of the plans *and* those of the Foreign Secretary. I tried to persuade Buchanan to give them to me for safe-keeping two days ago, but he wouldn't have it—can't resist trying to take all the glory to himself, you know. He's an excellent man—brilliant, in fact—but he has his faults, just like the rest of us. And he does like to play the showman. Well, it was a mistake on his part this time. I must say he's apologized handsomely for it, but that doesn't alter the fact that things are looking desperate for us at present. Klausen is dead, and if we can't find those documents, then his life's work will have died with him.'

Henry nodded gravely.

'I wasn't too keen on it before since it's such a long shot,' said the Earl, 'but I suggest we institute a search of the castle. They must be here somewhere—unless they've been destroyed, of course. But surely nobody would have done that?'

'Oh, no, I doubt it,' said Henry. 'Presumably the whole point of killing Klausen was to get the papers off him and pass them on to a foreign power.'

'Presumably,' agreed Lord Strathmerrick. 'You say he had been approached to work for the other side and had refused?'

'Yes,' said Henry. 'And since they couldn't get the man himself, I suppose they must have determined to get his research off him instead—even if it meant killing him.'

'It's a dreadful shame,' said Lord Strathmerrick gruffly, 'and we must do something about it. Now, what do you know about this Bagshawe fellow? Rather odd his turning up now, don't you think?'

'Quite a lot, as it happens,' said Henry. 'We've had our eye on him—or at least his organization—for some little while now. He is the third son of the Bishop of Tewkesbury, and is rather the black sheep of the family. At Cambridge he threw himself into a number of radical causes, but eventually seemed to settle on Socialism. He was a member of the Labour

Party and had intended to stand for Parliament, but he got chucked out of the party after he decided that traditional politics were too tame for him and joined a militant group known as the Young Bolshevists, who amuse themselves by going along to political meetings and causing a disturbance. You may have read about some of their recent activities.'

'I believe I have, yes,' said the Earl. 'They set off fireworks and overturn chairs, that sort of thing.'

'Yes,' agreed Henry. 'Naturally, we have been keeping an eye on events, but until today I should have said that there was no real harm in the group— or in St. John Bagshawe. They are an excitable lot, but they appear to lack any sort of coherent organization. As a matter of fact, we sent an undercover chap along to one of their meetings, and it was rather a tame affair—seemed to consist mainly of squabbling and bad poetry. It looks as though we may have been wrong, though. Perhaps there is more to them than we thought. Perhaps they have been influenced by someone in the group who knows what he is doing.'

'You think Bagshawe may have been sent here, then?' said Strathmerrick. 'I must say, it's damned odd the way he just happened to be found today, hiding in a barn. He *says* he was here on a walking-tour. Apparently he decided at the last minute to come and see Gertie, got lost in the snow and ended up inside the castle during the dance, but it sounds like a thin story to me—and that reminds me, I really must speak to the servants about taking more care. We can't have just anyone walking into the place whenever they feel like it.'

'It does sound rather unconvincing,' agreed Henry. 'Once he was inside the castle why didn't he join the dance, or at the very least tell someone he was here?'

'He says he fell asleep and didn't wake up until it was nearly finished,' said the Earl, 'but then why go running about in the snow afterwards, in the middle of the night, when he might have stayed? It all sounds damned fishy to me. I think we may have found our murderer, Jameson.'

'I think it's possible, yes.'

'A hot-head who sympathizes with the other side, and who was here uninvited in the castle at the fatal hour last night?' exclaimed the Earl. 'Why, it's more than possible—it's practically certain, I should say. As soon as we can get through to the village, we'll have him arrested. In the meantime, we'll just have to keep an eye on him. I don't suppose he can get very far for now.'

'But don't you think it looks rather too good to be true?' said Henry. 'Yes, he has the right political sympathies and was in the right place at the right time, and it's certainly a pretty big coincidence that he happened to turn up today, but there are one or two things that point to his being innocent—of murder, at any rate.'

'Such as?' demanded Strathmerrick.

'Well, to start with he doesn't seem to have been carrying a gun—or at least if he was, he didn't think to use it against Lady Gertrude and Mrs. Marchmont this afternoon.'

'Pfft!' said the Earl. 'A gun's easy enough to get rid of. It's probably at the bottom of a pond or a stream somewhere. We shall have to conduct a proper search for it once the snow starts to melt.'

'It's not so easy to get rid of a dead body, though,' said Henry. 'If Bagshawe did shoot Klausen then presumably he also put the body in the chest.'

'Yes, and what of it?' said Lord Strathmerrick.

'Well, how did he know where to put it?' said Henry. 'Lady Gertrude has admitted the man is a friend of hers but you have said yourself that he has never been invited to Fives before. If that is the case, how did he so conveniently know where to put Klausen after he'd shot him?'

'I don't suppose he did,' replied the Earl. 'He probably came across the chest by chance.'

But Henry was shaking his head.

'Hardly,' he said. 'What, do you really suppose Bagshawe just *happened* to be wandering around the castle, a dead body in his arms, and just *happened* to go into the billiard-room, which just *happened* to contain a chest big enough to hold a corpse? It's most unlikely. Dead bodies are heavy, and tend to draw attention to themselves, and there were a lot of people about last night. It would have been foolish in the extreme—not to mention almost physically impossible—for the murderer to haul the thing about while he looked for a hiding-place. No: whoever dumped the body in the chest must have known the chest was there, and since Bagshawe has never been here before, that is a point in his favour.'

'Someone might have told him where to find it,' said the Earl. 'One of our other suspects, for example.'

'You mean Mrs. Marchmont or Freddy Pilkington-Soames? It's possible,' conceded Henry, 'but when did it happen? It must have been after they arrived, since neither of them has been to Fives before either, so they wouldn't have known about the chest until they'd had a chance to explore the place. No, I'm not convinced of that theory. First of all, it supposes that the professor's murder was premeditated, since why else would Bagshawe need to know about possible hiding-places for a body, if he were not already planning to kill Klausen? Secondly, when was the information passed on to him? By all accounts, Bagshawe spent most of yesterday getting lost in the snow. How did he arrange to meet his associate or accomplice if they were unable to communicate with each other beforehand? Remember, the telephone lines came down on Friday night.'

'True,' said Lord Strathmerrick. 'I dare say a means could be found, however.'

'By the way,' said Henry, 'I don't know if there's any significance to this, but a few minutes ago I bumped into Freddy Pilkington-Soames, and he told me that Bagshawe didn't have the brains to murder anyone. I asked him why he was telling me this and he looked uncomfortable and said he thought Bagshawe was unlikely to make a good impression when we questioned him, and it would be a shame if the chap got hanged merely for being an ass.'

'Do you suppose he was being sincere?'

'It's difficult to tell with that young man, but I had no reason to doubt him,' said Henry.

'He's a slippery fellow,' said the Earl. Henry correctly deduced he was referring to Freddy.

'Something else has been bothering me, too,' he went on, 'and that is that we still don't know at what time Klausen arrived.'

'Does it matter?' said Strathmerrick. 'The first we knew of his arrival was when he was found dead, by which time it hardly seemed relevant.'

'Of course it matters. If we can trace the

professor's movements, then we can get a better idea of who killed him. If he turned up at one o'clock, for example, then you are in the clear—as am I, since we can confirm each other's alibis from before that time until the body was found.'

'What do you mean, I am in the clear?' said the Earl, spluttering slightly. 'I take it that is your idea of a joke, Jameson. Why, even the very thought of—'

'Of course I'm not being entirely serious, sir,' said Henry hastily. 'I was merely pointing out that the time of the professor's arrival might prove to be of vital importance in establishing who killed him.'

'Hmm,' said Strathmerrick suspiciously. 'I suppose you're right. We shall have to look into that more carefully.' He fell silent, deep in reflection. Suddenly, a thought struck him. 'But what of the documents?' he said. 'Jameson, while everybody is at dinner you must have this Bagshawe fellow's things searched for the missing papers. I can't believe that Klausen turned up without them, so whoever killed him must have taken them from his body.'

'I've already searched his things myself,' Henry assured him. 'He doesn't have them.'

'How provoking,' said the Earl. 'Then where on earth can they be? They can't simply have disappeared into thin air.'

'I don't know,' said Henry, 'but that's another thing: St. John Bagshawe might have shot the professor and taken his copy of the documents, but who took the Foreign Secretary's? It can't have been Bagshawe, since he couldn't possibly have known about the second copy.'

'No,' said Strathmerrick. 'I assume the papers were stolen by an accomplice.'

'But who?' said Henry. 'Who knew that Buchanan had the second set of documents?'

He waited for the Earl to consider this and reach the inevitable and uncomfortable conclusion. The Earl did so and his face darkened.

'Why, no-one,' he said. 'Except us, of course.'

'Quite,' said Henry. 'That is, you, myself, Buchanan, Burford, the Ambassador and Gabe Bradley. We are the only people who knew that the Foreign Secretary was carrying a copy of Klausen's plans. So, then, who stole them?'

EIGHTEEN

MRS. MARCHMONT SAT before the glass at her dressing-table, holding her head still as Marthe carefully fastened a jewelled head-dress to her hair. When the girl had finished the task to her satisfaction she stood back to regard her handiwork and gave a little sound of approval.

'Shall I do, do you think?' said Angela, turning her head this way and that to judge the effect.

'Yes, *madame*, you look very chic,' said Marthe.

'You don't think it's a little too daring, perhaps? Lord and Lady Strathmerrick are rather old-fashioned.'

'Yes, but they have three daughters of their own, *madame*. They are surely accustomed to the modern style of dress. Be assured, there is nothing about your person that could possibly offend anyone.'

'You are right, of course,' said Angela. 'I am just a little wary after the events of the last day or two. I believe the Countess does not approve of my conduct with respect to the men of the house.'

'Why, what have you been doing?' said Marthe with sudden interest.

'Nothing at all,' said Angela.

'Oh,' said Marthe, disappointed.

'But Lady Strathmerrick has rather unfortunately misinterpreted one or two—er—incidents.'

'With the American Ambassador, yes?' said Marthe, then as Angela looked up in surprise, she continued, 'I have seen the way he looks at you.'

'Does he look at me? Dear me. This is all becoming rather awkward. Selma is supposed to be my friend.'

'Oh, do not worry,' said Marthe. 'She knows all about it and does not care.'

'All about it? There is no "it," Marthe—at least, not as far as I'm concerned.'

'A pity,' said the girl. 'A woman ought to have lovers. You have been on your own for too long.'

'I like it,' said Angela. 'I can go where I please and do as I please. I can have second helpings of pudding without having to worry about what it will do to my hips. I can spend thirty guineas on a frock and another thirty on a diamond necklace to match it. I can ask Freddy to take me out dancing and let him flirt with me as much as he likes. I can sit in a cupboard drinking whisky out of the bottle and then stay in bed until eleven o'clock the next day if I choose. I can play at investigating murders without the fear that someone will disapprove of me for being unladylike. I can do anything I want.'

'That is why you ought to take a married man as your lover. He will have no hold over you and you may continue to live as you choose.'

'I thank you for your concern, Marthe,' said

Angela, 'but I broke off the engagement with Aubrey for very good reasons and I have no wish to revisit the past. Now, let's talk about something else. I want to know what you have found out about Eleanor Buchanan.'

Marthe grimaced.

'I am sorry, *madame*, but I have not been able to find out very much at all. Her maid keeps her mouth tightly closed. All she would tell me is that Mrs. Buchanan met her husband at Baden-Baden, where they were both staying, and that she is the daughter of a doctor who is now dead.'

'Dear me, a discreet lady's maid,' said Angela. 'How inconvenient.'

'I am also very discreet,' Marthe assured her.

'I have no doubt of it,' said Angela. 'Very well, then, I shall have to think of something else.' She rose and adjusted her dress. 'Don't wait up, Marthe,' she said, and went out.

Downstairs in the hall she met Henry Jameson as he emerged from the passage that led to the study.

'Ah, Mrs. Marchmont,' he said. 'Might I speak to you for a moment?'

'Why, of course,' replied Angela.

Henry glanced about him. They were quite alone. He coughed and lowered his voice.

'I have spoken to St. John Bagshawe, who informs me that when you and Lady Gertrude chased him through the woods, you pointed a gun at his head and told him to—er—"put 'em up."'

'I did no such thing!' exclaimed Angela. 'What do you take me for?'

'Then he was lying?' he said.

'Oh, I pointed a gun at his head all right,' said

Angela, 'but I should never dream of saying anything so vulgar. I believe what I actually said was, "Don't move."'

Henry seemed to be trying not to smile.

'Mrs. Marchmont,' he said, 'you know what I am about to say next, don't you?'

Angela sighed.

'I suppose you want the gun,' she said.

He nodded.

'I have no reason to suppose you shot the professor,' he said, 'but the fact remains that we have a dead body and a missing weapon, and I should be neglecting my duty if I did not at least take a look at yours, if only to eliminate it from the inquiry. I'm sure you understand.'

'Oh, very well, then,' she said reluctantly. 'I'll give it to you, but I want it back. It's not the same gun that killed the professor, I promise you.'

'How can you be so certain?'

'Because I brought it with me fully loaded and there are no bullets missing,' she replied.

'Where is it now?'

'My chauffeur has it. I thought that you—or some of the others, at least—might jump to the wrong conclusion if you found it in my suitcase, so to save you and myself any unnecessary worry I decided to give it to someone else to look after. Very well, then, take it if you must. Go to the servants' hall and ask for William. You may tell him I sent you.'

'Thank you. If it turns out that it was not used as the murder weapon, you shall have it back as soon as possible.'

'Just as I'm about to leave, I imagine,' said Angela under her breath, as Henry went off shaking his head.

'Angela!' said a voice just then, and she turned. It was Selma Nash, who was descending the stairs with difficulty, dressed in a long sheath dress that was quite dazzling and far more daring than Angela's frock. 'You look quite divine! Where have you been hiding all day? I've been dying to talk to you.'

Angela was seized with a sudden urge to run away, but she merely stood and waited until Selma reached the bottom of the stairs.

'I don't know what possessed me to wear this,' said Mrs. Nash with a rueful smile. 'I can barely walk in it.'

'You look quite stunning,' said Angela. 'Where did you find it?'

'Oh, the most awful little woman, darling,' said Selma, taking Angela's arm as they proceeded towards the drawing-room. 'Do you know Madame Estelle? Ghastly old witch with fingers like bird's claws and a voice that quite goes through one, but she makes the most gorgeous gowns, so I can't bear to leave her. Did you see Edrys Lawrence's outfit at Ascot this year? It caused quite a stir. That was by Estelle.' She went on in this vein for some minutes, and then said, 'But, darling, that's not what I wanted to talk about. I want to know what exactly is bothering Aubrey. He won't tell me, but I'll just bet you know all about it.'

'Is something bothering him?' said Angela rather feebly. 'And why should I know what it is?'

'Because I happen to know that the two of you were seen having a *very* intimate conversation in the breakfast-room this morning.'

Angela inwardly cursed the loose tongues of the Fives servants, but merely said cautiously, 'Yes, I believe he did come into the breakfast-room while I was there, but I don't remember what we talked about.'

Selma snorted delicately.

'Don't be ridiculous, Angela. You were holding hands and talking with your heads close together—practically kissing, in fact.'

Angela reddened.

'Look here,' she said, 'that's how it may have looked, but I can assure you—'

'Oh, I'm not interested in that,' said Selma with a wave of the hand. 'All I want to know is: what is this secret that everybody seems to know about except me? Of course, I knew there was something afoot when we came here—we were all set to start for the Riviera on Friday, but then right at the last minute Aubrey said we had to come to Scotland instead, so I had to repack my trunks in a hurry, since naturally the clothes I'd packed for Cap Ferrat would have been no good at all up here at the North Pole.'

'Naturally,' said Angela.

'So I knew there was something going on, but I thought it was the usual kind of thing—you know, an unexpected visit to Fives by the King, who'd decided it was a matter of urgency to summon the Ambassador and ask him some stupid question or other.'

'Does that happen often?' said Angela.

'You'd be surprised,' said Selma darkly. 'Anyhow, it was obvious when we arrived that there was some kind of political discussion going on, and Aubrey was his normal self—except maybe a little more excited than usual—but of course, that might have been because you were here—'

Angela disclaimed all credit for this with a shake of

the head.

'—but now something's happened, hasn't it? I know it has, because Aubrey's manner has changed completely. He's gone all quiet and brooding, and will hardly speak to me. And he and Gabe have been rushing around looking like thunder and ignoring me all day.' She laughed. 'In fact, I was so lonely I spent a whole hour this afternoon making polite conversation with Lady Strathmerrick, although I'm pretty sure she disapproves of my behaviour.'

'Really?' said Angela.

'Well, I guess I may have been just a *little* obvious with Freddy,' said Selma, considering. 'But anyway, whatever this thing is, it must have happened last night or early this morning, I'm certain of it. What was it, Angela?'

Angela hesitated. Although the secret could hardly be called a secret any more, she was still uncertain as to what she was allowed to say, and to whom. Fortunately, her dilemma was resolved by Clemmie, who just then rushed up to the two women and said to Angela breathlessly:

'I say, Angela, is it true what they're saying about Professor Klausen? Has he really been murdered?'

'Well I'll be—' said Selma in astonishment. 'Is *that* what it is?'

'Yes,' said Clemmie. 'They're saying he was shot through the heart last night while we were all at the dance. All the servants are talking about it. Someone broke into the castle and killed him, then dumped him in the billiard-room. He's still in there now and nobody is allowed in until they have taken him away. Is it true?'

'I'm afraid it is,' said Angela.

Clemmie gave an exclamation of dismay and Selma said, 'So that's what all the hole-and-corner stuff was about, was it? But why are they being so secretive about it? Why aren't we supposed to know?'

'I have no idea,' said Angela untruthfully. 'Perhaps it's because we're snowed in and they didn't want to cause unnecessary panic before the police could be informed.'

'Then how come you know about it?' said Selma suspiciously.

'Because I was hiding in a cupboard in the billiard-room when the murderer dumped the body. Sardines,' she explained in answer to Selma's inquiring look.

'Oh, yes,' said Selma. 'I remember now. We *grownups* were playing whist.'

'I rather wish I'd joined you,' said Angela.

'But who did it?'

'I didn't see,' said Angela, 'and as far as I know, neither did any of the other five people who were hiding in the cupboard with me at the time. Freddy was one of them,' she added, as a door opened and the young man himself sauntered out into the passage. Selma immediately detached herself from Angela and took Freddy's arm.

'I hear you've been shooting professors in the billiard-room, you naughty boy,' she said. 'Why don't you tell me all about it?'

They strolled off, and Angela turned to Clemmie.

'Look here,' she said to the younger girl. 'I've been meaning to talk to you. What can you tell me about Professor Klausen? I'm ashamed to say I don't know anything about him, even though he's meant to be famous. What exactly was he famous for? You explained it yesterday but I didn't really understand. And why would anyone want to kill him?'

'I don't know why he was killed,' said Clemmie, 'but I've read all about his work and it's terribly fascinating and important. He is the greatest authority in the world on atomic physics. I don't pretend to understand all his theories—although I'd like to one day—but I do know that he has been researching the possibility of harnessing the radio-active properties of certain substances in order to create enormous amounts of energy.'

'I see,' said Angela, who didn't.

'And that energy could be used for all sorts of purposes,' went on Clemmie with enthusiasm. 'Why, just think—it could be used to make cars and trains go faster, or to make machines that will manufacture things at great speed—far more quickly than we can produce things at present. Or it might be used for street-lighting, or—or to power ploughs, or to fire guns, or to make bigger bombs—practically anything, in fact.'

'It sounds very useful,' said Angela.

'Of course, most of this is theoretical at the moment. Nobody's yet found a way of putting it into practice, but Professor Klausen had announced publicly that he was determined to do it himself. He wanted to turn down the International Prize, you know—he said he didn't deserve it because his theories remained unproven. In the end they persuaded him to accept the prize by promising to award him another one if he proved them.'

Atomic science was not Angela's strongest point, but she was beginning to get the idea that something very important was at stake.

'So, then, am I to understand that if the professor's theories could be demonstrated in practice, a lot of people would be interested in knowing the secret?'

'Oh, yes,' Clemmie said. 'Why, it would be the biggest discovery since the invention of the steam-engine. Everybody would want to know about it. Klausen would be very rich indeed if he decided to sell his knowledge—would have been, I mean,' she corrected herself dolefully. 'It's an awful tragedy for science that he's dead.'

'So it appears,' said Angela. 'I'm only sorry I didn't give him the credit he was due while he was still alive. Perhaps I shall read something about his theories one day.'

'I can help you,' said Clemmie. 'Wait here.'

She darted off and returned a minute or two later with a book.

'I don't suppose you'd be interested in the really dry stuff,' she said, as she handed it to Angela, 'but you might like to read a novel about it instead. It's a bit more palatable than the real thing.'

Angela read the title.

'*The World Set Free*,' she said, intrigued.

'Wells isn't a physicist, you understand, but he's been following developments for years,' said Clemmie. 'I rather like him.'

'Thank you,' said Angela. 'I shall certainly take a look at it. When do you go to university, Clemmie?'

'Not until next year,' said Clemmie. 'I have a few months to persuade Mother and Father to let me do it. Gertie has promised to help me. Of course, it helps that Mother thinks I want to train to be a nurse. I'm not sure they could take the awful truth.'

Angela laughed.

'I hope you can convince them,' she said. 'Perhaps one day you will complete Professor Klausen's research for him.'

'I should like that,' said Clemmie, her eyes shining.

'Always assuming that he didn't complete it himself before he died,' said Angela to herself. 'I must say, it's starting to look as though he might have done.'

NINETEEN

As GERTIE HAD promised, the Fives New Year's feast was a magnificent occasion, during which the presentation of the food took precedence over that of the guests. The table in the grand dining-hall was laid according to the most exquisite etiquette and elegance, with a brilliant white, starched cloth and a quite bewildering array of knives, forks, spoons, glasses, finger-bowls and napkins. Careful arrangements of dried flowers, nuts and silver-painted fir-cones were placed to great aesthetic advantage, but these were as nothing to the main *chef d'oeuvre*: a three-foot-high representation of Fives Castle, carved in ice and placed in the centre of the table as though to remind everybody of exactly where they had eaten this truly spectacular meal, lest they should forget it in the inevitable haze of post-prandial indigestion.

And then there was the food. The guests watched in something like awe as a seemingly never-ending procession of dishes piled high with mouth-watering meat, game, poultry, lobsters, pies, potatoes, vegetables and other delicacies arrived one after the other, to be placed with solemn ceremony on the table. After that came sweets and savouries, ices, cheeses, meringues, fruit salads, mousses, *petits fours* and a gigantic fruit-cake. Even Angela, who had attended many private and public banquets in her time, had to admit that they had made a good job of it.

St. John was in his element, and bent his attention to his task with a single-mindedness that was quite remarkable to behold. Angela, who was sitting next to him, watched as he put away mouthful after mouthful of food, pausing only to take the occasional gulp of wine or water or to dab his mouth, and wondered how on earth he remained so thin with such an appetite. She herself, despite her earlier protestations to Marthe, was no more wedded to her principles than the next woman and, mindful that the dress she wore clung more than was perhaps strictly necessary, decided with regret not to have second helpings of pudding after all.

Once he had replenished his stomach to his satisfaction, St. John sat back with a great sigh, took a sip of coffee, which had just then been served, and indicated that he was available for conversation.

'I must say, they put on a good spread here at Fives,' he began. 'It was awfully sporting of Gertie to invite me to stay after I made such a fool of myself. Perhaps she doesn't despise me as much as I thought.'

Angela forbore to point out that he had been invited more for convenience than for anything else, given his present position as the chief suspect in a murder case.

'Have any of the men—er—spoken to you yet?' she said.

St. John stifled an indelicate noise with his hand and nodded.

'Yes. Old Strathmerrick and that Jameson fellow button-holed me and demanded the low-down, so I put on my best honest face and told them what I told you—that I knew nothing and was merely here to see Gertie.'

'Did they believe you?'

'I couldn't tell you,' he said. 'They didn't say they didn't, but I have the feeling they were looking at me rather askance.'

'Well, you must admit that your arrival was somewhat unorthodox,' said Angela.

'I suppose it was,' he said. 'It was just my bad luck I happened to turn up when I did, though. By the way, I was rather surprised to find out that Jameson knew all about me already. Who is he, anyhow?'

'He works for the Intelligence service,' said Angela.

'Does he really?' he said in surprise. 'He doesn't look the type, does he?' An idea struck him. 'Then they must have been spying on us,' he said. 'I thought our activities might be of some interest to the authorities, but I didn't expect them to send in the undercover chaps.' He drew himself up and his face assumed a pleased, almost flattered expression. It might even have been said that he preened. 'I say,' he said, 'just wait until I tell the chaps back at H. Q. They'll be tremendously bucked that we're being taken seriously at last. We've always had the feeling that most people consider us to be rather a joke.'

He tossed back a glass of liqueur and looked about

him for the bottle.

'Did they ask about your alibi?' said Angela. 'I suppose they wanted to be certain that you did leave the castle just after midnight, as you said.'

'Oh yes, and I told them I was quite sure of the time, as I happened to look at my watch just after I bumped into young Bobby, and it was twenty past twelve, or possibly twenty-five past, but certainly not later than half past. From something Jameson said, I gather the murder took place after that.'

'I don't think they know exactly *when* it took place,' said Angela. 'However, the body was deposited in the chest in the billiard-room at some time after two o'clock.'

'Well, then, that lets me out,' he said cheerfully.

'I suppose it does,' said Angela.

Shortly afterwards, the ladies retired to the drawing-room as gracefully as they could, given that most of them were feeling distinctly heavier than they had before dinner.

'Oh, how I should like to lie down and groan,' announced Gertie, throwing herself into a chair, 'but I suppose it won't do.'

'If you do it, I declare I'll join you,' said Selma. She went up to the Countess and clasped both her hands. 'Lady Strathmerrick, I'm speechless,' she said. 'Why, that was the most divine banquet I ever saw or ate— and I guess I've been to more banquets than any of you. It quite deserves to go down in history.'

The other ladies joined in the chorus of compliments. Lady Strathmerrick blushed a little. She rather prided herself on the New Year's feast, but it was always pleasant to have one's hard work appreciated.

'Oh, we've been doing it for years,' she said, 'and we couldn't give it up now—although we don't do it on as grand a scale as we used to before the war, of course.'

Angela rather wanted to lie down and groan herself, but she saw the dangers of a sleepy lull in the conversation and made an effort to talk. She was assisted by Freddy and St. John, who came in after a few minutes. St. John, in a rare display of diplomacy, went to make himself agreeable to his hostess, and Freddy joined Angela.

'Ass,' he said, with a scowl.

'Thank you,' said Angela.

'I meant St. John, of course,' said Freddy. 'He wanted to stay in the dining-room and talk to the other chaps and wouldn't take my hints that we were most likely *de trop*, so I pretty much had to whisper in his ear and tell him that Gertie wanted him in the drawing-room.'

'I shouldn't like to be in your shoes when she finds out,' said Angela.

'Oh, Gertie will forgive me anything. She's half in love with me, although she doesn't know it herself.'

'Is that why she hit you with a cold sausage at the Copernicus Club, that night you all got arrested? It seems rather an odd way of demonstrating one's love, don't you think?'

'Mere jocular high spirits,' said Freddy blithely.

'She told *me* she was rather keen on the Foreign Secretary,' said Angela.

'Nonsense. He's ancient and probably ga-ga. Besides, he's married.'

'That doesn't seem to stop you. And that reminds me,' she said. 'Go and work your charms on Priss again. I'm finding her engagement to Claude rather a mystery, especially after what I saw last night.'

'Why, what did you see last night?'

'Oh, didn't I mention it?'

She told him of her encounter with Eleanor Buchanan on the stairs, and he whistled.

'So they were sneaking about together in one of the bedrooms, were they? By Jove, I never should have thought it of either of them.'

'Has Priss said anything about Claude to you? Does she love him at all?'

'What do you think?' said Freddy.

'I think she finds him rather a crashing bore,' said Angela.

'She does,' said Freddy.

'Then why did she agree to marry him?'

'As far as I understand it, because it seemed like a good idea at the time. She's desperate to get away, you know—finds home life terribly dull, and she's always been under pressure to make a good marriage—I mean good from a political point of view.'

'I see. And presumably he is also marrying *her* for political expediency. I must say, it doesn't sound like the ideal match.'

'It doesn't, does it? I dare say she'll break it off sooner or later, when someone better comes along.'

'Well, then,' said Angela. 'If she's so indifferent to Claude, there shouldn't be any difficulty in finding out whether she knows anything about him and Mrs. Buchanan.'

'Why are you so interested in the perfectly harmless private affairs of two people who are of no importance to you?'

'Because I'm not so certain they are perfectly

harmless,' she said. She turned to him and went on seriously, 'Look here, you must have realized that a simply enormous scandal is about to blow up at Fives, once the news gets out about the murder. They can't possibly keep the thing quiet, and so we are all of us going to be under very close scrutiny for a while. I hope you have nothing to hide.'

'I have plenty to hide,' said Freddy. 'As do you, no doubt.'

'Then go and talk to Priss. Perhaps we can solve the mystery before the word spreads and we have reporters following us everywhere.'

'Oh, I'm not worried,' said Freddy. 'I shall follow myself and give myself an exclusive scoop. That will be one in the eye for Corky Beckwith at the *Herald*. He's been dying to do me a bad turn ever since I beat him to the story about the Archbishop and the collection-plate.'

'Go,' said Angela, and Freddy went. She saw him take a seat next to Priss, who tossed her head but did not seem unwilling to speak to him.

Eleanor Buchanan was standing in her customary spot by the window, staring out into the darkness and fidgeting with her gold locket. Angela went to join her.

'I don't suppose I shall need to eat again for another week or two,' she said pleasantly, by way of beginning the conversation.

Mrs. Buchanan smiled faintly.

'Yes,' she said, 'I feel rather like that myself.'

Angela watched as the woman's long fingers twined unceasingly in and out of the gold chain.

'That's a very pretty locket,' she said. 'I've noticed that you wear it often. Is it a favourite of yours?'

'Yes,' replied Eleanor. Her fingers stilled for a moment as she took the pendant in her hand and glanced at it. 'It was a present from my father shortly before he died.'

'Do you keep his picture in it?'

Eleanor regarded Angela with narrowed eyes, as though assessing her.

'No,' she replied at last. She opened the locket and held it up. Angela saw that it contained a photograph of a dark young man, taken perhaps a few years earlier. 'It's my brother,' she said in reply to Angela's questioning gaze.

'Oh. Is he—?' said Angela delicately.

'No, he's still alive, but we haven't seen each other for some time.' She looked at the floor. 'There was a—a disagreement, you see. I very much hope that one day we will be able to patch things up, but at present that's not possible.'

'Oh, why?' said Angela. She was being inquisitive, she knew, but could not resist asking the question.

'The situation is a little—complicated, let us say,' said Eleanor.

'Couldn't you pay him a visit?'

'Oh, no, I couldn't do that,' said Eleanor with finality. 'That would be quite impossible in my position.'

Angela longed to ask another question, but Mrs. Buchanan fixed her with such an intense gaze that she dared not risk it.

'I know why you're asking me these questions,' Eleanor said after a short pause. 'I'm not stupid, you know.'

'I beg your pardon?' said Angela in surprise.

'But you're wasting your breath,' went on the other

173

woman. 'I've had enough of it all now. I've done what you asked and I won't do any more. There's nothing more I *can* do, is there? If you don't leave me alone I shall tell my husband everything I know. I'm sick of it all—sick of it, I tell you!'

She turned on her heel and walked off, leaving Angela quite astonished and wondering what she had said that had offended Eleanor so much.

TWENTY

IT WAS GROWING uncomfortably warm in the drawing-room, and despite everyone's best efforts, the conversation was flagging. Angela, standing by the window, could feel her limbs growing heavy and had the almost irresistible urge to sit down on a nearby divan and fall into a light doze.

'Now, Angela, this won't do,' she said to herself at last, and decided to go and seek some cooler air. The cold passage outside the drawing-room soon revived her, but she was reluctant to go back in and have to face Eleanor Buchanan's hostile stares again. She stood there, glancing to the left and right and wondering idly if she might sneak up to bed without being accused of neglecting her social duties. Her mind began to wander over the events of the day, and she wondered if poor Professor Klausen was still in the chest. A poor excuse for a coffin! They would have to bring him out soon, and then she supposed the sombre formalities would begin: the identification, the post-mortem, the inquest, the police presence, the questions, and finally, perhaps, the arrest. But who had done it? Was St. John the man they sought, or was he just an unfortunate scapegoat who happened to have been on the spot at the right time? If not he, then who? Who?

Almost unconsciously she found herself drifting down the passage in the direction of the billiard-room. Once outside the door, she tried it gingerly. It was still locked. Of course it was still locked. What had she hoped to achieve by coming here? Perhaps to get a sense of what exactly had happened last night, when she had hardly been thinking straight. Now her head was clear and she could reflect objectively. Had anybody been thinking clearly today? After all, the situation was hardly a normal one: they were trapped in a castle with no means of communicating with the outside, and perhaps with a murderer in their midst. There were no police to begin an official investigation, and so the people in charge had been left to muddle along as best they could. Henry Jameson struck her as being quite as capable as his brother, but he was only one man and, furthermore, almost certainly had other things on his mind, given the purpose for which most of the male guests had presumably gathered here. He was probably more concerned with the fate of whatever it was Klausen had been carrying with him, than with the identity of the professor's murderer. Plenty of questions had been asked, but were they the right ones? For example, had anybody thought to investigate where exactly the murder had taken place? Some people seemed to think that the professor might have been shot almost anywhere in the castle, and that the killer had wandered around aimlessly with his body, looking for a hiding-place, but of course that was nonsense. One could not simply carry a corpse about, slung gaily over one's shoulder, without attracting attention. Dead bodies were heavy, and there had been people about last night. No, of course that was not what had happened. Obviously Klausen had been killed somewhere nearby and then hidden as quickly as possible.

Angela looked about her. To the right of the billiard-room a door opened into the portrait-gallery. She stood in the doorway and looked along it to the other end. It would have been foolish in the extreme for the murderer to come this way, given that it was brightly-lit and had windows on one side which looked onto the garden and the outer door of the ball-room. Had he brought Klausen's body along here he would have been visible to anyone who happened to be passing outside after the dance. No, that was no good at all. To the left of the billiard-room was the library, which was studiously avoided by most of the family. Angela turned and saw another door in the wall opposite. She opened it and discovered it was a store cupboard, stacked high with pails, brooms and assorted possessions long since forgotten about. It might be big enough to hide a body, but was an unlikely spot for a murder.

It must have taken place in the library, then. Angela hesitated outside the door for a moment, then turned the handle and went in. The room was dim— lit only by a green lamp which stood on a desk nearby. She gazed around at the walls, which were entirely covered with bookshelves. In the far corner was a large globe on a wooden stand. Angela went over to it and spun it gently. As far as she could judge from the countries represented thereon, it appeared to be at least fifty years old. She turned her attention to the books. This section seemed to be devoted to military history. Farther along was a complete set of encyclopaedias. She picked up a volume at random.

'Bashi-Bazouk—Bashkala,' she read. 'Hmm, very helpful.'

She straightened up and turned round, and began to try and picture the scene.

'Now, what happened, I wonder,' she said to herself, screwing up her eyes.

But it was no good—it was too dim and she could not see the room clearly enough. No sooner had this thought passed through her mind than there was a click and a light went on. Angela jumped.

'I suppose I ought to have expected to find you here,' said Henry Jameson from the doorway. 'Why didn't you switch the ceiling light on? You'll find it much easier to see.'

'I didn't think of it,' said Angela. 'But thank you—that's much better.'

'Is there any use in my asking you nicely to leave the room?'

'Look here,' said Angela. 'You are aware, aren't you, that practically everyone in the castle knows perfectly well that there's been a murder?'

'I suspected they might,' said Henry with a sigh. 'It's almost impossible to keep a secret in a place like this.'

'Well, then,' said Angela, 'what's the use in sneaking about and pretending nothing's happened? You may as well come out and admit it at once—that way you can question people quite openly, without having to think up silly reasons why you're suddenly interested in what they were doing last night.'

'You're probably right,' he said with a faint smile. 'You'll have to excuse me—I'm an Intelligence man and I'm not used to telling people things. As you can no doubt imagine, I've spent most of my working life trying to do the exact opposite.'

Angela laughed.

'And of course, politicians are a suspicious lot,' he continued.

'Yes, especially of me,' said Angela dryly.

'What makes you think that?'

'Common sense,' she replied. 'If I were in their position I should suspect me too.' She did not think it expedient to mention what Aubrey had told her that morning. 'I know Gabe saw me rooting around in the chest—oh, I quite admit it,' she said as she saw his look, 'but it was curiosity rather than guilt that made me do it.'

'I'm glad to hear it,' he said.

'I can imagine the conversations you've all been having today, asking each other whether I'm to be trusted. You probably told them what you knew about me ten years ago, and then I dare say Aubrey told you that we were once engaged and he would vouch for my honesty, and then someone mentioned that they'd read about me in the newspapers, and someone else wondered what the world was coming to, if women were allowed to go poking their noses into murder cases, and then Lord Strathmerrick probably piped up and said it was a damned nuisance and can we *really* be sure she's not a spy?'

This was such an accurate summary of the conversation that Henry had to smother a laugh.

'At any rate,' continued Angela, 'I guess I ought to

be thankful that St. John turned up this evening and deflected all the attention away from me. But I didn't do it, I promise you.'

'Very well, then,' said Henry. 'Let's accept for the moment that you are in no way involved in all this.'

'Oh, do let's—just for the moment,' said Angela slyly.

'In that case, presumably you have your own ideas as to what *did* happen. You didn't wander into the library to look for an improving book, I imagine.'

'Certainly not,' said Angela. 'I came here because I assume this is where the professor was killed. That's why you're here too, isn't it? Since the idea of someone carrying his body along miles of corridors to the billiard-room is frankly absurd, it stands to sense that he must have been killed somewhere close by, and as far as I can tell, this is the only room that is suitable.'

Henry nodded in agreement.

'Yes,' he said. 'I think it is.'

'Then why haven't you investigated it sooner?'

'We have had—er—other things to think about,' he said.

'Ah, yes, the missing documents,' said Angela.

'Now, how in heaven's name do you know about that?' said Henry. 'Don't tell me you know where they are.'

'No, I'm afraid I don't. I don't even know *what* they are, as a matter of fact, but I can make a pretty good guess.'

'Very well—tell me what you think they are.'

'I think they are the practical results of Professor Klausen's research into radio-activity. I assume he has proved his theories and was coming to tell you all about it.'

'I didn't know you took an interest in science, Mrs. Marchmont,' said Henry.

'I don't—Clemmie explained it to me.'

'Does she know about the documents?' he said half-fearfully.

'Oh, no,' she assured him. 'She doesn't know anything except that Klausen is dead.'

'Who else knows about them?'

'Only Freddy and I,' she said. 'And Gertie,' she added.

'Gertie!' he said in horror.

'But as far as I know, I'm the only one who has deduced what's in them. I'm right, aren't I? I can't think of any other reason why the British and American Governments should be meeting Klausen in secret during the Christmas holidays. He must have finally succeeded in finding a way to obtain energy from atoms and was dying to show you all his research.'

Henry would not confirm it, but he did not deny it either, and Angela guessed she had pretty much hit the nail on the head.

'So, then,' she said after a second's pause, 'I guess you need to find the papers before the snow melts and they can be smuggled out of the castle.'

'We do indeed,' said Henry. 'I don't know if you have any idea of just how important they are, Mrs. Marchmont, but let us just say they could mean the difference between peace and war.'

'Good gracious!' said Angela. She knew of old that Henry Jameson was not given to exaggeration. If he really believed what he said, then clearly much was at stake. 'I'm only sorry I can't help you,' she said. 'I rather wish now that I'd peeped through the cupboard door when the mysterious visitor came into the billiard-room. I take it whoever killed Klausen also stole the papers from him, then?'

'I assume so,' he replied. He looked at the floor for a moment, as though debating something with himself, then in a rare fit of indiscretion went on, 'but they're not the only papers to have gone missing.'

'Oh?'

Henry looked as though he regretted saying even as much as he had, and Angela had to prompt him to continue. He went on reluctantly:

'The Foreign Secretary persuaded Klausen to give him a copy of the documents before he arrived, for the purposes of security. They have gone too.'

Angela stared at him.

'But where were they?' she asked.

'Apparently Buchanan kept them locked in a secret compartment of his trunk. Someone broke the lock and made away with them—probably some time last night or today.'

'Who knew he had them?'

'That is a very good question, Mrs. Marchmont,' said Henry. 'For certain: I, Lord Strathmerrick, the Foreign Secretary, Claude Burford, the Ambassador and Gabe Bradley. Other than that I don't know. Naturally, everyone denies absolutely having told anybody else about them.'

'Then either one of you is lying or one of you stole the papers.'

'That's about the size of it,' he agreed.

'Dear me,' said Angela, after a pause. 'Things aren't going well for you, are they? If you don't want all this to get out you have to solve the murder *and* find the two sets of missing documents before the snow melts and the police start tramping all over the place and getting cosy with the newspapers.'

Henry grimaced at the mention of the newspapers.

'Yes,' he said. 'It's going to be big news, all right. I only hope we can keep a lid on the part about the missing documents, in the national interest. Your reporter friend, Freddy, now—do you suppose he can be trusted?'

'Occasionally,' said Angela without thinking, then went on hurriedly as she saw his alarm, 'Yes, I think he can in matters of this sort, but you'd do better to ask him outright. He's not a bad boy, really.'

'I shall speak to him, then, and impress upon him how important it is that as little as possible gets into the papers.'

'If you give him first go at whatever *can* be published then I'm sure he'll be as silent as the grave on everything else,' said Angela.

'And what about you, Mrs. Marchmont? Shall you be as silent as the grave, too?' said Henry with a meaningful glance at her.

Angela smiled at him.

'Mr. Jameson, you trusted me once, ten years ago, when I was young and untried,' she said. 'It was a risk then. I should like you to take that risk again. I don't like murder, and I'm as keen as you are to see that whoever killed Klausen is brought to justice and that his life's work is kept safe. I'd like to help you if you'll let me. Besides,' she went on in a more practical tone, 'what have you got to lose? I don't suppose the situation could get any worse if it tried. The professor is already dead and the papers are already missing. What else could go wrong?'

'We don't know what happened to the gun that killed him,' said Henry. 'Someone else might get shot.'

'Then you do believe it wasn't my gun?'

'I shall accept it for the moment,' he said solemnly.

'Admirable caution,' she said. 'Well, then, *I* shall accept for the moment that you want my help in solving the mystery. Now, I don't suppose you have found out at what time Professor Klausen arrived at Fives Castle?'

'No,' he replied. 'I should guess that it was some time during the dance, however, since one would assume that had he arrived at a reasonable hour then he would have immediately made himself known to his host and joined us for dinner.'

'That still leaves a period of about three or four hours. Did no-one see him? Not even one of the servants?'

'Not as far as we have been able to find out. You must remember that most of the servants joined the dance, and so nobody would have been there to welcome him.'

'Yes, that's true,' said Angela. 'One can't deduce anything suspicious from his unseen arrival.'

'He was a pretty secretive sort anyway,' said Henry. 'It would have been like him to sneak in when he knew nobody was looking.'

'So, what did he do after that? How did he end up in the library? Had he been to Fives before?'

'I don't think so.'

'Then he won't have known his way around,' said Angela. 'So, then, either he wandered about for a bit and just chanced upon the library, or—'

'—or someone brought him here,' said Henry, nodding.

'His murderer, presumably,' said Angela. She glanced around her. 'Does that mean that the killer knew exactly when Klausen was going to arrive? If so, then perhaps they had made arrangements to meet separately before the professor showed himself to the rest of the guests. But why?'

'I don't know,' said Henry.

'The alternative is that the murderer came upon Klausen by accident, brought him here and then killed him, intentionally or not. Either way, it seems fairly certain to me that our culprit was after the papers. Even if he didn't intend to kill the professor, getting hold of the documents was still his ultimate aim.'

'Yes,' said Henry. 'Perhaps whoever it was originally planned to steal them without any violence during the course of the weekend and then leave the castle quietly, but the snow put paid to that.'

'I wonder what happened,' said Angela. 'Can we be absolutely certain that the murder took place here in the library, do you think? Have you searched this room at all?'

'I've had a quick look round,' said Henry, 'but there hasn't been time today for me to search it properly.'

'Then let's do it now,' said Angela. Before Henry could reply she went down onto all fours, to the great detriment of her frock, and began examining the carpet closely. After a second's hesitation, Henry hitched up his trouser legs carefully at the knees and joined her. They crawled about the floor with great solemnity and concentration.

'By the way, I don't suppose you heard anything yourself while you were hiding in that cupboard in the billiard-room?' he said, after their initial search had revealed nothing.

'Not a thing,' she replied, frowning at a speck of dried mud. 'The walls are very thick here, so I imagine any gunshot sounds would be quite muffled anyway. He must have been fairly recently dead when I found him, though, as he was quite warm and not at all stiff when I felt his pulse.' She sat back on her heels and reflected for a moment. 'Now, if I wanted to shoot a man in this library, where should I do it?' she wondered aloud. 'Unless the murderer was a crack shot, then he was most likely standing quite close to the professor, since he was killed with a single bullet to the heart.'

'True enough,' said Henry. 'They must have been within a foot or two of each other, surely.'

He stood up, then wandered over to the globe in the corner and spun it absently as he glanced around, thinking. Angela watched him.

'That's exactly what I did when I came in,' she said. She stood up too and joined him next to the globe. 'It's a beautiful object, isn't it? I imagine the first thing everybody does when they come in here is to spin it.'

They glanced at each other as the same idea struck them both and with one accord bent down and began to scour the carpet around the globe. It was not long before they found what they were looking for.

'Look!' exclaimed Henry, and held something out for Mrs. Marchmont to examine. 'It was just by this shelf here.'

'Why, it's a coat-button,' said Angela. 'Is the professor missing one? I'm afraid I didn't notice.'

'As a matter of fact, he is,' said Henry in something like triumph. 'I happened to notice it particularly at the time, as I wondered where it had got to. I shall compare it with the others, but I'm pretty certain this is his.'

'Is there anything else? I suppose a bloodstain is too much to hope for?'

'I think it is,' said Henry. 'There was very little blood. I think the damage was mostly internal.'

They scratched about for a while longer but without any luck.

'Well, then,' said Henry at last. 'That seems to confirm our theory, at any rate. He was killed in the library.'

'And now we return to the question: who did it?' said Angela.

'This St. John fellow,' began Henry. 'Do you know him personally?'

'No. He's a friend of Freddy's. I met him for the first time today. I expect you've heard all about his political activities, though.'

'Yes,' said Henry. 'That might be a coincidence, and to speak to him one wouldn't exactly credit him with the greatest of intelligence, but firing a gun doesn't take a great deal of brain-power. We've questioned him briefly, of course, and his story is an odd one but might well be true.'

'It might, or it might not,' said Angela. 'I don't know if you noticed, but he was lying about his alibi.'

'Ah, you spotted that, did you? He might have made a mistake about the time, I dare say.'

'If he did then he's done it three times: once to me, once to you and then again to me. I asked him for the second time at dinner, and he was quite certain that he had left the castle before half past twelve—said he'd looked at his watch, in fact. But of course that's simply not possible, since Bobby bumped into him when we were playing Sardines, and we didn't begin that until well after one o'clock, as I recall.'

'Yes,' said Henry, 'and he made a mistake about the fallen tree, too. If he had left when he said he did, he would inevitably have found himself walking along the path to the village with several of the villagers—and most of them managed to get home at that time. As far as we can tell, the landslide didn't happen until closer to one o'clock. Where is he now, by the way? He and Freddy didn't stay in the dining-room for long after the ladies left. I hope they're not getting up to mischief.'

'It depends on how you define mischief,' said Angela, 'but I think we're safe. When I left the drawing-room, St. John was in deep and earnest conversation with Miss Foster about their respective literary efforts. It was touch and go as to who would manage to recite the worst poem to the other before things turned nasty.'

'If these militant types would only stick to the bad poetry then my job would be a great deal easier,' said Henry with a sigh. 'I ought to have known we hadn't rooted them all out. I fear the next few weeks are going to be difficult for the Government.'

'What do you mean by "rooted them all out?"' said Angela. 'Rooted all *who* out?'

There was no use in trying to hide things now, Henry was forced to admit.

'The spies,' he said.

TWENTY-ONE

'IT ALL STARTED a couple of years ago,' began Henry. 'You may remember all that industrial unrest we had—the strike and what-not, and the political activism that went on at the same time. There was a real worry within the Government during that period that we were about to suffer the same fate as Russia—or at least that Communism would shortly become a force to be reckoned with—and of course, those concerns were voiced on many occasions during meetings of the Cabinet. At a certain point, however, it was noticed that confidential decisions taken at Cabinet meetings appeared to be getting out, and that the information was making its way abroad. Stories about Britain's intransigent attitude towards its Eastern neighbours began to appear in the foreign press, and certain statements were attributed to our politicians as a demonstration of our lack of faith. Of course, we denied absolutely that anyone had ever made such statements, and demanded in the strongest possible terms that the accusations be withdrawn immediately. In reality, however, there was much consternation within the Government, for almost everything that had been published was true.

'Once our attention had been drawn to this, we started paying closer attention to what was going on abroad, and found that a surprising amount of information which ought to have been known only to a tiny number of very senior politicians in London was seemingly also known elsewhere: things about trade treaties and suchlike—dull stuff to most people, I dare say, but highly important in its own way. It was immediately obvious that somebody must be passing this information on, and we began investigating discreetly. We soon found the culprit: a young man called Stephen Golovin, who had recently begun working for the Cabinet Secretariat. He was the son of a doctor who had fled Russia with his family during the unrest of 1905 and had come to live in England. The Golovins settled down and lived here quietly and respectably for many years, but at some point—we don't know exactly when—young Stephen must have fallen in with some bad company. We learned from his family that there was a period of a year or two in which he was estranged from them, and they were at a loss to understand why—nor did they have any idea what he was doing during this time. Eventually, however, he seemed to grow out of his youthful rebellion, came back into the fold and began looking for work.

'As it happened, the Golovins were neighbours of Beresford Ogilvy, the then Home Secretary. He had always had a liking for the boy, and in the interests of helping his old friends offered Stephen Golovin a junior position in the Cabinet Secretariat which he accepted. The young man was a hard worker and had never raised in anyone the slightest doubt of his loyalty, until the very day he was intercepted in the act of smuggling a copy of the minutes to the latest Cabinet meeting out of the office and arrested.

'I, personally, believed it was a mistake to have him arrested immediately, since I thought it would be wiser to keep him under observation for a while and find out whom he was passing the information to, and who, if any, were his accomplices. However, some of the more—shall we say—easily startled members of the Cabinet insisted on having the police called as soon as they found out what was going on. Golovin was arrested, tried and sentenced to twenty years in prison.'

'I remember the case well,' said Angela. 'It was in the newspapers for weeks. And of course, the Home Secretary was forced to resign his ministry and his seat in Parliament, given the part he had unwittingly played in the affair.'

'Yes,' said Henry. 'It was most unfortunate. As a matter of fact, although it wasn't put about then, there was some talk of the whole Government having to resign which, as I'm sure you realize, would have been highly injurious to national security given the political mood at the time. Fortunately, it survived the crisis and a new Home Secretary was appointed. Meanwhile, Claude Burford, who was Ogilvy's former secretary, was chosen to contest Ogilvy's old seat and just scraped in by the skin of his teeth. He's not as clever as Ogilvy was, but no doubt he'll do well given his connections.'

'No doubt,' agreed Angela dryly.

'At any rate,' went on Henry, 'the whole thing gave

the Intelligence department an awful headache for months. It seemed to have died down in the past year or so, but I always rather wondered whether Golovin was working alone. He swore he was a lone agent, but I was never entirely convinced.'

'Did he confess to the crime, then?'

'Oh, yes. Was quite unashamed of it, in fact. He said his loyalties had never lain with Britain, and that his father had been a traitor for ever having left Russia in the first place. He refused to give us the names of the people to whom he had been passing on secrets, however, and we never found them out. Nor did we ever discover whether he was indeed telling the truth when he said he had been acting alone. Now and again we received a hint from our agents overseas that there was an entire ring of spies working here in Britain, but we were never able to confirm it.'

'But now it looks as though your agents may have been right,' said Angela.

'Yes, it does,' said Henry soberly.

'Who knew that Professor Klausen was coming here, and why?'

'As far as I am aware, only ourselves on the English side,' said Henry. 'On the American side, I don't know. Buchanan first spoke to the Secretary of State, who sent the Ambassador to take part in the preliminary talks. I assume the need for secrecy was emphasized, but undoubtedly a few people know over there. This meeting at Fives was arranged only last week, however, so there would have been no time for a spy to travel here from the United States.'

'Plenty of time to send a telegram to an activist in England, however,' said Angela. 'St. John Bagshawe, for example.'

'True enough,' he replied.

'Has the professor been removed from the chest yet?' said Angela.

'I'm almost ashamed to say he hasn't,' said Henry. 'I know it's not exactly a decent thing to do to a dead man, but we've had to leave him where he is until the rigor mortis wears off. We shall bring him out tomorrow, and then send someone out to fetch a doctor and the police. It seems to have stopped snowing, so with any luck the men will be able to move the fallen tree and clear a path through to the village. After that, the cat will be pretty much out of the bag, no doubt. I suppose I oughtn't to take it too much to heart: after all, from what you say, everybody in the castle knows all about it already, so a few million more people around the country won't make the situation any worse than it is.'

He looked so crestfallen that Angela could hardly help laughing.

'What should you have done if you had been the one to find the body?' she asked curiously.

'I?' said Henry. 'If I had found the body, then we should certainly not be having this conversation now, Mrs. Marchmont—and I should not be worrying about the story's getting into the papers.'

'I can well believe it,' said Angela. 'I am only sorry you have been forced to accept my help.'

'Oh, it could be worse,' said Henry. 'At least I know I can rely on your good sense.'

'And my honesty, of course,' said Angela.

'Of course,' he said.

Angela smiled to herself, then said, 'Is there anything else I can do to help you this evening? If there isn't, then I'd rather like to go to bed now, if you don't mind.'

'Oh, please do,' said Henry. 'I should like to go myself, but I suppose there will be more talking late into the night tonight. Politicians have the most extraordinary ability to talk for hours, without ever saying much to the purpose.'

'I think it's part of the job,' said Angela in some amusement. She bade him goodnight and went upstairs. She was feeling very tired after the adventures of the night before and did not suppose she would be missed in the drawing-room. Once she reached her room she undressed and slipped into bed. She was about to switch off the lamp when she saw the book that Clemmie had lent her earlier, lying on the table by the bed where she had put it. She took it up and began to read. After a few minutes, however, her attention started to wander and she could not prevent her mind from reviewing the events of the day and attempting to make sense of them. Why had St. John lied about what time he had left Fives Castle? There seemed to be only one logical answer to that question, and that was that he wanted to establish an alibi for the murder. But how had he known that an alibi was needed? As far as Angela could recall, when they had first questioned him in Freddy's bedroom none of them had mentioned the murder at that point. In that case, why not admit straight out that he had been wandering around the castle until after one o'clock? There was no reason to lie about it, since the truth would not have made him look any more foolish than he already did—unless, of course, his presence at Fives had a more sinister purpose. Could St. John have murdered Professor Klausen? He did not *seem* the type, but all the evidence was pointing that way: his political affiliations, his membership of a militant group, his previous violent activities—all of those would look bad for him if placed before a court. Perhaps they ought to give him a chance to account for himself before it got that far; it seemed only fair, after all.

'Oh,' said Angela, sitting up suddenly as she remembered something. She had meant to tell Henry about her strange conversation with Eleanor Buchanan earlier that evening, but it had slipped her mind. What had Eleanor meant when she said that she had done what Angela had asked of her and would not or could not do any more? Angela was at a loss to understand it. She thought back to their conversation. Eleanor had seemed to become agitated when they were talking about her locket—or, rather, its contents. Angela could picture the way Mrs. Buchanan wound her fingers in and out of the gold chain, pausing only occasionally to stroke the pendant absently. Perhaps she had been a little too inquisitive about Eleanor's brother: after all, family disagreements were a very personal matter and it was hardly good manners to insist on being told the whole story.

Angela yawned and glanced back down at *The World Set Free*. She was finding it slightly depressing and decided she would rather go to sleep. In the interests of remaining in Marthe's good books, however, she slipped out of bed first to pick up her evening things, which she had left on the floor. She draped them as neatly as possible across a chair, moving her handbag to do so. The bag seemed unusually heavy, and she glanced inside it in puzzlement, then froze, staring at what she had found.

'How very odd,' she said at last. She reached inside and brought out a gun—a small revolver not unlike her own. Angela did not even need to open the cylinder to know how many bullets it would contain, but she did anyway. As she had expected, one chamber was empty. Angela gazed at the gun and thought very hard. This was evidently the weapon that had killed Professor Klausen. Why had the killer suddenly decided to plant it on Angela? To incriminate her, presumably.

'I take it this is your idea of a joke, Mr. Murderer, whoever you are,' said Angela to herself. 'Well, I don't think it's funny. You had better watch out.'

Then she went to bed and slept for nine whole hours with the gun under her pillow.

TWENTY-TWO

WHEN ANGELA WENT into the breakfast-room the next morning she found only Aubrey Nash and Gabe Bradley there, laughing about something. When he saw her, Gabe glanced at the Ambassador, drained his cup and excused himself tactfully.

Angela took a seat across the table from Aubrey, helped herself to coffee and began buttering a roll.

'It's snowing again, I see,' she said by way of a greeting. 'I suppose that means we'll be cut off for another day at least.'

'Maybe not,' replied Aubrey. 'Lord Strathmerrick has sent out some men to begin clearing away the tree and the landslide. I don't know how bad it is, but I guess we'll be able to get through to the village by this afternoon.'

'And then the police can be fetched at last.'

'I don't think that's what Jameson has in mind,' he said. 'I believe he's planning to telephone Scotland Yard directly—that is, if the lines aren't down in the village too.'

'I see,' said Angela. 'Have you seen Mr. Jameson this morning? I want to speak to him.' She had been tempted to remain quiet about the gun she had found in her bag, given that she was presently without her own, but after reflecting on the matter a while she had reluctantly decided to tell Henry about it, even though it was bound to make her look even more guilty in the eyes of some of the more suspicious of the men. After all, Henry had taken her into his confidence last night, so it would be discourteous of her at the very least to act in bad faith.

'I think he and Lord Strathmerrick are busy with Professor Klausen,' said Aubrey.

'Have they moved him?'

'Yes. I guess the rigor mortis wore off and they were able to get him out. I'm glad of it—it's hardly fitting to store a dead body in an old chest like so much cast-off laundry.'

'No,' agreed Angela. 'He deserves some decency after the way in which he died. I don't suppose I'll get an opportunity to talk to Mr. Jameson until later, then.'

'I guess not.'

'What shall you do today, if you can't get away from Fives? I dare say you and Gabe have plenty of affairs of state with which to occupy yourself. Or are you doing some detective-work?'

Aubrey grimaced.

'No,' he said. 'Nobody has told me anything. The British Government fellows have taken charge and are doing it all their own way. Hardly to be wondered at, I guess—after all, it's their show and their dead body.'

'Yes,' said Angela. 'I imagine it must be rather

embarrassing for them to have invited the official representative of another country to meet their pet celebrity, only to have him be murdered before the introduction can take place. It doesn't exactly give a good impression of their efficiency, at any rate.'

'True—although it was hardly their fault. I'm only surprised they haven't placed Bagshawe under lock and key yet.'

'I imagine they'd like to,' said Angela, 'but there's no real evidence of his guilt—he wasn't carrying a gun, for example—and they can't just lock him up on suspicion. If they went around shutting away people they thought *might* have done it, then no doubt Freddy and I would have been locked in our bedrooms since yesterday, too.'

'I only hope they find the evidence they need,' said Aubrey. 'Lord Strathmerrick was talking last night about searching everyone's rooms today, although I don't know how he's going to explain that to everyone, seeing that we're meant to be keeping quiet about the murder.'

'He needn't worry about that,' said Angela. 'Everybody in the house seems to know more about it than we do.'

'Is that so?' he said in mild surprise. 'It just goes to show how hard it is to keep a secret in a place like this.' He was silent for a moment, then said regretfully, 'I'm sorry I never got to meet Klausen— I'd have liked to hear what he had to say. I've missed my chance now, though. I was only sent here because the meeting was arranged at the last minute and there wasn't time for anyone to get over to Scotland from Washington. But there's no urgency any more, and by the time everything has been resolved here, the matter will have passed out of my hands and will be the responsibility of the Department of State.'

'I expect Selma will be pleased to get away,' said Angela. 'I think she was looking forward to the Riviera.'

'Yes, the snow doesn't agree with her,' he said. He hesitated uncomfortably, then went on, 'Angela, I'm sorry I mentioned our old engagement to the others. I told them because I wanted to convince them that you're not a spy or a criminal, but I think it might have had the opposite effect.'

'I think you might be right,' said Angela.

'Believe me, it's not what I intended. I guess all my years in the diplomatic service never prepared me for something like this.'

'No, I don't suppose you encounter many murders in your job,' said Angela with a smile.

'Still, at least we know who the real killer was now, so you ought to be out of the picture.'

Angela thought of the gun in her room, but said nothing, and instead took a sip of her coffee.

'I'm sorry things ended between us, Angela,' said Aubrey suddenly.

Angela looked up at him, but did not reply.

'You never did tell me exactly why you broke it off. I hope it wasn't anything I did.'

'No,' said Angela, a little sadly, 'it wasn't. You didn't do anything wrong, I promise. But I had other things to think about then, and I realized that getting married would be a mistake and that you were better off without me. But don't let's talk about it now. All that is in the past, and you must admit we've both done very well for ourselves apart.'

'I guess so. Selma's a great girl—and she's good

for me too.'

'She's much better for you than I should have been,' said Angela.

'Why, that's nonsense,' he said. He glanced at her sideways. 'Although you did always like to do things your own way.'

'That's true enough,' she said. 'And I still do. I imagine I always will. You had a lucky escape.'

He laughed and shook his head.

'You're a good man, Aubrey,' said Angela. 'Selma is very lucky to have you.'

She reached across the table and took his hand, and they smiled into each other's eyes as old friends.

With her by now customary sense of timing, Lady Strathmerrick just then entered the room, causing Angela and Aubrey to withdraw their hands abruptly and gaze at their plates with great concentration. But the Countess was not interested in what her guests were getting up to; at that moment her head was filled with one thing and one thing only.

'Oh, Mrs. Marchmont,' she said. 'I have just heard the most awful news! I can hardly believe it. My husband has just informed me that poor Professor Klausen has been shot dead, and that you were the one to discover his body.'

'Er—' said Angela, but Lady Strathmerrick went on,

'I am very sorry indeed that anything so unpleasant should happen to a guest of mine. Please allow me to apologize for it—it must have been quite dreadful for you. I do hope you haven't been too upset. My husband's intentions are good, but of course he's a man and has no idea how to comfort a woman in distress. And then to leave the body in a chest—why, it's all most unsuitable. I assure you that such a thing has never happened here at Fives before.'

She seemed to take the murder as a personal reflection upon her housekeeping.

'I thank you for your concern, Lady Strathmerrick,' said Angela, 'but please don't worry yourself about it. I am quite all right—really, I am. I am only very sorry about what has happened to poor Professor Klausen.'

'Oh, so am I,' said the Countess, in some relief that Mrs. Marchmont did not appear to blame her personally for the catastrophe. 'I only hope we can speak to the police today. They must send someone after the man responsible. You know he escaped across the fields? He must have been truly desperate to do it, but I suppose that means he might be anywhere by now.'

Angela was pleased that at least one person in the house did not suspect her of involvement in the crime. Evidently Lord Strathmerrick had told his wife an expurgated version of the truth—either that, or she had taken it upon herself to believe that the murderer had escaped without inquiring too deeply into the matter. Angela wondered how the Countess would react if she knew what was really going on at Fives.

'At any rate,' went on Lady Strathmerrick, 'the men have been sent out to clear a path to the village this morning, and after that I dare say they will start clearing the worst of the drifts on the drive, and then we can all get away from this place. In the meantime, I do hope you aren't *too* disturbed at the thought of staying here for just a little while longer.'

Angela and Aubrey reassured her kindly and Angela pressed a cup of sweet tea onto her, for she saw that her hostess was very upset and agitated. Lady Strathmerrick smiled gratefully and took a few sips. After a moment or two she declared she was feeling much better, and shortly afterwards she went out again, since she wanted to speak to all her guests, she said.

Angela was rather sorry for her, and thought it rather a shame that the Countess felt the need to apologize to everyone for a murder she herself had not committed. Still, it looked as though they would soon all be able to leave Fives Castle, now that the men were clearing a path. On the one hand, it would be something of a relief to get away, but on the other it did now mean that the murderer of Professor Klausen would also be able to escape, and then how would they catch him? And even if they did, it might be too late, since he would no doubt have passed on the papers to someone else by then. Was Klausen's research doomed to fall into the hands of the enemy?

TWENTY-THREE

As ANGELA LEFT the breakfast-room she saw Freddy coming towards her.

'There you are,' he said. 'Come in and feed with me.'

'I've just eaten,' said Angela.

'Well, then, come in and talk to me while I eat. I want to know where you disappeared to last night.'

Angela followed him back into the room, which was empty, since Aubrey had left a few minutes earlier.

'You don't miss much, do you?' she said.

'Frederick Pilkington-Soames, the amazing boy-reporter, at your service,' he said. He wrinkled his nose fastidiously at the choice of dishes on offer and began to pile his plate high. 'These hawk-like eyes of mine see everything and miss nothing. What would be a mere casual brush of the hand to lesser mortals becomes a secret signal between hardened gangsters to me; a glance and a nod across a crowded ball-room, and Freddy P.-S. is already back at his desk, reporting on the scandalous *affaire* between Lady Jones and her butler. I see everything and know everything.'

'In that case I wish you'd tell me where I left my grey gloves,' said Angela. 'I haven't seen them in weeks.'

'Gloves? Are they a dove-grey suède with silver buttons at the wrist and a sort of perforated pattern on the back?'

'Why, yes, as a matter of fact they are,' said Angela.

'They're at my mother's,' he said. 'You left them there last time you visited.'

'So I did,' said Angela. 'Very well, then, I shall restrain my scornful laugh at your hubris on this occasion.'

'Splendid. Now, about last night,' he prompted.

'I was doing a little detecting in the library.'

'The library? Is that where Klausen was shot?'

'It looks like it. We found a coat-button of his on the floor.'

'Who is "we?"'

'Henry Jameson and I.'

He raised his eyebrows.

'Oh yes?' he said. 'Did you meet there by arrangement, or did he follow you there to arrest you? Incidentally, does the fact of having a brother in Scotland Yard give one the power of arrest?'

'I don't suppose so, but he's from Intelligence, so he's probably allowed to do whatever he likes in the interests of national security. Anyway, the answer is no to both questions. I went there of my own accord and he just happened to find me there, so we had a look around together.'

'Then I gather he's stopped suspecting you,' said

Freddy.

'Temporarily, at least. He reserves the right to change his mind, though.'

'Sensible chap. What about me? Am I still under suspicion?'

'No more than usual,' said Angela. 'I told him you could probably be trusted.'

'Thank you for that "probably"—I shall do the same for you one day.'

'I think he wants to have a word with you about not shouting things all over the newspapers,' said Angela. 'I suggested that you might be more amenable if he were to offer you a scoop.'

'That's more like it. Yes, that would be most acceptable. Very well, let it be hereby understood that my mouth is well and truly closed on this matter until such time as I am permitted to open it. Now, what did he tell you?'

Angela related to him the occurrences of last night, including Henry's admission that Klausen was bringing some papers with him, and that these, as well as the Foreign Secretary's copy, had both gone missing—although she did not mention what they were thought to contain. She also told him the story of Stephen Golovin and about Henry's concern that he had not been acting alone. Freddy listened as he ate, frowning occasionally.

'I see,' he said when she had finished. 'So they think there's a spy ring operating in Whitehall, do they? That's rather bad for them, given that they'd only just got over the shock of the last one. It looks as though there's going to be the most awfully big scandal—especially if they can't get the papers back. I assume they contained some important invention of

Klausen's.'

'Probably,' said Angela carefully. 'At any rate, I don't suppose they can keep the news of Klausen's death a secret, but they might be able to hush up the fact that it was murder—especially if they can get the papers back before the whole thing blows up.'

'Are we quite certain that they haven't been spirited away?' said Freddy.

'How is that possible? If the murderer is still here, then surely the documents are too.'

'But where?'

'I have no idea,' said Angela. 'Fives Castle is so big that they might be almost anywhere. It would be easy enough to hide them so that no-one would ever find them.'

'Of course, if we knew who'd taken them we could just follow him about until he goes to get them from their hiding-place,' said Freddy. 'And he'll have to do that sooner or later, since they're of no use to anyone stuck in a hole somewhere.'

'That's true enough,' said Angela.

Freddy put down his knife and fork.

'I wonder,' he said thoughtfully.

'What?'

He glanced at her and resumed eating.

'I was just thinking about where I should hide the papers if I were the murderer.'

'Where?'

'Well, for a start, I should want to put them in a place where I could get at them quickly and easily if I needed to make an immediate escape.'

'That seems reasonable,' agreed Angela.

'And then I'd want to put them somewhere they'd never be spotted, even if someone happened to come across them accidentally.'

'Such as where?'

'Why, with lots of other things that look like them, of course.'

'Do you mean the library?'

'Don't you think it's the perfect place?' said Freddy. 'It's full of musty old books and papers. It would be the easiest thing in the world to slip the documents in among the books or inside a periodical or something like that.'

'Yes, it would, wouldn't it?' said Angela. 'Do you mean that the murderer shot Klausen in the library, removed the papers from his pocket and then quickly hid them somewhere in the same room?'

'It's as good an idea as any, don't you think?'

'It makes sense, certainly,' said Angela. 'The most pressing matter at the time would have been to hide the professor's body. Presumably the papers could wait until later, so the killer shoved them in among the books somewhere with the intention of coming back for them at some point. Do you suppose they're still there, though?'

'There's no harm in searching,' said Freddy. He pushed his half-empty plate away. 'Come on, let's go and look now, shall we?'

Angela agreed and they went out. In the library she showed him the spot in which the button had been found.

'So he died here, did he?' said Freddy. 'I don't suppose there was any blood?'

'Not that we could see,' said Angela. 'He didn't bleed much, if you remember.' She spun the globe once again. It was a large one, and the wooden stand on which it rested was solid and massive. 'I wonder: if the murder took place some time during the dance—which it may well have done—then perhaps the killer shoved the body behind the globe for a while and came back for it later, once most people had gone home and the coast was clear.'

'Mm,' said Freddy. He was busy pulling books off the shelves in the corner where the professor had lain, flicking through the pages and then replacing them. 'How many books does this library contain, do you suppose?'

'Oh, many thousands, I should have thought,' said Angela.

'Well, then, don't stand there talking—give me a hand.'

Angela joined him in searching the bookshelves, but after a few minutes clicked her tongue impatiently and straightened up.

'It will take us weeks at this rate,' she said, 'and the dust is making me sneeze.'

'Why don't you go and look among those binders over there, then?' he replied. 'That might be a likely place.'

She did as he suggested and set to work. For some time there was no sound but that of rustling paper and the scraping of books on wood. Freddy worked his way gradually along the shelves until he had done the whole of the back wall, while Angela flicked through seemingly hundreds of old copies of *Blackwood's* and *The Quarterly Review*, wrinkling her nose at the pungent smell of old paper and trying not to tear the pages of the older issues, which were becoming somewhat fragile.

After spending some time in this manner with nothing to show for it but a painful paper cut, she sighed and threw down the binder she had been examining, then took up a stray copy of an illustrated newspaper from a few months earlier and began to glance through it.

'I don't believe the documents are here at all,' she said, gazing idly at a photograph of a scowling young man. 'Or if they are, they're too well hidden for us to find in the time we have.'

Freddy was rapidly reaching the same conclusion. He shoved a heavy tome back in its place with a bang and flung himself into a chair grumpily.

'It was such a beautiful idea too,' he said. 'How could I possibly have been wrong?'

'Perhaps you're not,' said Angela, 'but that doesn't mean we're going to have any luck. Why, they could be anywhere in here.'

'Hmph,' said Freddy, and lit a cigarette.

'By the way, you didn't tell me whether you managed to find out anything about Claude and Mrs. Buchanan,' said Angela.

He shook his head.

'Not much,' he said. 'Priss was pretty surprised when I broached the subject, in fact.'

'Not offended, I hope?'

'Oh, no. I don't think she much cares what he gets up to—and to be fair, it's not as though she has any right to, in view of her own goings-on.'

He paused in complacent reflection. Angela prodded his arm.

'You were saying,' she prompted.

'Ah, yes. No, as I said, Priss was surprised at the idea of Claude getting up to mischief with anyone— thought he was far too dull to do anything of the kind, she said. As a matter of fact, I almost had the feeling that she was looking at him in a new light when I suggested that he might have been misbehaving with the wife of his superior. She seemed almost interested in him. Perhaps I have accidentally done them both a good turn and they will now rediscover their love for one another.'

'*Re*discover?'

'Well, then, discover,' said Freddy. 'As you so rightly point out, it's not as though they had much interest in each other to start with. She has been thinking of breaking it off, you know.'

'Well, that's hardly a surprise,' said Angela. 'It's obvious she doesn't like him all that much. Or anyone, for that matter. Tell me, is she really as sulky as she seems?'

'No,' said Freddy, 'she's just terrifically bored at home and dying to get away.'

'Then I shouldn't have thought that marrying a man she finds dull would be the wisest thing to do on her part.'

'Yes, I think she's begun to realize that herself,' said Freddy. 'Come on, let's go somewhere else. I'm tired of looking at all these books. They remind me reproachfully of my incorrigible laziness at school, and I've been half-expecting old Spotty the Latin master to emerge from behind a bookshelf and threaten me with six of the best if I can't give him the first-person singular pluperfect subjunctive of the verb *terrere* here and now.'

'*Terruissem*,' said Angela after a moment's thought.

'Sometimes I quite hate you, Angela,' said Freddy.

In the passage outside they ran into Gertie, who had a wild, hunted look about her.

'Freddy, I insist you do something about that

211

friend of yours,' she said. 'He simply won't leave me alone. I've tried everything, I do believe. I've tried being politely negative; I've tried being distant; I've tried being vulgar and over-familiar; I've tried being wan and feeble, but none of it's worked. He just sits there gazing at me like a half-witted sheep and nodding. Just now I cracked and shouted "Oh, for Heaven's sake, please just leave me *alone!*" and then I swear he started *whining.*' She shuddered. 'I had to leave the drawing-room in a hurry before I lost my head, whacked him on the skull with a poker and dumped him in the chest with Professor Klausen.'

'Oh dear,' said Angela, trying not to laugh. 'Still, at least he hasn't followed you.'

'No,' said Gertie. 'I've left him with Clemmie. She won't thank me, but she owes me for that fancy galvanometer I gave her for Christmas, so she'll just have to put up with him. Why are all the men in this house being so tiresome at the moment?' she went on. 'Claude was pestering me at length earlier, too, wanting to know whether I'd seen anything through the cupboard door the other night. I said I hadn't, although quite frankly, even if I had I wouldn't have told him about it anyway—I should have told Father. Give me a cigarette, Freddy—no, best make it two. If anybody wants me, I shall be out in the garden, hiding behind a tree.'

She ran off, glancing about as though fearful that St. John would suddenly jump out from behind a pillar and start whining again.

'The man's an idiot,' said Freddy. 'He hasn't the faintest idea how to talk to women. All that mooning about and carrying their photographs next to his heart stuff just irritates them.'

Angela was only half-listening.

'Freddy, I've just remembered something else,' she said. 'Did you know that St. John was lying about his alibi?'

'No,' said Freddy in surprise. 'Was he really? In what way?'

'He said he left the castle before half past twelve, but that wasn't true. He left much later than that.'

'How do you know?' said Freddy.

Angela explained, and he whistled in dismay.

'I say,' he said. 'That looks bad for him, doesn't it?'

'It does, rather,' said Angela. 'I'm sorry.'

'Oh, don't be. If he did do it, then he's even more of an ass than I thought. I take it, then, that Jameson thinks he's more or less a dead cert for the murderer?'

'I don't know what Mr. Jameson thinks, but I imagine he'll be keeping a close eye on St. John from now on.'

'I dare say they'll have him arrested as soon as the snow is cleared.'

'Do you think so?' said Angela. 'It would make more sense to have him followed. If he has the documents he will presumably have to pass them on to somebody, but if they arrest him, then they won't be able to find out who that somebody is. This is their chance to break up the spy ring once and for all.'

'Yes, I see what you mean,' said Freddy. 'Well, then, perhaps he is safe for the moment. Come on, let's go and rescue Clemmie. She may one day represent the next generation of brilliant scientists now that Klausen has gone, so we don't want St. John to bore her to death before she can fulfil her potential.'

But Angela had stopped dead and was staring at

him.

'*What* did you say?' she said.

'I said we don't want—'

'No, no, before that.'

'I've no idea. Was I being brilliant, as usual?'

'I believe you were,' said Angela slowly.

He waited, but she said no more. She was biting her lip and gazing into space.

'Well, are you going to tell me what I said, so I can make a note for posterity?' he said impatiently.

She glanced at him.

'No,' she said. 'I should like to speak to somebody first. I may tell you later, if you're a good boy.'

She walked off purposefully, leaving him standing in puzzlement.

'Well, I'll be damned,' he said. 'What on earth is she up to now?'

TWENTY-FOUR

ANGELA FOUND ELEANOR Buchanan sitting in a
window-seat in the little sitting-room, quite alone,
gazing out of the window and playing with her locket
as usual. She turned as Mrs. Marchmont came in and
a frown crossed her face.

'What are you doing here?' she said. 'I thought I'd
made it quite clear that I didn't want to speak to you.'

'You did,' replied Angela, 'but I think you may
have been labouring under a misapprehension. I
wasn't trying to blackmail you last night, you know.'

Eleanor glanced up, startled, but said nothing.

'As a matter of fact, I was at a loss to understand
then why you were so angry with me,' went on
Angela. 'Of course, I realize now. You thought I
knew all about you and was hinting at it slyly, trying
to threaten you—but I promise you I wasn't. I hadn't
the faintest idea of it until today.'

'Hadn't the faintest idea of what?' said Eleanor,
half-fearfully.

'May I see the locket again?' said Angela. 'Ah, yes,

CLARA BENSON

I thought I remembered the initials inscribed on the front: "E. G." They're yours, I believe.'

Mrs. Buchanan nodded.

'They're the initials of my maiden name,' she said.

'Eleanor Golovin,' said Angela, and it was not a question.

Eleanor looked down.

'Did someone tell you?' she said.

'No,' said Angela. 'I saw a photograph of your brother in a newspaper this morning, but it wasn't until Freddy said something just now that I realized I'd seen his face before, in your locket. Please believe I have no intention of causing you harm, but somebody dangerous is at large and I think the time has come for you to tell what you know before the murderer can strike again.'

'I'm not proud of the fact that my brother is a traitor,' said Eleanor. 'I don't want you to think I am. But he's my brother, and the only family I have left since my father died. He did a bad thing, but I can't forget him and pretend he never existed—although I must keep him a secret from everyone, including my husband.'

'Do you mean he doesn't know?' said Angela in astonishment. 'But surely—'

'No, he doesn't know a thing,' said Eleanor. 'How could I tell him? We met last year in Baden-Baden and I fell in love with him and he with me. I never meant to keep it a secret, but the scandal was still in all the newspapers at the time—Stephen had just gone to gaol and the Home Secretary had had to resign his seat, and for a little while the Government had looked like toppling. Then when we met, Sandy kept on saying how happy I'd made him, and how marvellous it was that he could forget all the cares of state when he was with me. I meant to tell him who I was, but in the end I couldn't bring myself to do it. I know it was wrong of me, but I was in love with him and, perhaps foolishly, I thought that no-one would ever find out.'

'But didn't he realize the truth when he heard your surname?'

'He never knew me as Eleanor Golovin,' said Eleanor. 'When we first came to England we found that people often anglicized our name to Garvin, so that was the name we mostly used. When he grew up, Stephen started using his Russian name again, saying that we ought to be proud of it, but I was used to Garvin by then and saw no reason to change back.'

'When did you last speak to your brother?'

'I visited him in prison before his trial. I wanted to talk to him and find out what had possessed him to spy on the country that had been his home for most of his life, but he wouldn't talk to me about it. All he would say was that he was a true patriot and proud to be one, and that he would do the same again if given the opportunity.' She glanced up at Angela. 'I knew he'd fallen in with some odd people for a while, but I thought he had got over all that. It seems not, though: I suppose they were Radicals from the old country who got hold of him and convinced him that what he was doing was right. At any rate, he was angry and stubborn, and we—we had a row and I came away, and shortly afterwards he was sentenced to twenty years in prison. He was lucky not to be hanged—had it been wartime he certainly would have been—but the prison doctors said he was mentally unsound and ought merely to be locked up. After the trial I went abroad to Germany to think about things for a while, and that's where I met Sandy.'

'And you haven't heard from your brother since then?'

'No,' said Eleanor. 'He won't write to me, and I can't write to him any more. Can you imagine the sensation if it was discovered that the wife of the Foreign Secretary was the sister of a notorious spy? Why, it would be worse than the original scandal.'

'And so you have kept silent about it all this time,' said Angela, not unsympathetically.

'Yes,' said Eleanor. She seemed almost relieved to have unburdened herself of her secret. It must have been hard to keep it from her husband for a year or more. 'I've been a coward, I know,' she went on. 'I couldn't bear to tell Sandy about Stephen, as I knew I should lose him—of course he could never have married me had he known about it. I meant to be a good wife to him, truly I did. And I was, I promise you I was, until—' she stopped, and tears came into her eyes.

'Until Claude Burford began blackmailing you,' said Angela gently.

Eleanor nodded. She could not speak.

'How did he know who you were?'

Mrs. Buchanan took a deep breath and forced herself to be calm.

'He was the secretary of Beresford Ogilvy, the old Home Secretary, who was a friend of ours and gave Stephen his job in the Cabinet Secretariat. He lost his seat in Parliament after it all came out. I glimpsed Claude once or twice at the Ogilvys' house, but we were never introduced and I didn't think he would recognize me when he saw me here at Fives.

Unfortunately, I was wrong.'

'When did he approach you?'

'On New Year's Eve, before the dance. He found me alone in the drawing-room and said he had something he wanted to discuss with me in private, so we came in here. I'd only seen him once or twice before and hadn't thought much of him, but he seemed polite and honest enough, at least, so I didn't understand what he was saying to me at first. As a matter of fact, I thought he was—was making an impertinent proposal, and was about to brush it off and leave, but then he got hold of my arm and said he wouldn't let me go until I'd heard what he had to say. It was only then I understood that he remembered me perfectly well and meant to use the knowledge to his advantage. At first I tried to pretend that Sandy knew exactly who I was, but Claude laughed and said that was nonsense—he would never have married me in that case. Of course, I knew that was true so in the end I had to admit it.'

'And that put you in his power,' said Angela. 'What did he want?'

Tears were rolling down Eleanor's cheeks, and she brushed them away.

'He said Sandy had brought some secret papers with him to Fives, and that I was to get them for him. I said I didn't know anything about any papers—which was true—and Claude said that was all the better for me then, since once the theft was discovered Sandy wouldn't suspect me of having taken them.'

'Did he say why he wanted them?'

'No,' said Eleanor. 'Of course, I asked him, but he told me it was none of my business—it was important political stuff that I wouldn't understand. Then he said that in any case, surely the papers would be safer in his hands rather than in the hands of a man whose wife was the sister of a traitor. That was a low thing to say, and I told him so and said I should never betray my husband by doing such a thing. Then he got hold of my arm and sort of pushed me against the wall, and I became quite scared. He said I'd better do as I was told, or he would tell everybody who I was, then Sandy would lose his seat just as Mr. Ogilvy did, and did I want to be responsible for doing such a thing to my husband?'

'So in the end you did as he asked,' said Angela.

'Yes,' she said. 'At the party Claude made me dance with him, and told me he wanted the papers as soon as possible. Once the dance was over and we'd all gone to the drawing-room I excused myself for a minute and ran upstairs. Claude was waiting for me, and came into the bedroom with me while I fetched them.'

'If you didn't know about them, how did you know where they were?'

'Sandy has a secret compartment in his trunk, which he uses to carry confidential documents about with him,' she replied. 'I knew the papers would probably be in there, and I was right. I took them and gave them to Claude. He said something hateful—I can't remember what—then laughed when I told him he ought to be ashamed of himself. I couldn't bring myself to look at him after that. At any rate, I hoped against hope that that was the end of the matter, but then you came and started asking questions about my locket, and I thought you must be in league with him, and that the blackmail would continue.'

'I see why you must have thought that,' said Angela, 'but to be perfectly truthful, when I spoke to you I was trying to find out whether *you* were in league with him.'

'No!' said Eleanor. 'Never. I did what he asked, but only because he threatened me with exposure. I should never, never have done it otherwise.' She looked stricken, and when she next spoke it was almost in a whisper. 'I've betrayed my country and my husband,' she said. 'I'd never thought of it in that light until now, but I'm a traitor too, aren't I? Just like Stephen—except I'm worse than he is, because I did it out of cowardice, not conviction. Oh, Mrs. Marchmont, what shall I do?'

Angela felt genuinely sorry for the woman, but had no good news for her.

'I'm afraid there are bigger things at stake than your own concerns,' she said gently. 'It is vital that those papers are recovered as soon as possible. You must confess the whole thing to your husband before it is too late and Claude gets away with them. At present, he believes nobody suspects him, so there is still time to act.'

'How can I tell Sandy?' said Eleanor. 'He will never forgive me.'

'Does he love you?' said Angela.

Eleanor lowered her eyes.

'Yes,' she said. 'I believe he does.'

'Then I'm sure he will forgive you, even if he is angry with you at first. You must remember that what your brother did was not your fault.'

'I know that,' said Eleanor, 'but you can't deny I'm tainted because of it.'

'Still, that is no reason for you to go down the

same path as he did. You have made a mistake but you still have the chance to put things right. These papers are more important than you or your husband. You must be brave and tell him—otherwise, I'm afraid I shall have to do it. Do you truly want to be a good wife? If so, you must stop living in fear and start fighting for what you know to be right.'

Eleanor drew herself up a little and set her jaw.

'Of course, you're right,' she said suddenly. 'Very well, then, I'll do it. I won't let Stephen or Claude or anyone else drive a wedge between Sandy and me if I can help it. I shall go and confess to him the dreadful thing I've done, and pray that he will forgive me for it eventually.'

'Well, there's the lunch-bell,' said Angela. 'That will give you a little extra time to decide exactly what to say to him.'

They went out of the room together. On their way to the dining-room they encountered Sandy Buchanan. The Foreign Secretary's face lit up in a smile as he caught sight of his wife. Eleanor glanced at Angela and ran to her husband, and the two of them went in to lunch arm-in-arm.

TWENTY-FIVE

LUNCH WAS A tense affair. Half the guests were preoccupied, while the other half seemed to be waiting for something. Angela supposed that the news of Professor Klausen's death—which was now known to all—had done little to improve the mood of the party, although everybody was far too polite to mention it. Gertie was sitting glumly next to St. John, ignoring his attempts to engage her in conversation. Eventually he was forced to speak to Miss Foster instead, who launched into an interminable description of a story she was planning. Other than that, nobody said very much that did not relate to the meal.

Angela felt the mood as much as anyone, although she was pleased and slightly relieved to see Aubrey and Selma smiling at each other fondly across the table. At least that was one thing she need no longer worry about. She toyed with her food in some anxiety, wondering how best to act on the information she had learned from Eleanor Buchanan, and decided that the best thing to do would be to speak to Henry as soon as she could. Accordingly she stared at him until she caught his eye, then by her expression let him know that she had something to tell him. He nodded slightly in understanding and looked away.

Freddy was regarding her with narrowed eyes. She gave him her most innocent smile, which did not fool him in the least, and then went back to reflecting on her astonishment at the events of the past hour or two. What a morning of revelations it had been! Could it really be true that Claude Burford was their man? It seemed almost incredible: after all, he was a Member of Parliament—a junior one, it was true, but one who had the ear of some of the highest representatives of Government—was engaged to one of their daughters, in fact—and yet all the evidence indicated that he was passing secrets to a foreign power. Of course, his position made it all the easier for him to do it: in the normal way of things nobody would have had the faintest suspicion of his guilt, but here at Fives, where there were only a few of them, all trapped by the snow, it was more difficult to conceal his illicit activities. If he really were a spy, though—why, then, it was the most shocking of crimes for a man in his position.

And not only a spy, of course; it must not be forgotten that he was also a murderer. Angela glanced across the table at Claude, who was exchanging remarks with Priss imperturbably. In his impeccable suit and with his neatly-parted hair, he looked the very picture of staid and self-satisfied respectability. Could he really have killed Professor Klausen? Leaving aside the difficulty in reconciling the idea with the reality of his demeanour, Angela was forced to admit that there was no practical reason why he could not have done it. After all, as one of the men invited to the meeting he had known Klausen was coming, and why. Furthermore, he had been seen by Bobby walking around the castle on New Year's Eve. And he had been most curious to find out whether anybody had seen anything through the cupboard door—yes, most curious indeed. They had all assumed that that was because he was keen to find the murderer, but of course if Claude himself were the killer then he would be doubly anxious to make sure that nobody had seen him when he came to dump the professor's body. What a shock he must have had when he found out that there had been six people in the billiard-room at the time! He must have been terrified at the thought that someone had seen him.

Yes, Claude certainly might have done it. How had it happened? Presumably he must have seen Professor Klausen arrive some time that evening, either during the dance or afterwards. Angela could easily imagine the scene: Claude greeting the professor heartily and inviting him along to the library where they could converse briefly in private. Perhaps he had even said that the Foreign Secretary was waiting there to speak to him. Once in the library, Klausen, completely unsuspecting, had wandered over to the globe—just as she had done herself last night. Then what had happened? Angela saw in her mind's eye Claude taking the gun out of his pocket and coming up behind the professor. Possibly he had intended to shoot him in the back, but Klausen, perhaps suspecting something, had turned around suddenly and Claude had shot him in the heart instead. Angela pictured Klausen's shocked expression just before he slumped to the floor, dead. Claude immediately bent down and rifled through the man's pockets and brought out the papers. Had he put them in his own pocket or had he hidden them there and then? She and Freddy had not succeeded in finding anything in the library, but that was not to say the documents were not there. However, she was more inclined to believe that Claude had taken them away with him. Then what? It depended on when the murder had taken place. If it were earlier in the evening, then Claude could not afford to be away from the dance for too long, or he would be missed. In that case, he must have hidden Klausen's body behind the globe, planning to come back and hide it properly afterwards. If it were later—perhaps after the game of Sardines had begun—then presumably he immediately picked up the body, carried it next door and put it in the chest, intending to dispose of it at his leisure once the snow had melted. The Fives estate covered hundreds of acres, and there were plenty of places to conceal a body where he could be sure it would never be found.

It was the oddest thing. Angela had not thought much of Claude, but she would never have believed him to be a traitor and a killer. But Eleanor's evidence—if she was telling the truth—confirmed it beyond doubt. Mrs. Buchanan's odd manner had made Angela suspect originally that Claude might be in her power, but as it turned out, it was the other way round. He had known her secret and had blackmailed her into handing over the second copy of the papers. That meant he must have both of them in his possession. Were they the only copies in existence? If so, then it was vital that they be found as soon as possible.

Sandy Buchanan was saying something to Lady Strathmerrick. Angela caught Mrs. Buchanan's eye and Eleanor gave her a wan smile in return. What would the Foreign Secretary say when he found out the secret that his wife had been hiding from him? Angela supposed the next hour or so would be an uncomfortable one, to say the least, for both of the Buchanans.

Lunch was soon over, much to everyone's relief, and the guests went off to their various pursuits. Freddy wanted to speak to Angela but was waylaid by Priss and Gertie, who bore him off into the depths of the castle for some mysterious purpose. Henry caught Angela's eye as they left the room and made a sign to her to wait. She watched as he went up to Lord Strathmerrick and murmured something into his ear. The Earl glanced over at her and nodded, and Henry returned to her.

'Lord Strathmerrick says we may use his study,' he said.

The study was a comfortable, informal place, set about with several easy chairs and newspapers. It looked more like a refuge to which the Earl came to get some peace from his family than a room in which important business was done.

'Is this where Lord Strathmerrick holds his meetings?' said Angela, looking about her.

'Some of them,' said Henry. He went over to a connecting door and opened it, and Angela saw beyond it a more spacious chamber with a big table in the middle, around which were placed about twenty chairs. 'The more formal ones take place in here.'

'Ah, yes, that's more how I imagined it,' said Angela with a smile. Henry closed the door and came towards her.

'I gather you have something to tell me,' he said.

'Yes,' said Angela, immediately serious, 'and I'm afraid it's rather dreadful.'

Without further ado she told him what had happened that morning, and about her conversation with Eleanor Buchanan. His expression grew as serious as hers but he showed no surprise; nor did he make any comment until she had finished her tale.

'Do you think she was telling the truth?' he said finally.

'I have no reason to doubt her,' replied Angela. 'Of course, she may have made it all up on the spot and may herself be the person we are looking for, but it didn't strike me like that—and of course, if she was telling lies then it will be easy enough to disprove them. At any rate, I suppose we shall know soon enough, when we find out whether she has confessed all to her husband, as she promised.'

Henry said nothing, but he was thinking hard. He was not a man who took action precipitately in general, but this was clearly an exceptional case.

'I don't need to tell you that this is a very serious and delicate matter, Mrs. Marchmont,' he said.

'No indeed,' said Angela. 'To be perfectly frank, I can hardly believe what I have heard—but the fact remains that a man is dead and some very important documents are missing, so *someone* has evidently been up to no good, and that *someone* must, when all is said and done, have been somebody who knew what was going on here.'

'Yes,' said Henry slowly.

'What exactly do you know about Claude Burford, Mr. Jameson?' said Angela. 'Presumably he was thought to be above suspicion until now. If he is guilty, then there must be some reason for it. Why is he spying for another country? Of course, I only know what I have read in the newspapers and what you told me last night, but it looks to me as though this scandal goes much further than you thought.'

'Yes,' said Henry again.

'I believe Ogilvy was thought to have no idea of what was going on under his nose,' said Angela hesitantly.

'There was some suspicion at the time that he might have known more than he would say,' said Henry at last. 'The idea did cross my mind at the time. But if anything, I thought he perhaps suspected Golovin but was induced by friendship to turn a blind eye. After all, the man was the Home Secretary. It was inconceivable that there was anything more to it than that. It's still inconceivable, in fact.'

'Where is Ogilvy now?' said Angela.

'After he resigned his seat he went to live abroad,' said Henry. 'I believe he and his wife went to Switzerland. She was ill at the time of the Golovin scandal, and Ogilvy had been spending much of his time at her side. He claimed that was the reason for his not having been aware of Golovin's activities.'

Angela considered a moment.

'It really does seem absurd to think that Ogilvy knew what was going on,' she said, 'and, you know, there is no reason to suppose that he was involved in any way. The Golovins and the Ogilvys were friends, and Mrs. Buchanan had seen Claude once or twice before. It is quite possible that Claude was recruited by Stephen Golovin, don't you think?'

'I hope so. That would make the situation marginally less outrageous,' said Henry dryly. 'A spy in the House is already bad enough without his turning out to be the Home Secretary. Dear me,' he went on. 'If Burford is indeed our man, then it looks as though someone has slipped up rather badly in my department—and since to all intents and purposes I *am* the department, then it looks as though I will shortly be hauled over the coals.'

'Poor you,' said Angela in sympathy.

'Still, that's not important at present,' said Henry. 'The question is, what ought we to do now? First of all I suppose we ought to confirm Mrs. Buchanan's story, since we will need her evidence—if it ever gets that far. Then we will need to decide what to do about Burford.'

'If he is the killer then it may be too dangerous to confront him directly,' said Angela.

'Yes,' said Henry, 'and since the most important thing is to retrieve the papers, it may even be necessary to let him go for the moment.'

Angela was about to reply when there was a soft knock at the door and Sandy Buchanan entered. One look at his face was enough to tell them that Eleanor had kept her word and confessed all.

'Strathmerrick told me I should find you in here,' he said. Angela made a move to leave the room but he held up a hand and said, 'No, no, stay, I beg of you. I gather my wife has told you everything, and I have you to thank for the fact that she has now told me.'

Angela and Henry glanced at each other but said nothing. Buchanan went on:

'I shan't trouble you with my own feelings on this matter, except to say that sometimes women can be extraordinarily foolish—I beg your pardon, Mrs. Marchmont. No, the most important thing now is to decide what to do. Clearly, it is of prime importance that we find the papers.'

'Presumably Burford has both copies,' said Jameson. 'If he has any sense at all he will have hidden them in two different places, although of course we only need to find one of them.'

Buchanan shook his head. For a second he looked almost sheepish.

'I'm afraid that's not true. Unfortunately, our job is a little more difficult than that.'

'What do you mean?' said Henry.

The Foreign Secretary sighed.

'The two sets of documents are not the same,' he said.

TWENTY-SIX

'WHAT?' SAID HENRY.

'I suppose I had better explain,' said Buchanan. 'You see, when Klausen told us that he was ready to present his research, I insisted that he give me a copy of it for additional security. As you know, Jameson, Klausen had received warnings from one or two somewhat—er—excitable foreign organizations to say that if he refused to work for them then his life was no longer safe, and that they were determined to get hold of his research by hook or by crook. Naturally, we were equally determined that they should not, and in order to prevent any disaster of that nature, Klausen and I agreed that he should make two copies of the documents and give one of them to me to carry up to Scotland, so the enemy should know that it was useless to attack him. Of course, since he believed himself to be under observation at all times, this plan would only work if he gave the papers to me somewhere in full view of the public. Accordingly, we met on the Embankment last week and the hand-over took place.

'It seems, however, that this was not enough for Klausen. He firmly believed that nobody except himself was to be trusted in the matter—and he extended this mistrust to those in government, as he informed me quite openly. Therefore, he said, he had taken additional precautions on his own initiative, by making one real copy of the documents and one dummy one that contained fake calculations and conclusions, and putting them in identical envelopes. He himself had no idea whether the copy he had given me was the real one or the fake one. Thus, if anything did happen to him, then nobody in Whitehall would know whether the documents were valid, and the enemy was as likely as not to have gone to the trouble of killing him for nothing. Of course, it never occurred to either of us that anything would happen at Fives itself—we thought that once we were here we should be quite safe. How wrong we were. I'm sorry I didn't tell you earlier, Jameson,' he said, 'but Klausen insisted on my not mentioning it to anybody.'

Henry shook his head.

'He really ought to have trusted us,' he said. 'Then we might have protected him.'

'Do you think so?' said Buchanan. 'I should say that in view of what has happened, his suspicions were entirely justified. Now,' he went on briskly, 'we must act. There will be hell to pay soon enough, for us and for the Government, but first of all we must find those papers. Where is Burford now?'

'I've no idea,' said Jameson.

'He was talking to Lady Strathmerrick when we left the dining-room,' said Angela.

'Very well,' said the Foreign Secretary. 'I shall find him and hold him in conversation, Jameson, while you go and search his room. Mrs. Marchmont, wait here if you please.'

The two men went out and Angela was left alone in the study. She was not a little impressed by the Foreign Secretary's ability to put aside personal catastrophe in order to deal with more pressing affairs. It must have been a terrible shock to him to discover the secret that his new wife had been hiding from him. Once the news got out it was likely to deal an enormous blow to his political career, and it would be a wonder if he could survive it—but nevertheless he had shaken it off in order to concentrate on the thing that mattered the most at present: the return of Klausen's documents. Few men could have done the same, Angela reflected, and she began to see why people had spoken of Sandy Buchanan as being one day likely to become Prime Minister. He was immensely capable, there was no doubt of it, and if anyone could weather the scandal of having unwittingly married the sister of a foreign spy then Sandy Buchanan was that man.

An hour passed, and Angela was growing rather bored alone in the study and wondering whether she might leave, when Henry and the Foreign Secretary returned, this time in company with Lord Strathmerrick.

'Have you found the documents?' Angela could not help asking as soon as they arrived.

Henry shook his head.

'No,' he said. 'Either he's hidden them somewhere safe or he's carrying them about his person.'

'But this is terrible,' said the Earl, who had

evidently just that moment been informed that his prospective son-in-law was rather less of a suitable match for his daughter than he had supposed, and was still reeling from the shock. 'Are you sure of this, Jameson? Is there any proof? Forgive me, Buchanan, but are you quite certain your wife was telling the truth? After all, she has been lying up to now.'

'Yes, she has,' said Buchanan unemotionally, 'and naturally I'm extremely disappointed in her. I don't need to tell you that it has been a great shock to me to discover what my wife has done; however, given the circumstances it was perfectly understandable. She is young and easily swayed by a stronger personality, and I know she believed her actions to be the only way to prevent me from being forced to resign my position. Naturally, her biggest mistake was in not telling me who she was from the beginning, but whatever her mistakes have been, I know for a certain fact that she is not by nature a dishonest woman. At least I can comfort myself with that thought.'

'But she may well have ruined your career, Buchanan,' said the Earl.

The Foreign Secretary bowed his head.

'Perhaps,' he said. 'It was not intentional, however. But let us not talk about it any more. What's done is done, and now we shall both have to live with the consequences.'

He did not say that it had been foolish of a man in his position to marry a young woman of whom he knew nothing, but he did not need to: they all knew it. He was not the first great man to marry unwisely and nor would he be the last. He coughed and went on:

'At present, my personal concerns are unimportant. What is important is the recovery of the documents. Strathmerrick, how far have the men got in clearing a path to the village? Once they have got through, there is nothing preventing Burford from escaping. We must stop him before that happens. Can we overpower him, do you think?'

'Is there any need for that?' said Jameson. 'At present he doesn't suspect that we know, and so presumably doesn't realize that he needs to escape.'

'That's true enough,' acknowledged the Foreign Secretary. 'Well, then—'

Just then there was a knock at the door and Claude himself came in. He glanced around at the assembled company and his eye fell on Angela.

'I beg your pardon,' he said. 'I had no idea you were having a private discussion.'

'Oh, we weren't, my boy,' said the Earl heartily. 'Come in. Mrs. Marchmont was just telling us about a mysterious intruder she saw on the night of the murder.'

'Yes—' began Angela, thinking quickly, but Claude waved a hand and said,

'Don't worry, I shan't disturb you. I only came to give you this.' He brought out a key and handed it to Lord Strathmerrick. 'It's the key to the second-floor bedroom, where we have put the professor,' he said in reply to the Earl's questioning glance. 'I wanted to make sure that nobody would be able to get in and disturb the body.'

'Ah, yes, jolly good,' said Strathmerrick uncomfortably.

Claude smiled around at them all and went out. There was a strained silence.

'Well, if he didn't suspect it before, he does now,' said Henry at last. 'Did you say the men had finished clearing the path, sir?'

'Not yet,' said the Earl.

'Well, then, he can't get away,' said Sandy Buchanan. 'We have him where we want him.'

Angela opened her mouth as though to say something, but changed her mind.

'What is it?' Henry asked.

She turned to him.

'Just that—don't you think he might do something desperate if he knows he's in danger?' she said.

'I hope it won't come to that,' he said, 'but I think it's time we had a word with him, certainly.' He glanced around at the other two men. 'Do you suppose we can overpower him between us?' he said.

'We might,' said the Foreign Secretary, 'but I wouldn't say no to some help from the American chappies. They've got plenty of brawn on them.'

'Good God,' said the Earl, 'are you seriously suggesting that we restrain a respectable Member of Parliament by force on a mere suspicion?'

'Only if necessary,' said Henry grimly. He strode to the door. Slow to action, he was nevertheless determined once action was needed. Sandy Buchanan followed him, his jaw set. Lord Strathmerrick and Angela stood in hesitation for a moment or two.

'They can't arrest Claude,' said the Earl eventually. 'Why, he and Priss are supposed to be getting married next year. What is she going to do now?'

'Find someone else, I imagine,' said Angela. There seemed no other reply.

TWENTY-SEVEN

'I DON'T SUPPOSE anyone has seen Claude?' said Henry as he and the Foreign Secretary entered the drawing-room, where most of the other guests were assembled. Nobody had, it appeared.

'I thought he was with you in the study,' said Priss.

Aubrey Nash sensed immediately that something was up.

'What is it?' he said.

'I believe we may need some—er—assistance with something shortly,' replied Henry. 'I don't suppose you and Bradley would care to oblige?'

'Certainly,' said Aubrey, and Gabe nodded in agreement. They both rose and followed the other two men out of the room. Henry wasted no time in explaining the situation to them, and they both whistled in astonishment.

'Well, if that doesn't beat all,' said Gabe.

Lord Strathmerrick and Angela joined them just then.

'Where is he?' said the Earl.

'Nobody knows,' said Sandy Buchanan.

'We must split up and look for him,' said Jameson.

'He can't have gone far. Mr. Nash, you and Bradley start with the upstairs rooms if you please; meanwhile, Buchanan, Lord Strathmerrick and I will search downstairs. And please be careful—he may be very dangerous.'

'Phoo,' said Gabe Bradley. 'Why, I'm twice his size. We'll get him all right.'

'Don't forget he's already killed once,' said Buchanan. 'We don't want him to do anything desperate.'

They all went off, leaving Angela standing alone in the passage. She supposed they would catch him soon enough; in the meantime she decided to look for Eleanor Buchanan and try to offer her some comfort. At that moment, Freddy slipped out of the drawing-room.

'Have they gone?' he said. 'What was all that about? Come on, out with it.'

Angela told him everything as briefly as she could. His surprise was soon replaced by rapturous glee.

'I knew it!' he said. 'I always knew he was an absolute and unmitigated stinker, and I was right. This almost makes up for all those beatings he gave me. I say,' he said suddenly, 'do they still have the stocks these days? I should queue all night for the chance to land him one in the kisser with a nice, ripe tomato.'

'I confess the intensity of your resentment disturbs me somewhat,' said Angela.

'You weren't there,' he said. 'He threw a shadow over the best years of my promising young life. Have they gone to get him, then?'

'Yes,' said Angela. 'They're searching the castle now.'

'Well, they needn't bother, because he's outside. I saw him just now when I was looking out of the window.'

'Oh! Then we must tell Mr. Jameson quickly,' said Angela.

'Which way did they go?' said Freddy as they hurried off. 'We shall have to be quick, or he will get clean away.'

'But they haven't cleared a path to the village yet.'

'He wasn't going in that direction; he was going the other way, towards the East meadow.'

'Then we shall lose him,' said Angela in consternation. 'If he's determined enough, he will get across the fields and round that way. Now, where on earth has Henry got to?'

Freddy caught hold of her arm and she stopped.

'There's no time,' he said. 'Get your boots and your gun. We'll go after him ourselves. I'll meet you by the door in two minutes.'

'But I haven't got—' said Angela to his retreating back, then paused, remembering that she did in fact have a gun. It was not her own, but she supposed it would have to do.

After precisely one minute and forty-seven seconds they were tramping as fast as they could in the direction of the East meadow. It was easy enough to follow Claude's footprints, for the snow was no longer falling, although the sky was grey and heavy. For some distance they ploughed on in silence, then Freddy suddenly laughed and said:

'Haven't we done this before?'

'What do you mean?' said Angela.

'When we went to Dungeness. Don't you remember? We were chasing a murderer then, too.'

'So we were,' said Angela. 'The circumstances were rather different last time, though.'

'Yes,' said Freddy. 'Last time I wasn't spurred on by the desire to punch the criminal in the face.'

'You really don't like him, do you?' said Angela.

'Not much,' said Freddy, 'but not only on my own account; on Eleanor Buchanan's too. Blackmailing a woman is a filthy thing to do. He deserves everything he gets.'

Angela smiled at him.

'You're rather a dear underneath it all, aren't you?' she said.

'Yes, but if you tell anyone I shall never speak to you again,' he said. 'Look—there he is.'

They had now come out from under the shelter of some trees and could see the way before them quite clearly. Some way ahead of them, at the brow of a gentle incline, they could see the figure of a man climbing over a stile. At the same time as they spotted him, he saw them and stopped dead. He recovered himself quickly, leapt off the stile and disappeared over the hill and into the meadow.

'Damn,' said Freddy. 'He's on to us. We'd better hurry up.'

They scrambled up the slope as quickly as they could, and arrived at the top breathless and with snow clinging to their clothes. The landscape ahead of them was deserted: there was no sign of Claude, but a trail of footprints led across the meadow in the direction of the old barn in which St. John Bagshawe had taken shelter two days earlier.

'He's hiding in the barn,' said Angela. They climbed over the stile and set off.

'He must be cursing this snow,' said Freddy.

'Footprints are most inconvenient when one is trying to escape the law, don't you think?'

'I'm rather cursing the snow myself,' said Angela. 'My legs are still aching from yesterday.'

'The exercise will do you good after all the food you ate last night,' said Freddy.

'What do you mean, after all the food *I* ate?' said Angela indignantly. 'I don't suppose I ate any more than you. And nobody could possibly have eaten as much as St. John.'

'That reminds me, we must have a word with him later about his alibi,' said Freddy. 'Now, quiet.'

They were now approaching the barn, but it was soon evident that Claude was not hiding inside it, for the footprints led around to the back of the building and over the fence into the wood beyond.

'There's no way out through that wood,' whispered Angela. 'At least, not through the other side—the ground falls away too steeply. If he wants to escape he will have to come out this way or somewhere round there to the left. Perhaps we can cut him off.'

'Don't forget he has a gun,' said Freddy.

'I don't know that he does,' said Angela. She showed him the revolver that she had found in her room. 'I think this is his.'

'What? Isn't it yours?'

'No. Henry confiscated mine. I found this one planted in my handbag last night.'

'What? And you didn't say anything? Whyever not?'

'I meant to, but I got distracted. Anyway, never mind that for now. How can we flush Claude out?'

'Why, I suppose we'll just have to go in there and

tramp about until we find him,' said Freddy.

'Is that the best you can think of?'

'Do you have a better idea?'

'No,' admitted Angela.

'Let me see the gun again. I say, may I carry it?'

'Do you know how to use it?' said Angela, handing it to him.

He took the revolver and cocked it experimentally. There was a loud report, followed by a chorus of squawks and a great commotion of branches as a cloud of startled crows rose into the sky.

'No,' said Freddy weakly.

Angela waited a few seconds until her heartbeat had slowed, then carefully took the gun from his unresisting hand and put it back in her pocket.

'Perhaps next time,' she said.

But the crows were not the only thing to have been frightened out of the woods. There was a loud rustle and they turned to see a figure hurtle out from among the trees to their left and begin to plough across the meadow. In a flash Freddy was after him. The snow made the going difficult, but Freddy was young and energetic, and evidently fitter than Claude, for he soon began to catch up with him. Claude glanced behind him and realized that it was useless to try and escape. He turned suddenly and made back towards Freddy. The two men stopped a short distance from each other, regarding each other warily in silence, as Angela came up behind them.

'What do you want?' said Claude at last.

'What I *want* is to give you a jolly good kicking,' said Freddy. 'But I won't, as long as you come back to the castle quietly.'

'Don't be ridiculous,' said Claude. 'Why on earth

should I do what you say, you miserable pipsqueak? You really haven't come on all that much, have you, *Freddy*? Still the offensive little beast you always were.' He pronounced Freddy's name with exquisite disdain. 'Tell me,' he went on, 'do you still go crying to your mama when anybody is unkind to you? Such a shame she didn't believe you, isn't it? But then, who would ever take your word over mine? I dare say—'

His next words were lost as Freddy lowered his head and charged him full in the chest with a roar. Claude said 'Oof!' and then both of them were down, flailing at each other inexpertly in the snow. Freddy, who was on top, looked to be gaining the upper hand, but then Claude grabbed him by the neck and he began to go purple in the face. He eventually managed to prise Claude's fingers off and rolled away. The two of them stood up and faced each other breathlessly. They began to circle slowly. Claude was the first to get in a blow, and Angela winced as Freddy staggered back. But he was angry now, and determined to beat the man who had kept him in fear for so long all those years ago. He returned the blow with interest, and quickly followed it up with several jabs to Claude's body, then another punch to his face. Claude grunted in pain as the blow landed in his eye, and threw a couple of punches in return, which hit their mark. The two of them moved closer and grappled frantically in a furious embrace. It was an unequal struggle, for Claude was more solidly built than Freddy, who was unable to land any more blows while they were so close together. Suddenly Claude lunged at Freddy, and for one absurd moment it looked as though he were about to kiss him, but then there was a howl of pain and Claude pulled away and

Freddy was suddenly clutching his left ear, which was bleeding profusely all over his hand. Claude spat something into the snow and Freddy was left staring in horror. Claude had bitten off part of his ear-lobe.

'Why, you—'

Words were insufficient to express Freddy's outrage. He gave a blood-curdling yell and launched himself at his enemy. Down went Claude, and he gave a strangled cry and tried to protect his head as Freddy in his fury rained blow after blow on every square inch of his opponent's face and body that he could reach. Freddy in a boiling rage was quite an impressive sight, and Angela, just then remembering the gun, wondered whether perhaps she ought not to intervene and save Claude from being beaten to a pulp. Before she could act on her thought, she heard a shout and turned to see Gabe Bradley running towards them, with Henry Jameson following close behind. The two men pulled Freddy off the whimpering Claude with some difficulty, and then it was all over. Claude, bloodied and subdued, was borne away by the newcomers, and Angela was left to calm Freddy down and minister to his wounds with her handkerchief.

'We'd better go back and see to that ear of yours,' she said, once he showed signs of being in a state to listen and respond coherently.

'Did he get all of it?' said Freddy fearfully. 'Am I horribly disfigured?'

'Of course not,' said Angela. 'He just took a little piece, that's all. Think of it as a battle scar—a testament to your bravery.'

'Was I brave?'

'Oh, terribly.'

'You might have stopped it sooner, you know.' he said. 'You were the one with the gun.'

'Ah, yes,' said Angela. 'I—er—forgot about it in all the excitement. Besides, I thought you would relish the opportunity to put one over on your old enemy without anybody else's interference.'

Freddy glared at her accusingly.

'I believe you enjoyed it,' he said. 'Admit it—you did, didn't you?'

Angela put on her best disapproving expression.

'Of course not,' she said. 'I am a respectable woman. I am shocked that anything of the sort should happen here at Fives. Fighting ought to be kept for the East End.'

Freddy did not reply, but the old complacent look was beginning to steal back across what could be seen of his face.

'I did give him rather a drubbing, didn't I?' he said.

'You certainly did,' said Angela. She took his arm and they set off back to the castle, Freddy limping slightly.

'I dare say I look awful,' he said.

'Pretty awful,' she replied. 'But just think of all the attention you'll get from the ladies when they find out what a hero you've been.'

This thought appealed to Freddy, and he indulged it in silence for several minutes as they crunched onwards through the snow.

'You did enjoy it a little, didn't you?' he said, after they had gone some way.

'Perhaps just a little,' admitted Angela.

He let out a laugh, which swiftly turned into a groan, and they entered the castle as darkness began to fall.

TWENTY-EIGHT

ALL HIS YEARS of experience as a broker of civilized political agreements had not prepared the Earl of Strathmerrick in any way for the situation in which he now found himself. Until that morning he had been a man upon whom life and fate smiled benignly: he was a respected member of the House of Lords, and one to whom everybody turned in times of need. He was spoken of as the real power behind the Government despite the fact that he made little contribution himself to policy. His wealth was immense, and his family life unexceptionable—his second daughter's occasional escapades aside. Now, however, he found his painstakingly-constructed fortress tumbling about his ears. Not only had his prospective son-in-law turned out to be a traitor and a murderer (to the great detriment of the Earl's domestic happiness and that of his family), but that same prospective son-in-law, in view of his position as a Member of Parliament, now looked set to bring down the entire Government (to the great detriment of the country as a whole).

247

Faced with such a monstrous onslaught of misfortune, Lord Strathmerrick was quite at a loss to know what to do next. He shifted uncomfortably in his chair and looked round the table at the faces of his English and American colleagues, some serious, some thoughtful. He cleared his throat and addressed Henry Jameson.

'So you say there's no doubt about it?' he said, somewhat inadequately.

Henry glanced down at the sheaf of papers on the table before him and moved it an eighth of an inch to the right.

'Well, he was carrying the documents all right,' he said. 'Or at least one set of them.'

Everyone stared at the little pile of papers.

'May we have a look at them?' said Aubrey Nash at last. 'That's why we're here, after all.'

Henry glanced at the Foreign Secretary.

'I don't see why not,' said Sandy Buchanan with a sigh. 'Goodness knows, we've been to enough trouble to get them back. But don't expect to understand them—as I said, they're in code and they may not be the genuine article anyway.'

'Then we still have no idea where the other copy is?' said Aubrey.

'No,' said Henry, handing him the papers. 'Burford won't tell us. As a matter of fact, he claims he doesn't know where they are.'

'What?' said the Earl.

'Yes,' said Henry thoughtfully. 'It's rather odd. He admits to having blackmailed Mrs. Buchanan, but says he knows nothing about what happened to the other copy of the documents.'

'Do you mean he didn't think to search Klausen's

body after he shot him?' said Aubrey.

'No,' said Henry. 'He says he didn't shoot Klausen at all.'

There were one or two exclamations of surprise and disbelief.

'But that's nonsense,' said Gabe Bradley. 'He must have done it. Who else could have dumped the professor's body in the chest?'

'Oh, he did that all right,' said Sandy Buchanan.

'Then I don't understand,' said Aubrey. 'Suppose you start at the beginning and tell us exactly what he *has* admitted to. Where have you put him, by the way?'

'We've locked him in the bedroom next door to the one where we put Klausen,' said Henry.

'How is he?' said Aubrey.

'Somewhat battered. We've patched him up and made him as comfortable as possible. Young Freddy appears to have given him rather a pasting.'

'Odd, that,' said Lord Strathmerrick. 'I shouldn't have thought the fellow had it in him—he looks far too much of a milksop to me.'

'Far from it,' Gabe assured him. 'It took two of us to pull him off. He was quite beside himself. I dare say I'd be the same if someone had just taken a chunk out of my ear.'

'But going back to Burford,' prompted Aubrey.

'Go ahead, Jameson,' said the Foreign Secretary.

'Very well,' said Henry. 'Burford's story is this: he never intended to get involved in the whole spying thing, but two or three years ago he met Lady Priscilla and they became engaged. At that time he was a lowly secretary to Beresford Ogilvy, but he had strong connections within the party and planned to stand for

Parliament in a year or two once a safe seat could be found. He admits that when the engagement was first suggested, he—er—exaggerated the extent of his private wealth to Lord Strathmerrick, since he did not wish it to appear that he was a poor prospect for a son-in-law, even though at that time he would have been unable to support Lady Priscilla in the style to which she was accustomed. The deception did not worry him, since he was confident that once his ambitions had been realized, his fortunes would improve and they would be able to live very comfortably. However, not long after the engagement was announced, he became entangled in an unfortunate financial speculation and lost a large amount of money—almost everything he owned, in fact. As is the way of these things, he attempted to recover his losses by throwing good money after bad, and soon afterwards found himself in an even deeper hole than before and facing ruin.

'Naturally, if Lord Strathmerrick were ever to find out about this, then he would certainly not allow the wedding to go ahead; moreover, there was no chance of Burford's being able to stand for Parliament as a bankrupt. It looked very much as though all his ambitions were at an end. For some weeks he kept his troubles to himself, but one day he happened to be in company with Stephen Golovin, who had not yet come under suspicion for his spying activities, and accidentally mentioned that he had money difficulties, although he did not confess their extent. Golovin was sympathetic and they became friends—or so Burford believed. Of course, it is more likely that this was a calculated move on the part of Golovin, who presumably wanted to recruit more people to his cause.

'One day Golovin took Burford aside and said he knew of a way in which Burford could pay off his debts with very little effort. According to Burford, he had that very morning received a final demand for payment from one of his creditors, and so was in a somewhat desperate state of mind. He had only a week in which to find the money, or all would be revealed and his ambitions and his engagement would be at an end. Naturally, therefore, he jumped at the opportunity. It was very easy: all he had to do was to make a copy of some minutes to a confidential meeting that was due to take place between the Home Secretary and his American counterpart that day, and hand it to Golovin. He did so, and the next day received through the post an anonymous letter containing a cheque for almost half the sum of his debts.

'A month or so later, he was again approached by Golovin and asked if he would like to make some more money. Another creditor had begun to press for payment, so Burford said yes. This time the documents related to a secret meeting about overland trade routes on the Continent. Again, he received in return an anonymous letter containing a cheque.

'After two or three more incidents of this kind, Burford was back on a sound footing financially and had no need to hand over any more information in return for payment, so the next time Golovin asked for his help he declined. Shortly afterwards, Golovin was arrested and sent to prison. As we all know, the ensuing scandal ended in Ogilvy's resignation as Home Secretary and the end of his career in Parliament. Burford then stood for election in

Ogilvy's seat and won. With Golovin safe in gaol and all debts paid off, he believed he was safe. After a few months, however, he was horrified to receive an anonymous letter of the type in which the cheques had arrived. The writer of the letter politely requested that Burford send a copy of certain Government documents to a particular address, in return for which he would receive generous remuneration as he had done in the past. However, if he refused to do so, then the writer of the letter would have no choice but to report the fact of his previous spying activities to the proper authorities.

'Naturally, this put Burford in something of a tricky position, but after reflecting on the matter he realized that he was now involved too deeply and that there was no way out for him, so he did as the letter demanded and supplied the documents in question.'

'Good God,' exclaimed Lord Strathmerrick. 'Do you mean to say the fellow has been passing information to foreign powers ever since he was elected to Parliament?'

'And before that, too,' said Jameson. 'According to him, the whole thing started as a regrettable error but swiftly descended into an agonizing and shameful torture from which he could see no escape. Apparently, he has been beating his breast in misery for the past year and a half at least, and has been suffering from the most unbearable guilt.'

'He didn't feel guilty enough to turn down the money though, I guess,' said Aubrey dryly.

'No,' agreed Henry. 'His little—er—side-line appears to have been rather remunerative. At any rate,' he went on, 'the anonymous letters continued to arrive—not too frequently, of course; too often would have aroused suspicion—and each time Burford saw no choice but to do as he was told.'

Here the Earl snorted. Henry ignored him and went on:

'Now we come to our little incident here. Burford says that last week he received another letter, telling him that Professor Klausen would be bringing some important papers to Fives Castle, and that he was to get hold of them. As we all know, Klausen never turned up—alive, at least—and Burford started to get worried. What would happen if he couldn't get the documents? Would he be exposed? Fortunately for him, the Foreign Secretary then revealed that he had another copy, and so he determined to get that one instead and thereby save his skin—although, of course, he was unaware that the two sets of documents were not the same. He knew Mrs. Buchanan's real identity, although he had kept quiet up until then for reasons best known to himself—perhaps he was hoping to make use of her in some way—'

'He did that all right,' said Sandy Buchanan bitterly.

Henry cast him a sympathetic glance and went on:

'—so he approached her and blackmailed her in turn, threatening to reveal who she really was if she did not get the papers for him, which she duly did after the dance on New Year's Eve. Luckily, because of the snow, he couldn't pass them on to his correspondent and so here they are, back in our possession, thanks to some quick thinking on the part of Mrs. Marchmont and Mr. Pilkington-Soames. Had they not spotted Burford trying to escape, he might have got clean away. It was by the merest chance that

I happened to glance out of the window and see them heading after him. It took Bradley and me a little while to catch up, although young Freddy seemed to have the situation well in hand by the time we arrived.'

'So he stole one set of documents, but claims he didn't steal the other one,' said Aubrey Nash. 'Can that be true? He can't possibly deny having killed Klausen too, can he?'

'One would imagine not, and yet that is what he says,' said Henry. 'This is where the story becomes even stranger. According to Burford, after Mrs. Buchanan gave him the documents he put them in his pocket and went into the library, with some intention of finding a temporary hiding-place for them in case the alarm was raised and a search instituted. He initially saw nothing untoward, but after a few minutes of looking about him for a suitable place of concealment, he spotted what looked like a foot sticking out from behind the large ornamental globe in the corner. On further investigation he discovered to his astonishment that it was the body of Professor Klausen, who had evidently been shot.

'Burford then claims to have lost his head. He immediately assumed that somebody was trying to pin the murder on him and determined to hide the body so that it should never be found. He intended to bury it somewhere on the Fives estate once the snow had melted, but in the meantime hid it in what he considered to be the nearest safe place—the wooden chest in the billiard-room next door. The room is generally cold, and so he judged that there was little risk of anyone noticing a smell for some days at least. Naturally, he had no idea that six people were hiding in a cupboard there while he did it. I imagine it must have come as the most awful shock to him when he found out.'

'It did,' said Gabe. 'I remember it distinctly. He looked at me as though he'd seen a ghost.'

'Does he admit to having searched Klausen's pockets?' said Aubrey. 'He must have done, or he's even more of an idiot than I thought.'

'Yes,' replied Henry. 'He searched them as soon as he had got over the surprise of finding the body, but found nothing, he says.'

'Look here, this is all nonsense,' said Lord Strathmerrick. 'Why is he bothering to deny having murdered Klausen? Of course he did it. What you ought to be doing now, Jameson, is searching for the gun and the other set of papers.'

'I have the gun already,' said Henry. 'Mrs. Marchmont found it planted in her handbag last night.'

'Is that what she said?' said the Earl. 'Then why didn't she tell you before?'

'She didn't have the opportunity,' said Henry. 'She took it out with her this afternoon, intending to use it as a means of bringing back Burford, but has now given it to me.'

'Are you sure it's the murder weapon?'

'I believe so,' said Henry, 'although we won't be able to tell for certain until we've examined it properly and got the bullet out of Professor Klausen for comparison.'

Sandy Buchanan rubbed his eyes. The day had been a hard one for him.

'So, then, leaving aside the small matter of the murder, this is where we stand,' he said. 'We have the documents that were stolen from my trunk, but we are still missing the ones that Klausen was carrying. We don't know which documents are the right ones, so we need both copies in order to make sure Klausen's research doesn't fall into the wrong hands. How can we find the second set, if Burford won't admit to having taken them?'

'Do you want me to beat it out of him, sir?' said Gabe eagerly.

The Foreign Secretary's mouth twitched in amusement.

'Thank you,' he said, 'but we prefer gentler methods over here—and besides, I think he's taken enough of a drubbing for one day, don't you? I shall speak to him tomorrow, when he's had a chance to recover a little, and see if I can get anything out of him.' He looked at his watch. 'I suppose we ought to be thinking about dressing for dinner,' he said.

Aubrey was thoughtfully shuffling the documents that lay in front of him.

'If Burford is telling the truth, then I wonder how his anonymous correspondent knew that Professor Klausen was coming here with the papers,' he said. 'Presumably that means Claude is lying about the whole thing.'

'Unless, of course, another one of us has been passing on secrets,' said Henry lightly.

TWENTY-NINE

IN THE DRAWING-ROOM Lady Strathmerrick was suffering in a similar manner to her husband. Coming as it did on top of the shocks of the past day or two, the discovery that Claude Burford (whom she had not in truth liked much despite his ostensible suitability as a son-in-law) had been rampaging around the house, shooting her guests, had proved almost too much for her. Although she wished for nothing more than to go and lie down in her room for several hours, the ingrained manners of a lifetime prevented her from seeking that succour, and she was forced by the demands of her own upbringing to sit with the rest of the guests—although to make polite conversation was impossible. Instead she sat, pale-faced and staring straight ahead, while Miss Foster flapped about ineffectually and tried to rally her. Meanwhile Gertie, who deep down was very fond of her mother, sat by her, holding her hand and gazing at her in concern. Eventually Gertie jumped up, poured a large glass of brandy and forced the Countess to drink it.

'Thank you, dear,' said Lady Strathmerrick, as the colour slowly began to return to her cheeks. She looked about her as some semblance of awareness returned, and was relieved to find that nobody appeared to require her attention at that moment. Priss and Clemmie were sitting with their heads together, whispering in agitation—although in truth, Priss looked more surprised and angry than upset, while Eleanor Buchanan was talking to Mrs. Marchmont, and Mrs. Nash was clucking in concern over Freddy Pilkington-Soames, who appeared to be bleeding from one ear all over the cushions. Gus and Bobby were staring at Freddy in fascination, and Mr. Bagshawe was gazing pathetically at Gertie as usual.

'Have some more,' said Gertie, pouring another slug into the glass.

'Oh, no, I mustn't,' said the Countess. 'I shall never stay awake until dinner. No, I am quite recovered now, thank you.'

'Then I shall drink it,' said Gertie, swallowing it in one gulp. 'I think I need some brandy too, after the events of this afternoon. I must get hold of Angela once she's stopped talking to the Buchanan woman. I want to know exactly what happened.'

Over in the corner, Angela was listening to what Eleanor Buchanan had to say. Naturally, her husband had been shocked when she had confessed to him her secret and told him about Claude's blackmail.

'Was he very angry with you?' said Angela.

'Yes,' said Eleanor. 'At least, he was at first. But then he started blaming himself for having let me fall prey to a blackmailer and asked me to forgive him. That made me feel even worse, of course, because naturally he has been completely blameless throughout the whole affair. Now he is going to suffer, and all because of me. Oh, Angela, I've been such a coward. I ought never to have kept the secret from him—ought never to have married him, in fact,' she added sadly. 'He would have been much better off without me.'

'Is that what he said?'

'Oh, no,' said Eleanor. 'He said he still loved me and was quite determined to stand by me. But how can I live with the guilt? I can't help thinking that the best thing I could do would be to leave.'

'And betray him again, after he has placed his trust in you a second time?' said Angela gently. 'I hardly think that would be a just reward to him, do you?'

Eleanor gave her a startled glance.

'I hadn't thought of it like that,' she said after a moment. 'Oh, Angela, all I want to do is the right thing—what's best for Sandy.'

'If that is the case then you must stay with him and face up to the consequences of what you have done,' said Angela. 'It is up to him to decide whether or not he can live with it—and from what you say, he has already made his decision.' She smiled. 'He obviously loves you very much.'

'Do you think so?'

'Of course—why, anyone can see it,' said Angela.

'And I love him so very much too,' said Eleanor. She straightened up and set her jaw. 'You're right again, of course. Very well, I shall stick with him for as long as he wants me, and if he should decide in the end that what I have done is unforgivable—well then, I shall accept his decision and try to live with it.'

'I hope it will never come to that,' said Angela. 'At any rate, I am glad you told him the truth. To continue with the lie would have been impossible.'

'In a funny way it was quite a relief,' said Mrs. Buchanan. 'Now there are no secrets between us, and if we can only get over this present difficulty then I almost feel as though we can start afresh. If only there were some way to hush up all this scandal—or at least suppress some part of the truth.'

'I shouldn't be a bit surprised if Mr. Jameson and Lord Strathmerrick manage something of the sort between them,' said Angela. 'All may not yet be lost.'

'I hope so,' said Eleanor. She glanced at the clock. 'And now I had better go and dress for dinner. I am on my best behaviour now, so I mustn't be late.'

She went out, and Angela was immediately joined by Gus and Bobby, who in a flurry of breathless whispers clamoured to know what exactly had been going on that afternoon, since nobody else would tell them. Angela gave them an expurgated summary of events, and they gaped at her in speechless excitement, then Bobby suppressed a whoop and tried not to caper about.

'Serves him right,' he said in a low voice, 'after the telling-off he gave us yesterday. We never liked him.'

'Yes, he was an awful sneak,' agreed Gus. 'If you ask me, we're well rid of him. Now Priss can get married to someone nicer.'

'Gabe,' said Bobby, nodding. 'Let's have him. I like him. He's jolly good at making snowmen. And I'll bet he's the sort who will play pick-a-back without worrying about getting shoe-marks on his clothes. Not like Claude.'

This seemed to be the summit of their wishes with regard to a prospective brother-in-law, and Angela readily admitted that in that respect at least Gabe

Bradley was an eminently suitable candidate, being big and tall enough to carry either of them on his back if required. They bounced up and down in excitement, then ran off to chew over the new information among themselves.

Angela smiled, then decided to follow Eleanor's example and dress for dinner. When she reached the top of the stairs she encountered Henry Jameson coming out of his room, frowning. He had almost walked past her before he noticed her and brought himself up short.

'Is everything quite all right?' said Angela, noticing his abstraction.

'Mrs. Marchmont, perhaps I am getting old and losing my memory, but I am right in thinking that you gave me the second gun, aren't I?' he said.

'Yes,' said Angela. 'I handed it to you in the hall when Freddy and I came in, don't you remember?'

'Yes, I thought you did,' said Henry. 'And I'm pretty sure I put it in the drawer in my room.'

'Are you telling me you've lost it?' said Angela.

'Either that or someone has taken it,' said Henry soberly.

They stared at each other.

'Ought I to look and see whether it has been planted in my handbag again?' said Angela, in a vain attempt to make light of the matter.

He did not reply, so she tried again.

'Who could have taken it?' she said.

'I don't know,' he replied. 'And I don't know why, either.'

'Who knew you had it?'

'Why, almost everyone, I should think,' he said. 'The whole house has been in an uproar since we all found out what Burford had been getting up to. I don't suppose there's one person who doesn't know the entire story by now.'

'Might Claude have taken it?'

Henry shook his head.

'No,' he said. 'We questioned him then locked him in a bedroom upstairs, and it was only after that that I went and put the gun in my drawer.'

'Perhaps someone took it as a joke,' said Angela, although it did not sound likely, even to her. 'At any rate,' she went on practically, 'surely it doesn't matter now that you've caught Claude. After all, he's the only murderer in the house—isn't he?'

'Not according to him,' said Henry. 'He says he didn't do it.'

'What?' said Angela.

Henry gave her a brief summary of Claude's version of events.

'I see,' said Angela. 'Do you think he was telling the truth?'

'I hope not,' said Henry frankly. 'If he was, then we are not much further forward than we were before, since presumably there is another spy on the loose somewhere—one who knew about the existence of the papers and was in a position to instruct Burford to steal them. But I should hate to think that was the case.'

'But what had Claude to gain by returning only one set of the papers once he was caught?'

'None, as far as I can see,' said Henry.

'Then perhaps he is telling the truth. Perhaps someone else killed Professor Klausen and stole the documents from his dead body.'

'I hope not,' said Henry again. 'It doesn't bear

thinking about.' He went off, looking grim.

At dinner everyone was in a state of suppressed excitement, eager to talk about the events of the day but prevented by good manners from doing so—since, when all was said and done, it would have been the height of bad taste to draw attention to the fact that Lady Priscilla's fiancé had turned out to be such a bad lot. St. John, it was true, could not resist whispering triumphantly to Angela about his presumed exoneration, but everybody else did their best to keep the conversation to unobjectionable subjects.

'I gather the men managed to clear a path through to the village this afternoon,' said Aubrey Nash.

'Yes, thank goodness,' said Lady Strathmerrick, 'although I'm afraid it will take some time until the drive can be cleared sufficiently to allow motor-cars to pass through.'

'Then we shall have to impose on your generous hospitality a little longer, Lady Strathmerrick,' said Selma with her most charming smile. 'I never thought I could enjoy being trapped in a place so much.'

'How very kind of you to say so,' said the Countess.

'You'll be able to return to the inn now, at any rate,' said Angela to St. John.

'Yes,' he replied. 'I'm going tomorrow morning, but I shall be back in the afternoon as I have some things to do for the ladies. Do you have any errands you'd like me to run? I've promised to post Miss Foster's latest chapter to her writers' circle, and—' (in a lower tone) '—Gertie wants me to get her some cigarettes—although you'd better not tell her Governor about that, as she's not supposed to smoke.'

'No, I don't think I need anything, thank you,' replied Angela. 'As a matter of fact, I may take a little walk into the village myself, before it starts snowing and we get cut off again.'

'Father says the weather is improving now,' said Clemmie. 'I dare say the drive will be clear in no time and we can all get back to London.'

They all talked of the snow with politeness and determination until everything had been said that could be said on the subject and a general silence fell. It was Gertie who eventually broke the embargo as the apple tart was being served.

'I say,' she said suddenly, 'has anybody taken Claude up something to eat?'

Nobody had, it appeared.

'I shall send up a maid with a tray,' said Lady Strathmerrick.

'Better not,' said Sandy Buchanan. 'We don't want him to overpower her and escape.'

'Bradley and I will take him something shortly,' said Henry. 'He won't get the better of us.'

He then found some other observation to make about the weather that had not already been made, and they all pursued the subject energetically until dinner had ended.

The ladies soon retired to the drawing-room to whisper in corners, while the men remained behind to mutter gruffly at each other. Angela was gazing out of the window, idly wondering whether the part she had played in bringing Claude to justice meant that she was now *persona non grata* in the view of her hostess, when she noticed that the fastening of her necklace had worked loose and the article in question was about to fall to the floor. Closer examination revealed that the catch had broken. Since the dress she was wearing required a neck ornament—according to Marthe, at least—Angela left the drawing-room and went up to her room to find a suitable replacement. As she reached the top of the stairs, however, she heard voices she recognized coming from the next landing. Something about their tone arrested her attention, and she moved to the bottom of the second flight and looked upwards. The first thing that caught her eye was a wide-open door and the sight of Gabe Bradley standing in the doorway with one hand to his forehead, in an attitude of shock. Without thinking, she hurried up the stairs to join him. He heard her coming and turned.

'Don't,' he said, but it was no use. Angela had already seen what lay in the room beyond. It was a small bed-chamber, simply furnished with a bed, a little table and a chest of drawers. On the chest was a tray of food. Henry Jameson was bending over the bed, on which lay a man who seemed to be asleep. It was Claude Burford.

Angela stared. She knew immediately what had happened. Henry straightened up as he saw her, and before he even opened his mouth she knew what his next words would be.

'He's dead,' he said.

THIRTY

'SHOT,' SAID ANGELA. It was hardly a question.

Henry nodded. He looked sick.

'Through the heart, just like Klausen,' he said.

Angela came further into the room and gazed down at the dead body of Claude Burford. His face was swollen and bruised from the fight with Freddy, but aside from that he might have been sleeping. Only a tiny round hole in the centre of his breast indicated that anything was amiss.

'What do we do now?' said Gabe, white in the face. 'Lord Strathmerrick and Mr. Buchanan will need to know.'

'Yes,' said Henry. 'Go and tell them, will you, Bradley? Tell them to meet me in the study as a matter of urgency. I shall lock the door then join you.'

Gabe needed no further instruction. He ran off. Henry was about to follow him, but Angela put her hand on his arm.

'Have you still got my gun?' she said.

'Yes,' replied Henry. 'I looked to make sure when I

discovered that the other one had been taken. It's still there, all right.'

'Then I suggest you get it. It looks as though you're going to need it.'

'I could kick myself,' he said, as they hurried downstairs. 'If only I hadn't been in such a rush this afternoon I should have put the second gun in a much safer place. I ought to have known that something was up when it went missing, but I never dreamed that Burford would be the target. Wait here.'

He went into his room and emerged a few moments later with Angela's revolver.

'You'd better keep it for now,' she said, and he slipped it into his pocket.

They arrived outside the dining-hall to find Lord Strathmerrick, Sandy Buchanan and Aubrey Nash emerging behind Gabe with shocked looks on their faces.

'Is it true?' demanded Buchanan of Henry. 'How did it happen?'

'I don't know,' said Henry. 'But there's no time to be lost. We must decide what to do next.'

'Now we shall never find the documents,' moaned Lord Strathmerrick, who was not quite wringing his hands but looked as though he would like to.

The men all disappeared in the direction of the study, leaving Angela standing alone once more in the passage.

'How they do talk, these politicians,' she said to herself. 'When disaster strikes, they like nothing better than to sit down and chat about it for an hour or two.'

For her own part, she could not decide what to do, and in the absence of any other ideas returned to the drawing-room. There she found the ladies in glum mood, which was only slightly enlivened by an animated debate currently going on between St. John and Miss Foster about the relative merits of Robert Burns and Sir Walter Scott. Angela sat down in an easy chair, her mind elsewhere, and gazed absently at Freddy who, with bandaged ear, was still enjoying the ministrations of Selma Nash. After a few minutes he glanced her way and laughed as well as he could.

'Why, Mrs. M, what on earth are you gaping at?' he said. 'If you're not careful someone will toss a penny into your mouth and make a wish.'

Angela, coming to, realized she had indeed been sitting with her mouth open, and shut it with a snap. She stood up and glanced significantly towards the door, then went out. Freddy narrowed his eyes, waited a few moments and followed her.

'What is it?' he said.

'Claude is dead,' she replied.

'Good God,' he said, staring. 'Do you mean he killed himself?'

'No. It looks like murder.'

Now he was even more astonished.

'But who did it?' he said. Angela said nothing, and he went on, 'Do you mean to say there are *two* murderers on the loose at Fives?'

'No,' said Angela, 'I don't think there are. Claude denied killing Klausen, you know, and it looks as though he may have been telling the truth.'

'I say,' said Freddy, and paused to digest this new idea. 'But why was he killed?'

'To keep him quiet, I assume,' said Angela. 'He was certainly involved in the theft of the papers, but once he was caught he became a dangerous burden, so he was put out of the way to prevent him from betraying his accomplice.'

'This gets stranger and stranger,' said Freddy. 'I feel as though I'm in the middle of the most extraordinary dream. I rather think I'd like to wake up now, though.'

'I feel the same,' said Angela, 'but perhaps we can put an end to it this evening.'

'You don't mean to say you know who did it?' said Freddy, impressed.

'Not exactly,' she said hesitantly, 'but I have a hunch about the papers. If they are where I think they are, then we have our murderer. If I'm wrong, then there's no harm done.'

'If you *are* right, you will naturally claim that you knew all along.'

'Naturally,' she said.

'Very well, what is the next step?' said Freddy.

'First of all, I'm going to talk to Henry, and then I shall need your help,' said Angela.

'How very kind of you to let me in on the thing,' said Freddy. 'What do you want me to do? Please don't ask me to hit anybody. I'm not up to fighting again.'

'Don't worry,' said Angela. 'It's nothing of the sort. I just need you to charm a woman. You ought to find that easy enough.'

She explained what she wanted in a few words and he raised his eyebrows but listened carefully.

'I say,' he said when she had finished. 'Are you sure?'

'No,' she replied, 'but I'd like to take a closer look. Now then, do you think you can do it?'

Freddy drew himself up.

'I should say so,' he said. 'In the service of my country and the delightful Mrs. M. I am prepared to do anything.'

'Excellent. I shall remind you of that promise one day, but this will do for the present. Now, I am going to fetch Mr. Jameson. I shall be back in a minute. In the meantime, perhaps you'd like to begin.'

He nodded and returned to the drawing-room, and Angela hurried along to the study and knocked on the door. To her dismay, she found only Gabe and Aubrey there.

'Where is Mr. Jameson?' she said.

'He went upstairs with Buchanan and Lord Strathmerrick, as they wanted to see Burford's body,' said Aubrey.

'Dear me, and I did need him rather urgently,' she said.

'I can fetch him if you like,' said Gabe, standing up.

'Oh, would you? I'd be most grateful,' she said. 'We'll be in the drawing-room—and please tell him to bring the gun. I think he might need it.'

She left Gabe and Aubrey glancing at each other in surprise, and ran back to the drawing-room. She paused a moment to get her breath back then slipped through the door quietly. Everything was much as it had been before, except that now Freddy was sitting on a sofa next to Miss Foster with an open book in his hand.

'—but I always thought Wordsworth was a terribly dull chap,' he was saying. 'All that whimpering about daffodils. If you want real feeling, then Coleridge is your man.' He struck an attitude and declaimed, '"The night is chill; the forest bare; is it the wind that moaneth bleak?" Marvellous stuff. It gives me quite a shiver whenever I read it.'

'Oh, yes,' said Miss Foster, clasping her hands together. 'I quite agree with you, Mr. Pilkington-Soames. I believe there is nothing quite like poetry for striking a thrill to the very heart, but the *subject-matter* is of the first importance.'

'I read one once in which the chap spent forty-seven verses describing the spots on the back of a ladybird,' said Freddy. 'If anyone ought to have been forced to wear an albatross around his neck, it was that poet.'

Miss Foster tittered, and the two of them bent their heads over the book while Freddy flicked through in search of something purple enough to satisfy the lady's tastes.

In the meantime, Angela had spotted what she was looking for. Miss Foster's notebook was lying on a small table just to one side of the sofa, but not quite out of Miss Foster's eye-line. Nobody else was taking any notice. Angela moved quietly behind the sofa. Freddy, who had not looked up but was perfectly aware of her presence, drew the poetry book towards him slightly and indicated a particular verse, so that Miss Foster was forced to turn further away from Angela in order to see it. Angela took her opportunity and quietly picked up the notebook.

'I say, Mrs. Marchmont,' said a loud voice just then, making her jump. 'I didn't know you were interested in literature too.' It was St. John, who had spotted what she was doing. He came over, took the notebook out of her hands and began flicking through it. 'Look, Miss Foster, Mrs. Marchmont wants to read your latest chapter. I said you ought to

271

let people have a look at it. No use in hiding one's light under a bushel and all that, what?'

Angela had frozen for a second, but now she glanced over and saw Freddy and Miss Foster both staring at the notebook in horror. Miss Foster quickly recovered herself and gave a little laugh.

'Oh, Mr. Bagshawe,' she said. 'I've told you before how *protective* I am of my notebook. Why, I hate to say it, but it makes me feel quite *anxious* to see the fruits of my imagination in anyone else's hands. May I have it, please? I should be only too glad to read one or two extracts to you if you like.' She rose and held out her hand to take the book.

'Nonsense,' said St. John jovially. 'If you're ever going to succeed as a writer then you must be prepared to let others read your stuff. Don't worry— we're all friends here, and even if it's a little rough around the edges, I'm sure everybody will be happy to suggest areas in which you might improve.'

'I really must insist—' began Miss Foster, and tried to take the notebook out of his hands, but St. John held it out of her way.

'Now, now,' he said in playful admonishment. 'There's no need to be shy about it—' he stopped in surprise as Miss Foster snatched at the notebook and he lost his balance. For a few seconds they fought over it comically, then there was a tearing sound and it fell to the floor, scattering loose leaves everywhere.

There was a brief silence, then Miss Foster made a dart at the floor and began picking up the papers.

'I'm awfully sorry,' said St. John. 'Do let me help you.'

'There's no need—' began Miss Foster, but St. John had already picked up several of the loose leaves and was frowning at them.

'I say, Miss Foster, you do write on jolly thick paper,' he said. 'Look, it seems to be made of two sheets pasted together. Yes, it is—look, you can see where the glue is coming away here.'

Everyone in the room was now watching the little scene with interest.

'St. John,' said Freddy in a warning tone.

Miss Foster glanced around and saw the expressions on the faces of Angela and Freddy, then turned back to St. John.

'Give the papers to me,' she said, and suddenly the soft, affected voice of Letty Foster had gone, to be replaced by something altogether colder and harder.

'What?' said St. John absently, still absorbed in pulling the glued pages apart. 'Why, they're all the same—and look, what's this? Somebody's put some other bits of paper between the layers. Dashed odd way of going about things, what?'

There was a click, and everyone in the room gasped at the same time.

'Give me the papers,' said Miss Foster, more loudly this time. St. John looked up and blinked as he saw the gun in her hand, pointing directly at his chest.

'Is that a gun?' he said.

'What on *earth* are you doing, Letty?' said Lady Strathmerrick in astonishment.

'Give her the documents, you ass,' said Freddy to St. John.

St. John, not the quickest of thinkers, finally seemed to realize that something was amiss, and handed the scraps of paper to Miss Foster. She seized them and hurried out of the room, just as Henry Jameson and Sandy Buchanan entered through a different door to a chorus of astounded voices. Sandy Buchanan held up his hands until everybody subsided.

'What's all this?' he said.

'Miss Foster has taken the papers,' said Angela to Henry. He understood immediately and ran towards the door through which Miss Foster had just left. 'Be careful!' Angela called after him as he went out. 'She has a gun.'

'I don't know where she thinks she's going in that evening-frock,' said Gertie. 'She'll have to stay indoors or she'll freeze to death outside.'

Sandy Buchanan started to say something, but he was immediately interrupted by the sound of a gunshot from somewhere nearby inside the castle. It was followed quickly by another, then silence. All the guests gazed at one another, wide-eyed.

'Do you suppose she's shot him?' said Gertie. 'Perhaps someone ought to go and find out. Freddy, be a sport, will you?'

Freddy was about to tell her exactly what he thought of her suggestion that he pursue, unarmed, a dangerous woman carrying a revolver, when Henry Jameson slipped back into the drawing-room. He said nothing, but exchanged significant glances with the Foreign Secretary. Buchanan was about to follow him out of the room when Gertie spoke up.

'You don't really think you're going to get away with that, do you?' she said. 'Come on, spill the beans. What have you done with Miss Fo? Did you shoot her?'

Henry hesitated, but saw that the weight of opinion was against him and that he would most likely be set upon by an angry mob of women in sequins and pearls if he did not 'spill the beans,' as instructed. He nodded briefly.

'Is she dead?'

'I'm afraid so, Lady Gertrude,' he replied. 'Unfortunately, I was forced to defend myself when she fired at me. Her shot went wide, but mine did not.'

He and Buchanan then went out, leaving the rest of the guests staring at each other. For some moments, it seemed as though nobody knew what to say, then Gertie, irrepressible as ever, spoke.

'I say,' she said. 'Gus and Bobby will be awfully disappointed to have missed all the excitement.'

THIRTY-ONE

'ARE YOU SURE they're the right documents?' said Lord Strathmerrick. He had insisted they sit in the little conference-room off the study, since the formality of its polished table and stiff-backed chairs enabled him to feel that he was at last regaining some measure of control over the situation after the chaos of the past three or four days.

'Oh, yes,' said Henry. 'I don't think there's any doubt. Look—you can see they're in the same handwriting as the ones we found on Burford.'

'Well, that's something, at any rate,' said Aubrey Nash.

'But how on earth did you know where to find them, Mrs. Marchmont?' said Sandy Buchanan.

Angela, who suspected that she was the only woman ever to have been invited to sit in this room and talk, was rather enjoying the feeling of being a pioneer. She thought for a moment.

'I didn't know for certain,' she said, 'but I'd been struck by one or two rather odd things. The first was the fact that St. John was lying about his alibi. He said he had left the castle before half past twelve on the night of the murder, but that was certainly not true—and I know it wasn't an honest mistake on his part because I questioned him about it and he repeated the lie. I didn't really believe he was the murderer, but it seemed he must have had some reason for hanging about the place late at night, and given his—er—political leanings, I wondered if perhaps he wasn't a member of the spy ring, and merely playing the part of a rejected suitor. If that were the case, then he must have been summoned to Fives for a particular purpose. Then at dinner this evening he happened to mention to me that he was intending to go into the village tomorrow and post the latest chapter of Miss Foster's novel to her writers' circle. I didn't think anything of it, but it reminded me of an incident a day or two ago when Miss Foster lost her notebook and Gertie and I found it. We looked at it out of curiosity, and I happened to notice then that the loose leaves she carried around inside it were much thicker and stiffer than ordinary paper.

'Of course, I didn't realize at the time that she had glued the edges together and concealed the missing documents inside them, but this evening I started to wonder about Miss Foster as a possible suspect. It seemed to me that her situation as governess and trusted companion to the Strathmerrick family put her in the ideal position to overhear many secrets of state. Lord Strathmerrick was accustomed to inviting important people up to Fives to discuss confidential affairs, and I could only imagine that he frequently did the same thing at his house in London. There would have been plenty of opportunities for Miss

Foster to listen at doors, get a glimpse of private papers and so on. Then I remembered something St. John said about having seen her wandering about the castle on New Year's Eve, long after she was supposed to have gone to bed, still carrying her notebook with her, and I started to put two and two together. It seemed incredible at first, but the more I thought about it, the less incredible it became, and I decided to try and get a closer look at the notebook.'

'Then she was using her writers' circle as a cover for her activities?' said Aubrey.

'That is my assumption,' said Angela. 'She told me herself that she frequently sent chapters of her manuscripts to other members of the group in order to elicit their opinion. I imagine that the chapters in question in fact consisted of information in code that she had picked up from the Strathmerrick household. She mentioned a Mr. Adams, who runs a small publishing-house in London. I shouldn't be a bit surprised to discover that he is the ringleader of this spy network, if indeed there is one.'

'Yes,' said Henry, 'I think you're right. I have had a quick look through Miss Foster's things and found a number of rather interesting letters which I shall look at in more detail later—perhaps tomorrow, since it is rather late now. At any rate, I certainly intend to send a man into the village first thing tomorrow to telegraph Scotland Yard. I very much hope that we will be able to put an end to this whole distressing affair at last.'

'Then it was Miss Foster who murdered Professor Klausen,' said Aubrey.

'Yes,' said Henry. 'I imagine she saw him arrive during the dance and took him to the library under some pretext or other. She then shot him through the heart, concealed his body behind the globe and stole the papers from him. I think she planned to have Claude Burford dispose of Klausen's body somewhere on the Fives estate where it would never be found; then when the professor was reported missing nobody would have known where to start searching for him, since he might be almost anywhere—might have remained in London or even gone abroad, in fact. Then the papers could be spirited away with ease, and nobody would ever connect their disappearance with Fives or Miss Foster, even if Klausen's disappearance did cause a stir. It was just her bad luck that the body was found at all.'

'Then she and Burford were in league?' said Aubrey.

'Not exactly,' said Henry. 'I don't think he was ever a leading figure in the organization—rather, it's more a case of his being forced to do what he was told for as long as he was useful. Burford might have been in a better position than Miss Foster to get the documents from Klausen, for example. It's just a pity he didn't tell us about Miss Foster as soon as we caught him—had he done so, then he might still be alive, albeit disgraced and in prison.'

'But what about this Bagshawe fellow?' said Aubrey. 'Oughtn't we to be putting him under lock and key if he's in league with them all?'

Henry coughed.

'We'll keep an eye on him, certainly, but I think we're safe for the moment. I spoke to him a little while ago and—er—put the fear of God into him. It's pretty clear that he has been a dupe in all this.'

'Are you quite certain of that?' said Lord Strathmerrick. 'What is his explanation? Don't tell me he really just came to moon about after Gertie.'

'No—although that was part of the attraction,' said Henry. 'His story is that he was leaving a meeting of the Young Bolshevists a week or two ago when he was approached by a stranger whom he had noticed sitting at the back of the hall during the meeting. The man did not give his name, but expressed admiration of a particularly fine, rousing speech that Bagshawe had made that evening. Bagshawe was clearly devoted to the cause, he said, and if he was amenable, the stranger would like to make him a proposal. The stranger explained that he was a member of another, much larger movement of people of the same political persuasion as Bagshawe himself. This movement had been so effective in its activities, and had exasperated the authorities to such an extent that it had been outlawed. However, it still continued to operate in secret, and was always looking out for new members who were wedded to the cause. From his performance that evening, Bagshawe looked an ideal candidate, and the stranger therefore wanted to invite him to join the group.

'Bagshawe, who despite his strong views does not appear to possess the sharpest of wits, was flattered by this, and asked for more information about this secret movement. The stranger replied that he would be only too glad to furnish Bagshawe with more details, but since the group was proscribed, he was forced to be very cautious when recruiting new members, for if the police were to find out about it then many innocent people would be arrested and thrown into prison purely because of their political beliefs. If Bagshawe really wanted to join then he would first need to demonstrate his trustworthiness by performing a simple task.

'It was known, the stranger said, that Bagshawe was friendly with Lady Gertrude McAloon, the daughter of the Earl of Strathmerrick, and that it was customary for the whole Strathmerrick family to spend New Year at Fives Castle. Now, an important member of the secret movement was also going to be at Fives at New Year, and would be carrying with him—or her—some highly confidential documents containing details of the group's membership and minutes of all its meetings. If he wished to prove himself, Bagshawe's task would be to go to Fives Castle, using his friendship with Lady Gertrude as a cover, collect these documents and bring them back down to London. If he was successful, then he would be admitted to the movement as a junior member.

'Bagshawe was all ears at this, and the first thing he wanted to know was the name of the person from whom he was to take delivery of the documents. At this point, the stranger shook his head and said that unfortunately the secrecy required and the fear of exposure to the authorities were such that he could not even reveal that information. However, there was no need to worry, since the correspondent in question would be looking out for Bagshawe's arrival and would make the approach personally.'

'What a ridiculous story. Did he really fall for it?' said the Foreign Secretary, half-laughing.

'Hook, line and sinker,' said Henry. 'He accepted the mission there and then, and came up to Scotland, as we know, a few days ago. However, what Bagshawe had not confessed to the stranger was the fact that his friendship with Lady Gertrude had been overrated, and that she actually considered him a confounded nuisance and was unlikely to be happy to see him. As a result, instead of coming straight up to the front door and knocking like any other visitor, he tramped around the grounds for a day or two, trying to be subtle in his approach but instead leaving footprints all over the place and making himself look highly suspicious. He then sneaked into the castle like a burglar on New Year's Eve, and hung around, hoping to find the person he was supposed to be meeting.'

'What? Without even having announced his presence?' said Lord Strathmerrick. 'How was anybody supposed to know he was there? Why, the man's an idiot.'

'Not the clearest of thinkers, certainly,' agreed Henry. 'At any rate, after a few hours of creeping around and not daring to approach anyone, he lost his nerve and sneaked away. By that time, the path to the village was blocked and so he ended up hiding in the barn. When Lady Gertrude and Mrs. Marchmont caught him and questioned him, he made a mistake about the times, and said he had left the castle earlier than he in fact did. However, once he had been told about the murder and knew that he needed an alibi, he had to stick to his story at all costs.'

'But he found his correspondent eventually, didn't he?' said Aubrey. 'He told Angela he was going to post the papers to London, so he can't be as innocent as he claims.'

'Well, that's the thing,' said Henry in some amusement. 'He swears he had no idea that Miss Foster was his correspondent, since he had been expecting to meet a man. He admits that she made one or two significant remarks to him which he now realizes he was meant to understand, but when she asked him to take the papers he truly did believe that they were chapters of a novel she wanted him to post in the village.'

Sandy Buchanan gave a shout of laughter.

'Why, she might have done that herself,' he said. 'Her superiors ought to have been more careful about whom they picked to act as a go-between.'

'Yes,' said Henry. 'Bagshawe's look of surprise when I hinted at what the documents actually contained was quite a sight to behold, and he was not at all happy at having been made a chump of, as he put it. Even now, I'm not sure he quite realizes how narrow an escape he has had, but I shall have another word with him and impress upon him the absolute necessity for good behaviour on his part from now on, on pain of future arrest.'

'Why did they choose him in particular, do you think?' said Aubrey.

'It's difficult to say,' said Henry, 'but from what I can see the members of the spy network seem to have been either people acting from conviction—who were presumably given the greatest responsibility—or people who were blackmailed or tricked into it. Burford, for example, had everything to lose if his financial dealings were revealed, and so felt he had no choice but to do as he was told, while St. John Bagshawe was the ideal recruit from one point of view at least, since his political activities would make him the perfect scapegoat if he were ever caught. It would have been the easiest thing in the world to pin the murder of Professor Klausen on him.'

'But what about Miss Foster?' said Angela. 'Why did she do it?'

'As I said, I found some rather interesting correspondence in her room,' said Henry. 'I haven't had time to read it all properly, but it includes some letters addressed to "My Darling Wife" from a man signing himself "Evgeny."' He paused to allow the others to digest this information.

'Do you mean to say she was married?' said Lord Strathmerrick at last. 'You're joking, aren't you? Why, the woman was a spinster through and through. One only had to look at her to see it.'

'What exactly do you know about Miss Foster, Lord Strathmerrick?' said Henry gently. 'She was with you for several years, I understand. Presumably you must have come to know her very well. What did she tell you about her family, for example?'

'Well, naturally—I mean to say—of course, we— she said—' said the Earl, then spluttered to a halt as it struck him that in fact he knew little or nothing about the woman who had lived under his roof for seven years, ostensibly as a member of his own family. 'Perhaps my wife can tell you more about her,' he said lamely, 'although it goes without saying that she knew nothing about all these goings-on.'

'Naturally,' said Henry. 'I didn't mean to suggest for a moment that she did. As a matter of fact, it appears that Miss Foster was able to conceal her thoughts and intentions extremely well. From the letters it looks very much as though she had a history of which you all knew nothing. If she was indeed married to this Evgeny—which, I am sure you have noticed, is a Russian name—then she may well have spent some time abroad and fallen under the influence of a foreign power. Indeed, who can say whether she was even born an Englishwoman? Why, anybody can assume an English name if they wish. That will be another thing for Scotland Yard to investigate.'

Lord Strathmerrick looked stricken—as well he might, thought Angela. For seven years he and his wife and children had shared a house with this woman without ever apparently bothering to inquire about her history. Instead, they had taken her appearance as a vague, untidy spinster of laughable literary ambitions at face value, and had unknowingly allowed her to pass important state secrets to a foreign power for who knew how long? Years, perhaps. This would be a severe blow to the Earl's reputation as a discreet broker of power, and who could tell whether it would ever recover?

At length the Earl collected himself with some difficulty. He gave a cough.

'Well, well,' he said brusquely. 'Let us admit our mistakes and learn from them. Now then, Jameson, I think it is safe to say that the next few weeks are going to be pretty uncomfortable for all of us—that is, unless we can think of some way of hushing this matter up.'

Here, Sandy Buchanan regarded Angela directly.

'Mrs. Marchmont,' he said, 'in the past few days you have proved yourself again and again as a woman to be depended upon. May I have your assurance that we can depend upon you again on this occasion?'

Angela understood him perfectly.

'Naturally, I have no desire to see the Government fall and the country plunged into chaos,' she said. 'Whatever story you choose to put about, I shall not say a word.'

'What about Mr. Pilkington-Soames?' said Buchanan. 'I understand he is a reporter at the—er—*Clarion*.' He spoke as one who had heard mention of the journal in question, but would never dream of having it in his house.

'As I said to Mr. Jameson, I imagine he will be perfectly happy to keep his knowledge of the true facts quiet provided that he is allowed to be the first to report whatever story you do choose to tell,' said Angela. 'However, I can't speak for him, so you will have to arrange it with him yourselves.'

'Very well,' said the Foreign Secretary. 'If we tread carefully, it looks as though we may be able to escape the worst of the scandal. Jameson, I shall leave the rest up to you.'

'Hmm,' said Henry. 'I think a simple explanation will be best. Lord Strathmerrick, I believe you always had some doubts about the mental stability of Miss Foster?'

'Ah—' said the Earl.

'I understand she had mentioned to Lady Strathmerrick several times that she was afraid of certain shadowy enemies who were planning to abduct her and lock her away. I gather you had some concerns that she was perhaps suffering from delusions—am I correct?'

'Oh—er—yes, absolutely, what?' said the Earl.

'What a pity, then, that she should act on her delusions, and in her derangement be responsible for the deaths of two such eminent men, don't you think?' said Henry. 'She must have been truly beyond help if she could mistake Professor Klausen and Claude Burford for abductors intent on harming her, and kill them in such a confused and tragic attempt at self-defence.'

There was a chorus of agreement from around the table and everyone nodded solemnly.

'Perhaps it will be wisest to draw a veil over what we know to the disadvantage of Claude Burford,' went on Henry. 'After all, the man has been duly punished for his sins and it won't do any good now to expose them to the nation.'

There was some shuffling of feet at this, especially from Lord Strathmerrick, who was still very angry at Claude's betrayal, but eventually he nodded reluctantly.

'Well, then, that seems to settle the matter,' said Sandy Buchanan briskly. He looked at his watch and stood up. 'It is very late,' he said, 'and I should like to get some sleep, since it looks as though we are going to be walking on egg-shells for the next few weeks and I should like to have a clear mind for it.'

There was no arguing with this, and they all filed out of the room.

'Shall you get away with it, do you think?' said Angela to Henry as they walked together along the corridor.

'I hope so,' said Henry. 'I suppose you think it's not quite the thing?'

'Not quite, no,' she replied. 'Don't worry—I shan't say a word, and I perfectly understand why you need to do it, but—' she paused.

'But what?'

'You'll think me odd, I dare say, but a small part of me thinks it rather a pity that such a cunning and clever woman should go down in history with a label of insanity attached to her name, when she was quite evidently nothing of the sort.'

'Unfortunately, a job such as mine requires me on occasion to—rewrite the truth, let us say,' he replied. 'I don't say I like it either, but I do what I must in the service of my country.'

'And nobody could ask more of you,' said Angela. She stifled a yawn. 'It's been a long night,' she said, 'and I am very tired, so I shall bid you goodnight.'

'I think I shall stay up for a while and read through Miss Foster's correspondence,' said Henry. 'I should like to be prepared when the police arrive.'

'Well, good luck, and goodnight.'

'Goodnight,' he said, 'and thank you.'

She shook her head, smiling, and went upstairs to bed.

THIRTY-TWO

THE NEXT DAY the news was received that the telephone lines had been repaired, and Fives Castle was once more able to communicate with the outside world. Furthermore, by lunchtime the long drive had finally been cleared, and the guests were informed that they might leave whenever they wished. The sense of relief at this development was almost palpable, although everybody was far too well-mannered to express their happiness in the form of anything other than a polite noise. The past four days had been trying ones for almost everyone—especially the Strathmerrick family, who had been faced with the unfortunate revelation that two of their peripheral members were dangerous criminals, and who now likely had several weeks of impertinent pestering by the press to look forward to (although Freddy had promised not to abuse his favoured position and was on his best behaviour until such time as permission was granted for him to unleash his pen).

Marthe was glad to be going, and was almost

cheerful as she packed Angela's things, while William was overjoyed to be reunited with the Bentley, and was preparing for the long journey ahead by digging about under the bonnet, checking each part with loving care. Angela was sitting by the window in her bedroom, paying some much-needed attention to her finger-nails, when there was a knock at the door and Gertie came in.

'You're going, then,' she said.

'Yes,' said Angela. 'We set off tomorrow morning—always assuming it doesn't snow again tonight.'

Gertie shuddered.

'It had better not,' she said. 'I've had enough of this place and I'm dying to get back to London.'

'I thought you were keen on a bit of excitement,' said Angela.

'Of course I am,' said Gertie, 'but I think three dead bodies in one weekend are quite enough for anyone, don't you?'

Angela stood up and joined Gertie at the window. A thaw had begun to set in—whether temporary or not nobody could say—and water dripped gently onto the window panes from above. In the distance Lord Strathmerrick could be seen directing the delicate operation to remove the mortal remains of Professor Klausen, Claude Burford and Miss Foster from the castle. Gertie grimaced as a little procession of men came into view, bearing three makeshift stretchers on which lay three covered figures. They were loaded as respectfully as possible into the grocer's motor-van, which had been pressed into service as the only suitable conveyance available, and then the doors were shut on them for the last time.

The Earl stood for a while, evidently giving instructions to the driver, who nodded, and then the vehicle moved off slowly—which had less to do with respect for the dead than with the fear of skidding off the road.

'Have the police arrived yet?' said Angela.

'Yes,' said Gertie. 'Mr. Jameson button-holed them as soon as they got here and herded them into the study before they could get any ideas about investigating. I've no doubt he's waving Scotland Yard at them and telling them in no uncertain terms that they're to keep their noses out of it for reasons of national security if they don't want to lose their jobs.'

'I should like to see that,' said Angela. 'Mr. Jameson is always so mild-mannered that one would never suppose him to have the strength of character to do what he does, and yet he is one of the most competent men I have ever met. I can only suppose he has a hidden firmness of purpose that he displays only on special occasions.'

'I shouldn't like to cross him, that's for sure,' said Gertie. 'Give me a cigarette, will you?'

'I see you have managed to shake off St. John,' said Angela, handing Gertie her cigarette-case. 'Where is he? Hiding in his room for fear of arrest?'

Gertie let out a short laugh.

'Hardly,' she said. 'Why, the man is formed entirely of brass. He's strolling about the place as though he hadn't a care in the world. Nonetheless, the message does seem finally to have penetrated into his thick skull. I told him yesterday to go and bother someone else, and he took me at my word. When I last saw him he was mooning about after Priss. He'll get no change out of her either, though—she's already got her hooks into Gabe.'

'And so you are left without suitors,' said Angela mockingly.

'Yes,' said Gertie. 'I remain in splendid solitariness, and can indulge my unrequited crush on Sandy Buchanan in peace. Or perhaps I'll marry Freddy, just to annoy Father.'

'Please give me plenty of notice if you do,' said Angela, 'and I shall take good care to move to a remote island in order to avoid the fireworks.'

They both laughed merrily.

A little while later Angela came downstairs to find Aubrey and Selma Nash in the entrance hall, preparing to depart, as they were going to visit friends in Edinburgh for a few days. There was much clasping of hands and kissing as they took leave of her, and then Aubrey went outside to speak to their chauffeur, leaving Selma and Angela together.

'You will write, won't you?' said Selma. 'I should hate to lose touch again.'

Angela readily agreed. She had enjoyed getting reacquainted with Selma despite a certain embarrassment with regard to Aubrey.

Selma took Angela's hand and lowered her voice.

'I want to thank you,' she said.

'For what?' said Angela in surprise.

'For keeping Aubrey at arm's length,' said Selma. Before Angela could reply she went on, 'I should have been awfully jealous, you know. I never would have said a word—fair's fair, when all's said and done—but I'd have hated it. I could stand anybody but you.'

She put a finger over her lips and ran out to join her husband. Angela stood for a second, eyebrows raised, then followed Selma out and waved the

Daimler off as it departed down the drive. When it had quite disappeared from view, she walked slowly back into the house, deep in thought. Her reverie was broken by the sound of stamping just outside the front door, and she turned to see Freddy kicking the snow off his boots and brandishing a shovel. His bruises were developing nicely and his ear was bandaged, but he was looking as cheerful as ever.

'Brr!' he said. 'Hallo, Angela. You'll no doubt be pleased to hear that I have managed to find my car and dig it out, although it went into a huff when I tried to start it. I don't think it has forgiven me for abandoning it in a snowdrift. May I borrow William, please? If anybody can fix it, he can.'

'Why, certainly,' said Angela. 'Are you going tomorrow? I suppose you'll have to get back to the paper soon and start work on your story.'

'Yes,' said Freddy. 'I'm to receive instructions from Jameson first, though. He's going to tell me what I can and can't write. Of course, I can't just palm off a work of fiction onto old Bickerstaffe—I mean, I know it's only the *Clarion*, but there are limits—so Jameson is going to square things with him before I start.'

'Do you think Mr. Bickerstaffe will be amenable to printing it?' said Angela.

'If it's a choice between that and losing the exclusive I should say he'll jump at the opportunity,' said Freddy.

'I wonder if the general public will fall for it,' said Angela.

'With Frederick Pilkington-Soames writing the story? Why, they'll lap it up! Once they've read my thrilling prose, gasped in horror and shed a tear over the terrible events at Fives Castle, and taken another good long look at that daring photograph of Gertie that was in all the newspapers last year, they'll be clamouring to believe it—will be most indignant at the mere suggestion that it might not be true, in fact.'

'I hope you're right,' said Angela. 'I know some members of the Government seem to have been wandering around with their eyes closed in recent months, but I'd rather be ruled by politicians who have the same weaknesses as the rest of us than have no rulers at all. And if nothing else, I should hate to see Eleanor Buchanan held responsible for the Government's collapse.'

'Well said,' said Freddy. 'I say, I wonder if they'll ever manage to decipher those documents now that Professor Klausen is no more. Why, they don't even know which are the real ones.'

'I dare say they'll set some of their tame scientists onto it,' said Angela, 'and besides, Klausen must have kept notes of his work, surely. I can't believe the papers are the only record of all those years of research. He probably has pages and pages of stuff locked away in a safe somewhere.'

'Oh, probably,' agreed Freddy.

'Well, then, everything seems to have been cleared up to everyone's satisfaction,' said Angela. 'The murder has been solved and the documents recovered, and I have begun to re-establish myself with Lady Strathmerrick as a respectable woman.'

'Why, has your chap gone?' said Freddy.

'Aubrey and Selma have left, if that is whom you are referring to,' she said.

'Very wise on Selma's part to take her husband away before you could steal him back,' said Freddy.

Angela was about to reply hotly when she saw his face and changed her mind.

'You really are the most awful tease, Freddy,' she said. 'My behaviour has been above reproach, as you well know.'

'Oh, but you don't want to be *too* respectable, do you?' he said. 'Why, people will think you're no fun. Personally, I prefer being naughty.'

'I'd noticed,' said Angela dryly.

Freddy was looking at something over her shoulder.

'In fact, I'm going to be naughty this minute,' he said mischievously, and before she could stop him he threw his arms around her and kissed her enthusiastically, then let her go and slipped away quickly, leaving her standing there gaping. It was a second or two before she could collect her thoughts enough to notice the startled expression on the face of Lady Strathmerrick, who was just then passing—as Freddy had been well aware. Angela blushed. The Countess quickly recovered herself and moved on haughtily.

'Bother,' said Angela, and lifted a hand to smooth her hair.

***

BOOKS IN THIS SERIES

The Murder at Sissingham Hall
The Mystery at Underwood House
The Treasure at Poldarrow Point
The Riddle at Gipsy's Mile
The Incident at Fives Castle
The Imbroglio at the Villa Pozzi
The Problem at Two Tithes
The Trouble at Wakeley Court
The Scandal at 23 Mount Street
The Shadow at Greystone Chase (coming soon)

NEW RELEASES

If you would like to receive news of further releases in the Angela Marchmont series of mysteries by Clara Benson, you can sign up to our mailing list at clarabenson.com/contact.

We take data confidentiality very seriously and will not pass your details on to anybody else or send you any spam.

Printed in Great Britain
by Amazon.co.uk, Ltd.,
Marston Gate.